T0167431

hyphen

in memory of Joyce Nield

First published in Great Britain in 2003 by Comma Press
www.commapress.co.uk
Distributed by Carcanet Press
www.carcanet.co.uk

A CIP catalogue record of this book is available from the British Library

ISBN 1 85754 731 4
The publisher gratefully acknowledges assistance from the Arts Council of England
North West, and the Regional Arts Lottery Programme.

Set in Bembo by XL Publishing Services, Tiverton
Printed and bound in England by SRP Ltd, Exeter

Contents

Introduction

Why ask poets to write short stories?

It would be spurious, not to say a little impertinent, to ask twenty of Britain and Ireland's finest versifiers to endure such a serious job-swap just to point out a few family resemblances between short fiction and verse – containment of narrative, potency of symbol, conciseness of language, and other ways of saying they're both short. It would be equally trite to ask them to do it for some campaign towards more 'poetic' prose in contemporary fiction. All good fiction is 'poetic', in the loose sense of the word.

Rather, Comma Press have commissioned, invited and compiled these stories in order to mark what we believe is a relatively new stage in the way poetry, or more precisely poets, regard themselves: a new looseness in what it means to *be* a poet (although we'd never pass up an opportunity to take a new spin on the short form, either).

The boundaries between literary disciplines have traditionally been fairly porous. Writers of the highest standard have migrated between novels and short stories, short stories and drama, often effortlessly. Before the beginning of the twentieth century, poetry also enjoyed a great deal of traffic between itself and its oral cousin, drama. It's only in the last century that verse has become too concerned with its own definition to fully communicate with the changes and insights of other, younger art forms - short fiction being just one of them. For a good century, poets have kept to themselves.

There is something about *being* a poet which fixes them. Indeed, since the introduction of free verse, many have found themselves bound, not just by their genre, but by the very techniques they chose to deploy. Seamus Heaney alliterates and uses lots of onomatopoeic monosyllables. Mark Doty goes for long, unrhyming couplets. Paul Muldoon prefers highly elaborate rhyme schemes and variable line-lengths. That's what they do. Even those famous for shifting forms like WH Auden or Thom Gunn find themselves still defined, as poets, in relation to form.

All writers have a style, but poetic style brings with it unavoidable technical decisions that in turn carry centuries' worth of use. This demands to be studied and imitated long before it can be subverted for the poet's own use. Inevitably this process binds itself to what poets regard as their true definition as writers, their voice, and over the last century thewholething has become an even greater hang up than normal. All thanks to a movement that ostensibly strove to renew things, Modernism.

In short fiction, Modernism had a relatively singular, one-off effect. Writers like Joyce and Chekhov nudged the short story's drama into the internal, psychological world of their characters. Traditional short stories were places where *things happened*. Mrs Marple found her killer. Fortunato got buried alive behind a cellar wall. That sort of thing. In post-Modernist stories the action is more subjective. It was Joyce who first applied the Christian notion of 'epiphany' to literature, and the internal arena it opened up has served literary short fiction pretty well. For the best part of a century, short stories have flourished in this internal space, without the need for any further, seismic upheavals, just the odd figurehead like Carver to rejuvenate it.

For poetry it's been a different story. Ever since Poe assailed the notion of longer poetry in *The Poetic Principle* (1850), the process of modernising verse has been inextricably linked to an awareness of form. Poe defined poetry as a combination of 'music' and 'idea' and, though it may always have been cleft in this way, separating the music or form of it so strategically set in play an argument that would end in revolution.

Modernism was driven by 'a feeling that form and subject-matter are [or should be] structurally identical,' to quote Robert Graves and Laura Riding's version of events. It was incumbent on their own generation to re-align the two where previous generations had let them slip. Tennyson's *In Memoriam* is always the villain. Section by section, it moved arbitrarily, critics insisted, from reminisced revelry, to prosy scientific contemplation to Miltonic elegy, each time without any deviation in the inflexible *abba* quatrains. The early Modernist responses of Paul Valéry and the French Impressionist poets went too far the other way - so the Modernist account goes - by over-prioritising the formal, musical quality of the poem until meaning and subject-matter became 'merely a historical setting for the music'. By the time we get to *The Wasteland*, of course, the two halves of the poetic brain - form and content - are back in sync. Metre, and other formal considerations, mutate from passage to passage throughout this long poem, precisely as the ideas do.

Or at least this is how the quieter exponents of Modernism tell it. The truth is, instead of a swift and unfussy realignment of form with content, what occurred was a tumultuous influx of entirely new forms. In the case of *The Wasteland,* this was to save the very epic poem Poe had set out to dispatch. It wasn't just an influx of new formal possibilities, either. It was deluge.

Form, on its own, is the vaguest of terms. It could be used to denote rhyme scheme and metre, or more broadly anything that constitutes surface, style, tonal value, rhythm, or vocal register. Across the arts, it can be applied to any aspect of process, medium or apparatus. Though when all other words buckle under the anxiety of influence, the single word suffices.

The ambitious, wannabe playwright Treplieff in Chekhov's *The Seagull* is forever harping on about 'forms'. He chides his mother's lover – the successful but mediocre novelist Trigorin – with tirades about form; the need for new ones in theatre and literature; his desire to run from outmoded ones 'like Maupassant from the Eiffel Tower'. We might also use the word, though again vaguely, when heaping praise. 'He reinvented the form,' we say, 'broke the mould.' But come the time of real artistic revolutions, it's a bashful creature.

Each time a new stylistic mode introduces itself, the genre it arrives in goes slightly further into isolation. Whatever the discipline, modernisations take their art in one direction, outwards. The whole corpus of art therefore expands, however complexly, like the creeping patterns of frost on a car roof. Consequently, with each new movement there's less common ground *between* the genres to enable artists to migrate.

The peculiar thing about such progressions is they actually win favour with the general reader through the pretence of doing the opposite. Instead of creating new forms and adding to the overall technical palette of future artists, they claim to be *shedding* form. Consider the recent attempt in filmmaking to absorb new low-budget filmmaking technology into a philosophy. Led by the Copenhagen-based filmmakers Lars Von Trier and Thomas Vinterberg, the Dogme 95 movement called for a 'Vow of Chastity' from its members: films should be shot on location with hand-held cameras, dispensing with lighting, props, and soundtrack; they should be set in the here and now, use improvisation and be directorially un-credited. Such strictures were explained as a reaction against the post-60s bourgeois 'myth of the auteur' in cinema, in pursuit of a democratisation of filmmaking. Yet Dogme's constant reference to the 'cosmetics' of conventional cinema implies that what you get with Dogme films is somehow a more stripped down, more naked realism.

The result was some very shaky, very grainy, very imaginative films. There was nothing 'realer' about them, nor were they any more transparent in their technique. For what *is* camera wobble if not an added layer of style? What is this sense of character involvement at the level of film production, if not another filter to watch the film *through*?

Bertolt Brecht made much the same claim when he removed the props and backdrops from the productions of some of his plays, exposing the ropes and scaffolding of the theatre house, the graffiti on the back wall. Likewise Brendan Behan when he sat in the stalls at his plays, shouting instructions to the actors, even complementing the author. 'This is a play here,' they were telling us, unavoidably, just as the camera wobble in Dogme films reminds us, like we need reminding, 'This is a film here'. In both cases the new style implies a greater honesty, as if it's taking some of the 'ifice' out of 'artifice', as if confessing its deception, baring its soul. But at what point does saying 'This is a film/play here' ever make it any *less* of a film/play here? Stripped stages and dodgy camerawork succeed in making us sneer at the previous generation's excesses - the pretence of costume, the conceit of high budgets - but the pretence or conceit of having a group of actors playing roles never alters a jot.

What is being exposed when Modernism strikes isn't the subject ever, or the truth, but the apparatus itself. Forms can only expose other forms, and the new ones seem transparent only by highlighting the opaqueness of the old. Yet both are still there. Nothing is replaced because the honesty of the new depends on the dishonesty of the old remaining implicit. To pursue the clothing metaphor, it's like a fashion designer bringing out a line in inside-out, seams-on-the-outside clothes - to escape the pretence of last year's smooth, figure hugging look. 'This isn't skin here,' it says, as if it needed to.

In Modernist poetry, examples of this were e. e. cummings' removal of capitals, or better still Elizabeth Daryush and Marianne Moore's simultaneous invention of Syllabics. The English ear doesn't count syllables, of course, only stresses, so asking the language to behave suddenly like it was actually French or Latin, is effectively to dress it up in purposefully unfunctional clothing. If poetry couldn't avoid the issue of line-lengths, why not make it deliberately arbitrary, Syllabics say, and thus exposed. Syllabics put the pipework on the outside of a poem; it makes a Pompidou Centre out of it.

In short fiction, 'form' hasn't accumulated with quite the same intensity. The lack of attention to it at the microscopic, syllabic level has rather allowed its writers to look at the process more holistically.

One thing all writers agree on is that good literature cannot be paraphrased. A work of literature has to be, by necessity, exactly as long as it is. The short story writer Flannery O'Connor pursued this belief by distinguishing between what she called 'abstract meaning' and 'experienced meaning' – the latter being the key to what literature does, and the reason why writers always answer the question 'What does it mean?' with an obstinate 'Go and read it'. Experienced meaning is untranslatable, O'Connor insists, it is solid and insoluble, being *what it is*. The reader attains it only by experiencing the art (and sometimes not even then), the artist only through an exact commixture of the explicable and the inexplicable. By contrast, *abstract* meaning is without physical property and can thus flit from one critic's wording to another's.

This provided O'Connor with her first definition of the short story. In her posthumously collected essays, *Mystery and Manners* (1972), she argues that a short story is first and foremost 'a complete dramatic event'. 'A story that is any good can't be reduced, it can only be expanded. A story is good when you continue to see more and more of it, and when it continues to escape you. In fiction two and two is always more than four.'

I'd argue this is no good as a distinction of short fiction because it could, or perhaps should, be applied to all the arts. The problem with certain visual arts, you might say, is that they take O'Connor's 'experienced meaning' as a given – ticked off by the sheer physical experience of looking at an artwork. What they confuse, the argument might go, is 'experienced meaning' with just plain experience – the meaning having departed for the abstract issues of the exhibition notes.

I'm joking of course.

What O'Connor provides with her two little phrases is a twin-head hammer to batter through all of the above. The picture we've drawn of genres piling on form with every development, and in doing so radiating further and further apart… is nonsense. Movements like Modernism neither add nor strip away form because both notions are founded on the misconception that form is in some way a layer and that subject or truth resides beneath it. Think of O'Connor's little phrase, 'experienced meaning'. Experience is both a mass and count noun. It can be atomic or continuous, unlike a work of art or a chosen form, which come as complete packages. By saying that, in art, meaning reaches us atom by atom *with* the experience, O'Connor is saving us from ever mistaking one as macroscopically clad in the other. Hence, once the initial shock of a movement's new experiences subsides, there's no reason why both traditional and modish experiences can't begin to blend into one - in good art seamlessly.

Such seamlessness is only recent in poetry. For decades making a choice constituted an act of allegiance to one or other of the backlashes or counter-backlashes to Modernism. Until only the last couple of decades that choice was binding in a poets' career. It bolted down their interpretation of poetry and bound them to continuing the fight, staying on the battlefield, and thus remaining at all times a poet. Free versifiers, even those who played with paragraph-long 'lines' like Geoffrey Hill, would have felt as disinclined to try their hand at fiction as the formalists, for the war against regularity (i.e. for *subtler* rhythms) required a faith in the principle of form *in general* – just as much as the defence of regularity did.

Now, at last, poets are beginning to let their hair down, and in experiments like this one, they can begin to start listening again to other genres. As they do so, they should bear in mind some of the *real* differences between verse and short fiction. 'I have decided,' O'Connor writes in a later attempt to define the short story, 'it is probably some action, some gesture of the character that is unlike any other in the story... both totally right and totally unexpected... both in character and beyond character.' For O'Connor, it is a fundamental (possibly Christian) notion of the mystery of personality, which centres any short story and sets the form apart; the way that for poets it is, by and large, the mystery of language.

All of the stories gathered here have some sense of this mystery. Some find it in the traditional climax: the small, private defiance of Joe Sheerin's put-upon-husband in 'The Man Who Moved Boulders'; the closing cruelty in Sinéad Morrissey's childhood recollection. These are utterly unpredictable acts. Other stories discover it earlier on, or in the set-up. For Gerard Woodward's Colin, it's the fact that anyone *can* make such a basic, biological category error. For Cliff Yates' riff on the Invisible Man scenario, it's the human reality that things really would carry on as normal.

Elsewhere, the mystery O'Connor speaks of comes in less obvious guises. The esteemed writer in Sean O'Brien's 'I Cannot Cross

Over' is haunted continuously by what he isn't, rather than the mystery of what he is. Likewise in Matthew Francis' 'Singing a Man Death', the denouement mirrors what O'Connor calls a character's 'moment of Grace' - in the negative.

These are all still poets, though, and much of the 'mystery' derives not from the characters but the imagery: the quivering, thawing water at the end of Gerard Woodward's story; the view of the night sky, from underneath a railway arch halfway through David Constantine's 'Under the Dam'; or countless other moments I've had the editor's honour of sharing first. Such passages are unadulterated poetry, whichever way you look at them.

No doubt some of these writers' mysteries will prove too localised to carry an entire short story, and may paradoxically best suit the wider landscape of a novel. Inevitably some of these pieces will also, at their heart, be poems. The titular hook and narrative irony of Steven Blyth's story closely resemble the ropes and leavers of his narrative-driven poetry. The delicious ticking over of Joanne Limburg's 'Best for Value, Best for Choice' is essentially a poetic structure, though perfectly executed here in prose. There is always the chance that other attempts will fail altogether, proving neither prose poems nor short stories, but rather dramatised rhetoric or personified discourse. All things considered, we'd venture that the strike rate is pretty high.

Short stories are never going to be poems. The genres will never regroup nor crash back into each other in some temporal rewind. The reason is we *read* prose, we *listen* (albeit internally) to poetry. As such, the prose world is forever, and not coincidentally, prosaic. It is dull, flat, quotidian. The prose writer has to go about actively searching for O'Connor's mystery, without evidence but with faith that it's there. The poet's universe, by contrast, is replete with the mystery - the mystery of music and of listening. In fact it's sodden with the stuff. Mystery is something poets should actively avoid. As Marianne Moore writes: when otherwise pleasant phenomena are 'fashioned/ into that which is unknowable,/ we are not entertained…'

As for what happens when you hyphenate the enigmatic with the mundane… that's a mystery.

The Blood-Blister

John Latham

Uncle Harry always wanted to give birth to a child. That's why, at eighty-eight, he's slipped an egg into the dry warmth of his buttocks, forcing him to tilt a little to one side on the stool on which he sits waiting for Professor Abdus Salam to make his next move in their chess-game.

I wanted it, too, when I was a child. But now I'm sixty, and the child I might give birth to is as old as I am. In fact, it's older than I am, as old as my mother, recently dead, who's here at my party, carrying her teapot with the broken spout from guest to guest. Older than her, perhaps, older even than her mother who abandoned her.

Are you ready for the journey, child-o'-mine? This will be no smooth transition, you'll come out in bits and pieces, and though the doctors will attempt a patching job, I have little hope of their success.

Mrs Campion is strumming on her harp with woollen strings. Alex is crawling through a nest of bracken. Wendy Eva, with no mouth or eyes, has upturned the pale oval of her face towards the sky. Ernest is on one knee in torrential rain, looking for Germany. Lionel scarcely crackles as he burns.

And as for you, my golden girl, I can't find you in the fog, but from time to time I hear you breathe.

★★★★★

The trial, at the far end of the corridor, is reaching its conclusion.

"Not guilty," rules Mr Maddock.

He thumps his gavel onto the bench in front of him, on which Mrs Capper, passing through a few minutes earlier, has left a paper bag containing the set of best false teeth she shares with Miss Bickerstaff, her sister, thinking they are the humbugs she's bought specially from Alick's, a gift to Mr Maddock who, seventy years ago, winked at her from the boys side of the room, in scripture, since when she's been trying to pluck up the courage to respond.

The teeth crack, splinter, fly in all directions. One fragment swoops, glinting, into the flames licking round Lionel's forehead, causing Miss Atkins to see an arrow from God, a sign from the Almighty that she would not be damned for looking at the burning man's nakedness, and so she does, secretly biting her dry old lips as she watches the play of dancing light around his testicles.

Another fragment lands on Uncle Harry's knee, as he sits waiting for Professor Abdus Salam's next move. He lifts it up, inspects it, looks perturbed.

"I'm falling to bloody pieces," he grunts.

He pushes it swiftly into his mouth, moving it around with his thumb until he finds a cavity into which it seems to fit.

A third fragment pings against an unplucked string of Mrs Campion's harp, producing a sound that only Ernest and Wendy Eva can hear, its pitch precisely that of the sorrow in Wendy's missing eyes, causing tears to well out of her forehead, and Ernest to remember his father's shoulders more clearly than ever before.

A fourth piece trips the mechanism that controls the scroll that is Mr Campion, unpeeled from the steam-roller that squashed him, causing him to wind up suddenly and Miss Atkins, distracted from the burning bush, to wonder who it is who's been called so peremptorily into the presence of the Lord.

"I appeal against the verdigris," screams Aunt Lil.

"Appeal sustained," shouts Shelley, who's taken Mr Maddock's chair.

He turns to Ernest, who's trying to will Wendy to stop crying.

"I find you guilty of giving a full bottle of lemonade to a girl with no mouth...."

"Bite his balls off," yells Mr Trolley.

"That's what makes the turnips grow," states Mr Maddock.

".....and I sentence you to be stitched inside the blood-blister on Robert Bratbury's lip."

"But I won't be able to see Germany," wails Ernest.

"I'll come with you," I mouth to him.

No-one else hears me, but Ernest looks pleased.

★★★★★

The entrance is through a curtain of purple flesh on the side of the blister facing the chaos that is Robert's mouth, which is why

I never spotted it before.

Before we enter I turn round and peer towards his throat's deep well, from which a warm breeze issues, laden with the fragrances of this week's meals. In the foreground is a drunken graveyard, his teeth, mostly listing, many chipped or black, some missing, some sunk so deep only their tops can be discerned, wedged in the pink and scarlet billows that enfold them. Drops fall randomly from his upper molars, flick against the lower ones or are sponged up by his tongue, which seems too large for his mouth, so that its every movement presses against the walls, threatens to block the air-flow to his lungs.

The blood-blister has fascinated and frightened me since the day I met him, my first day at junior school, two weeks into term because I'd been off sick with mumps, and this boy in the playground, giving Joyce Farrington's pale white arm a Chinese burn, ignoring her pleas and then her tears, had this great bruised thing wobbling on his lip, making him look indestructible and merciless, as indeed he was, twisting Joyce's flesh until Shelley rang the bell, leaving her with a crescent shaped weal whose origins she daren't explain when her mother noticed it at bed-time.

I think the emotional impact of the blister was heightened by the single thing I knew about Robert before I first saw him. Johnnie had called to see me a day or two before my return to school, and had told me about this boy from the tough part of our village, who had led a group of lads into the Victorian toilets at the edge of the school yard, whose smell I can still conjure fifty years after their demolition, and for a bet – from which he won three packets of chewing-gum and a matchbox full of earwigs – lowered the lavatory cover, squatted on it, and shat onto it through a hole in his trousers a turd which kept on coming throughout the first half of the playtime, rotating his buttocks so that it coiled into a perfect pyramid, glistening, steaming, enormous, flecked with green. Every boy in the school came to admire it, Marjorie Bickerstaff, too, but she was sick on Watty Hulse's foot.

Ernest's handcuffs had been removed, and we hold hands as we grope our way into the blood-blister. Once we're through the folds of flesh it opens out, becomes quite spacious, a basically spherical cavern illuminated with scarlet light, the origins of which I can't see, with beautiful stalagmites and slowly dripping stalactites, pulsing diaphrams, pools of foam, wells of black liquid, presumably blood. The ground is firm and sticky to our feet.

The only word to describe what my Aunt Lil is sitting on is a throne, a throne made of weeping flesh. She's large, fatter than before she died, but she's dwarfed by its vast, suppurating pinkness, its billows and declivities, its curves so gentle that its overall effect is innocent, benign. Not so Aunt Lil, her sequin-studded dress too young for her, too short for her, so that as Ernest and I stand in front of the dias on which the throne is mounted our heads are at the level of her knees, which are apart, I feel the draw of that dark region in which all I can perceive are albino thighs, varicosed and flabby, straps connecting her corsets to silk stockings, her knickers' baggy purple, and the shadow of a hungry creature that feeds on little boys and is hiding, waiting to pounce.

Did she know I was watching her, when I was little, hiding in the safe warmth of the airing cupboard, peering through the slats, while she sat on the stool of my mother's dressing table, turned away from the mirror, towards me, legs apart as now, skirt-line almost to her waist, squeezing a livid pimple on her thigh, crooking her finger underneath the black strap, stretching it then letting go, the smack of the elastic making me shudder, clutch the water-pipes to save me from her suction, she then turning to the mirror, applying thick lip-stick, kissing her white handkerchief, spitting on it, making some adjustment to her face, kissing the handkerchief again; and so on until she was ready, she'd stand up, snap her thighs again, smooth her rumpled skirt and go downstairs. I'd sneak out of the cupboard, sick with stomach ache, and sometime that evening steal the handkerchief from her handbag, take it upstairs with me, count the ghost-kisses she'd pressed onto it, work out the sequence of diminishing age and faintness, remember how the cambric clung to the underbelly of her lips as she pulled it away and I – not wanting to be pulled away – wound my arms tighter round the pipes.

Did you know, Aunt Lil, that I was watching you? That the stomach-ache that came as I peered at you through the slats has recurred throughout my life whenever I've felt the pull of purple places. That as I stand before you, Ernest's hand in mine, in the scarlet light of Robert Bratbury's blood-blister, I hate you and at last I'm understanding why.

"I was expecting you, our Jack," she says.

Her smile was perhaps meant to be ingratiating, but it looks like a smirk to me. I bridle, feel accused, defensive.

"I'm only here to keep Ernest company."

"Pah! Don't tell fibs. You've always told fibs. You're here because this is where your home is."

"I've never been inside a blood-blister in all my life."

"If you were small again I'd pull your trousers down and smack your arse until you told the bloody truth."

"What is the bloody truth?"

"The truth you won't face up to is that you've lived your whole life inside a blood-blister you've created yourself."

"I hate you, Aunt Lil."

To my surprise a wave of pain washes over her face. She bites her lip, and when she speaks again two of her teeth are covered in lipstick.

"I know you do, lad. It makes me sad, both for you and for me, and I want to talk to you about it."

She claps her hands.

"But all this is nowt to do with you, Ernest. Be off with you. Take that passage."

She points to a small cleft in the wall.

"Go down there, lad. It's too small to stand or crawl in, you'll have to wriggle on your stomach. But if you keep on past the drunken drums, you'll find him."

"My father?"

Ernest's face is ecstatic.

"Of course. Who else have you been searching for all your life?"

"I love you, ma'am," says Ernest.

"Pah! Now, don't raise your hopes too much. He's not in good shape. And don't look at him too hard or he'll dissolve."

"No. I won't. Can I go now?"

She nods. Ernest runs towards the tunnel, slips onto his face and his momentum propels him, sliding fast, through the small cleft in the flesh, out of sight.

"I bet the silly bugger gets lost," she says.

She says it affectionately, whereas most people tend to sneer at Ernest. I'd already softened towards her when I saw her pain, and now I feel sorry for hurting her.

"I don't really hate you, Aunt Lil."

She pulls a rather rueful face.

"I know you don't, lad. It's not hatred you feel for me. It's fear. With perhaps a touch of contempt because of my ignorance and uncouthness. Right?"

I start to deny it, but she sweeps my words away with an impatient flourish of her arm.

"Be honest. There's no point in lying when you're in a blood-blister."

"I suppose I do feel something like that."

"Good. Now we can start."

She beckons to me.

"Climb up here. Sit on my lap."

Nervous though I am, I obey her. Her lap is capacious and comfortable. Her breasts, most of which I can see, are freckled and smell of sweat. Her lipstick is so thick I could scrape it off with a knife to make a healthy sandwich. My legs dangle into the space between her thighs. She slips off my shoes and tosses them onto the floor.

"Let's snuggle for a minute before we talk," she says.

I don't want to, but I let it happen.

She folds me in, and I'm drowning in a feast of smells that were faintly present before, but are now pouring from every part of her. I turn my head to find fresh air, but I'm enveloped by her, I'm losing my identity. I try to struggle free, but the weight of her flesh has made me powerless. I start to gasp for air.

Her voice sounds as if it has percolated through a thousand blankets.

"Are you frightened, lad?"

I manage to nod, and her strong arms lift me out of her lap onto an arm of the throne, where the air is fresh, and I begin to recover.

"It's that fear of dark, moist places I want to talk to you about."

"Go on."

"It's not your fear. It's your mother's. It's not even hers originally. It belonged to her grandparents, who brought her up, who were terrified that she'd turn out bad, like her mother, get pregnant out of wedlock, so they fed her shame and fear of doing wrong, of having anything to do with dark, moist places; and she gave it to you in her milk.

I didn't understand this when I was alive. I thought she was prissy and that you were a little pervert, sitting in that cupboard spying on me, drooling through the slats. I couldn't tell her what you were doing, she'd have been destroyed, and I was damned if I was going to alter my life because of your sweaty palms. So I decided it was your problem, that you'd either grow out of it or you wouldn't.

You need to plunge in, Jack. Step out of your clothes, out of your skin, step outside yourself, jump off, and I bet you'll find that you can fly."

Oh, Alex! Where are you? I want to fly with you.

"I'll need someone to push me, Aunt Lil."

"Nah! Better if you do it yourself. Just close your eyes and let go. Chances are you'll find your wings before you hit the ground."

"And if I don't?"

"You'll get bruised. Break a bone or two. Mebbe your neck."

I know she's right. I've spent sixty years trying so hard not to break my neck, that I haven't found the time to learn to breathe.

"How do I do it, Aunt Lil?"

"Don't play games with me, lad. Tha knowst. Get on with it. Let go of the water-pipes."

And so, scared, naked, in scarlet light, in a dripping, sweet-smelling cavern in the blood-blister on Robert Bratbury's lower lip, I plunge headfirst into voluminous darkness smelling of sweat and stale perfume, where the air I breathe sends my senses reeling, and I am glad, where the skin of the dead woman I slither over is smooth and coarse and warty, and I am glad, where hair like brambles scuffs my cheek, clogs my mouth, and I am glad, where the ground throbs heartbeats and its moisture sucks on me, and I am glad, where I'm drawn into a torrid space in which I'm sucked away, and there is nothing left. And I am glad.

★★★★★

When I wake up Aunt Lil's not there, the throne looming above me as I lie curled on the floor is empty. I wonder if I've been dreaming, but then I see my clothes, neatly folded, by my head.

I dress slowly, not wanting to think, but rather to file all these experiences for examination when I'm calmer, and not in the middle of an adventure.

I remember Ernest, worry that he's lost, as Aunt Lil predicted, decide to try to find him. I crawl across the floor to the cleft into which he disappeared. It is roughly vertical, only about a foot high, so I have to lie on my stomach and wriggle in. Once through I find the floor slopes downwards, quite steeply, and since it's also slippery I can slither easily, somewhat like sledging in slow motion.

Like sledging at night, no moon, just a faint glow from the stars which here, deep in Robert's blood-blister, is vermilion, its source invisible and far away, as if the light had trickled through translucent jelly. It shows me nothing, for there is nothing to see, the flesh I'm sliding through being as featureless as jelly, parting easily at the pressure of my forehead, closing easily over the space my feet have just moved through.

But the light is important, because it signals the existence of some other world outside my body. At one stage it illuminates some growths that look like listing cylinders, and which I take to be the drunken drums. The light enables me to know, in some strange sense at least, where I am travelling.

So I'm filled with fear when the glow disappears, not suddenly but insidiously, so that for a while I can fool myself that its luminosity hasn't diminished; until I have to accept that it has slipped away to zero.

I'm slipping away too, perhaps to zero, nothingness, extinction, perhaps to some new stage on my journey. It helps me curb my panic that there's absolutely nothing I can do. I think the slope has become steeper, since I'm sliding readily, there's no way I can stop, let alone go back. I have to ride this flow, go with it wherever it will take me.

Then I realise that I'm enjoying myself. I'm quivering. I feel as if all my senses are engaged. Yet I hear nothing, I see nothing, I smell nothing, I taste nothing, and though I'm forging through warm jelly, it's formless, so I'm touching nothing, either. The flesh surrounding me is at body temperature, so there's neither hot nor cold. And so it seems to me that perhaps the most profound experience comes from sensory deprivation, not surfeit. That only when all associations with one's body have been lost, can the body find that stillness in its centre that enables it to totally embrace itself, its world.

Those are my feelings, formulated but at the time wordless, and I revel in them as I glide. This happiness is perfect. I need no-one else in order to achieve it.

But the experience is too profound, too pleasurable for me to bear for long. So I ease out of it, slowly, bringing my conscious mind into action, wondering if anyone, in the whole of history, has ever before found true enlightenment while journeying through a blood-blister. I wonder if Robert knows I'm here, if the blister has grown or been excised, if he's dead, if they masked it somehow as he lay in his coffin, to make him look beautiful, which he never did in life, if he remembers – and if so still feels proud of – that prodigious turd that caused Marjorie, who had no soul, to be spontaneously sick on Watty's shoe.

And so I move back to a more accustomed state of mind, in which I feel flawed and comfortable, and I'm grinning as the sledge levels off, comes to a halt in a small gallery, in which there is light, and I can see Ernest sitting with his father.

★★★★★

Ernest's father is horizontal, face down, suspended about four feet from the ground, arms and legs enmeshed in the silk cords of his parachute, which is dangling from something, I presume a tree, out of sight in the darkness above him. He is wearing a khaki battle-dress festooned with medals, all of which are bleeding. His body is swinging gently to and fro. Ernest is sitting directly underneath him on a fallen log, looking up at him, a rapt expression on his face. I sneak up, sit beside him. Ernest acknowledges me without removing his gaze from his father.

Although his father's eyes are open, they don't appear to register anything, and the conversation between Ernest and myself takes place in whispers, so as not to wake him.

'Is this your father?'

'Oh, yes.'

Ernest is biting his lip with joy and excitement.

'He doesn't look like the photograph.'

'That's because he's upside-down.'

'Has he spoken to you?'

'Oh, yes.'

'What did he say?'

'There weren't any words. Words get in the way when you're speaking to someone you love who you haven't seen forever.'

Ernest is crying now, silently, but the joy in his face is unabated. I feel abashed.

'Have you touched him, Ernest?'

Ernest nods.

'Where?'

'He let me touch his bullet-hole.'

'Show me.'

'I don't think he'd like me to.'

'I only want to see it. C'mon, Ernest.'

Ernest slowly stretches out his arm, points to a black circle just below the soldier's Adam's apple. I feel excited. My first bullet-wound. I have to touch it.

Ernest knows what I am feeling, doesn't try to stop me as I reach upwards, slide my middle finger all the way into the neat hole in his father's throat. It feels dry, almost powdery, and I'm disappointed. I try to slide it out but the hole has contracted, it locks around my finger and all I achieve as, panic rising, I tug harder and harder is making him jump up and down on his strings, like a puppet who's in control of me.

I look at his face, and whereas before it had seemed distant, dreamlike, now it seems to be leering at me.

'He won't leave go, Ernest!'

'Tell him you're sorry.'

"Sorry for what?'

'Sorry for making him remember.'

'I'm sorry, Mister,' I blurt out.

The grip relaxes. I remove my finger. His face is dream-like again.

It takes me a while to calm down. Then I examine my finger. It looks the same as before. I lick it. It tastes as usual. I hold it to my nose. It smells of gunpowder. It was worth it, after all.

'Did he hold on to your finger, Ernest?'

'I didn't put my finger in his bullet-hole. I touched it with my eyes.'

We sit quietly, his father gyrating gently above us, even though there's no wind.

I feel a splash of wetness on my head, then another, then a slow patter of drops. I look up. Ernest's father is dissolving, uniformly, all over his body, so that he grows pale and then transparent but remains recognisable. Drops are now falling steadily on me, but though I feel their wetness when they land, my clothes and skin are still dry.

I look at Ernest. His head is thrown back, unwounded throat exposed to his father above him. His mouth is open and he is drinking drops that fall into it. He is drinking his father.

I can't watch anymore. I put my head between my knees, close my eyes, doze a little.

When I wake Ernest's father has disappeared. Just his battle-dress remains, limp, swinging slightly. His medals have stopped bleeding.

'Time to go,' Ernest says.

He looks light and happy.

He takes my hand as we wander out of the gallery into the next. I lift my other hand to my face, sniff my middle finger. It still smells of gunpowder.

—

The Little Bomb

Anne Stevenson

The little bomb lay between them on the table where, sitting apart from the guests, they were making sandwiches and arranging them on a white oval platter with a rim of sailing boats, red, white and blue. A clipper ship at the centre of the platter was disappearing under the sandwiches, so that the concentration needed to arrange them - smoked salmon, ham and pickle on rye, cream cheese and cress - drew the two of them together, but she was still not sure she knew him well enough to ask about the bomb. A memento from the Second War, certainly, and she hoped fervently it had been the last big war, but she understood vaguely that it was there, too, for her protection, a present from the airlines.

The summer party was already in full swing. Gathered into groups that now and then released peals of silvery laughter, the women wore floating chiffons, the men, white linen suits and straw boaters. An old fashioned English garden party. Margaret, Bruce's mother, was ladling out Pims from the fruity depths of a punch bowl, a string quartet was silently in action on the terrace, the sun was laying familiar, bushy shadows on the lawn. As for the bomb, it looked like a toy. Its shiny metal casing - was it tinfoil? - pointed upward from a leaden base, painted orange. The whole of it was no bigger than her forearm, nothing to be afraid of, but now she was alone with it — he must be passing around the sandwiches — she noticed a flame flickering in a sort of cage, as if for lift off. If only she knew something about time bombs, or was it a rocket? Now it was making little grinding noises, like a flint lighter. What should she do? She must keep calm, not raise the alarm, but act. Surprisingly, it wasn't heavy at all. Grasping it, holding it out well away from her filmy white dress, she set off, running across the stony pasture for the lake. The obvious place to put out a bomb was the lake, though the path was much rougher than she remembered. And the fire in the little bomb was spreading. She would have to drop it, wherever she was, and hope to escape before it exploded. There, she was away and scrambling up a stony path in the cliff face...

★

Where did the sun come from? A June morning. Light already. Squinting at the alarm clock on her bedside locker, she saw that it was only a quarter to six. There was time to finish the dream if she could get back into it. Shutting her eyes, she looked for the path again, and for the lake, but all that remained was the faintly erotic spell of the scene that should have been a nightmare but wasn't. None of the dreams that flowed into and enlivened her nights, now that her days were spent in identical torpor, were nightmares. Why? Shouldn't she be scared to death of dying? The young man who had been helping her - who was he? Bruce? Not the Bruce she had married, or maybe, yes, it might have been - from a long time ago, the slender athlete who had somehow disappeared when he became the stout, balding professor who had addressed her fondly, 'yes, dear' or 'no, dear' - every day of her life for over sixty years. Was this Bruce at twenty-one, twenty-five? Was the party their wedding party?

No, it was earlier than that. In New Haven. Or Cape Cod, well before the war when the Scottish cousin - no relation, really, because he'd been grandmother Edith's younger sister's stepson - in queer-looking flannel shorts and socks, a blond mop of hair. God, how that naughty, devil-may-care air of superior daring had captured her heart at - had she been nine? Whatever. They had done everything together, and it went without saying that he always did everything better than she did. Climbing the ash tree, playing 'rugger' with a beech ball, playing cricket with a baseball bat, playing checkers, except that he called them draughts.

The swimming, though, was the thing! What a swimmer and diver he'd been! At the pool, there he was climbing to the very highest level of the diving board, waving from a terrifying distance, now balancing straight as a pole at the edge. Steady, steady, now a leap into the air, doubled like a dolphin, and now the arrow of his body plunged into the turquoise water with scarcely a splash.

Then or later? Cape Cod. Supper time. They had trooped into the kitchen, starving after a day at the beach. A large bowl of sugared blueberries lay on the counter, and she had volunteered to divide them into equal portions. Bruce looked about fifteen. So she must have been thirteen, old enough, anyway, to ache with desire for his approval. But of course she was making a fool of herself, spooning the berries absently into the glass dishes when Bruce, as always, assumed control. Back into the bowl went the dark blue berries, and now she was helping him count them, dropping them, one by one, to make absolutely equal portions. Equality, an equal distribution of the goods of life. And there had been goods. There had been assets and successes. Bruce had counted them, one by one, and dropped them, carefully measured, into every year of their prosperous life together, so there was nothing you could blame him for, he couldn't be blamed for not being there any more.

★

Now I won't get back into the dream, she thought, however much I hug it, the pain is too severe. The pressure on my bladder, my ridiculous, self-willed bladder, so annoyingly first person singular, possessive pronoun, my. If I could turn over, no, don't have the strength, have to ring. Damn, Esther's on duty, unpleasant girl – why did she choose to be a nurse if she doesn't like sick people. Or maybe it's just old people she hates. Can't blame her. I used to avoid the smelly old things like the plague, and now I'm old, I want to avoid myself? Well, there's a truth worth telling. Esther is prettier than Sue. She wants to be out and about and in bed with the boys, but the young doctors won't look at her. They won't look at Sue, either, though they should. I'll try to hold out for Sue, so gentle with her hands, that girl, a real gift for caring. They should look at her soul, not her face. She must want a family. I was probably more like Esther, conspicuous for a running sore of discontent. Sue deserves someone like Bruce who will give her kids. When does she come on duty, seven-thirty? I'll wait. Think about the young man at the party who could have been Bruce. Think of the girl counting blueberries for him, who once was me. Think about what she was hoping to do, the actress she was going to become, the novels she was going to write. Think of Miss Morris telling her how talented she was, and Doug Rosen accusing her of burying her talent when she married. Deaf old Dr. Lemon, one Sunday, preaching on the parable of the talents, me sitting there in the third pew from the front, crazy about a young man in the choir whose name I never did learn. He would be old now, older than me, must be dead, and never will I meet him or know what he did with his life. Who *was* that young man in the dream? Not Bruce. I so wanted him to take me in his arms, press me to him entirely, carry me away, and then the little bomb got between us.

Now, I'm going to tell myself something very odd. When I feel pain, I feel it in myself. I am all me when I'm sad and miserable, and it's not pleasant. Not nice at all. But when I think, I think 'her', and when I dream, I dream 'her'... and they are neither of them me now. They may be the same person, I'm not sure. Anyway, there is definitely a me-Helena. I know I'm an old lady called Mrs. Robert Bruce Dewar, but the other me, the her, is still Helena Burnside. Now, Mrs. Robert Bruce Dewar, as anybody might have read in the obituary pages, survives her husband, Commander R.B. Dewar, war-hero, specialist in Naval tactics, adviser to the Labour Government, etcetera, etcetera. A very respectable woman, Mrs. Dewar, by birth American, mother of four, grandmother of nine, former chairman of heaven knows how many global charities and local worthy causes. Though, unfortunately, disabled by old age, disposed of in the nicest possible home for the elderly by her dear children, none of whom have time or inclination to care for her in their own homes. Nor could they. 'Mrs. Dewar, approaching ninety, suffers from severe osteoporosis and crumbling vertebrae.' Contrary to expectations, however, this awful physical helplessness has secretly undermined my famous will power, on which, like a bank account, I must have drawn so extravagantly every day, week, month and year of my married life that now it's empty. Nothing in it at all. Sixty, seventy years spent and wasted, with nothing to show for them, not even reliable memories. Not even reliable affections. No wonder my children can't be doing with me. I can't be doing with them, and that's the truth. I hardly remember the names of my grandchildren. Nor my great-grandchildren. Heavens!

★

But the strangest thing is – and now that my bladder has decided to relieve me of that ghastly pressure, I have an interval to think about it – the strangest thing is that my other life seems to be happening, the life I might have led had I resisted Bruce and not been so frightened of British manners and at the same time so determined to brave out the war and be one of his crowd. How noble I felt, working through the war in London, refusing to run away to the States with the twins. And now something is happening – maybe not to me, but to her – in dreams that give her a choice again. Maybe she is being given another chance. That's why it's so important to identify him – that young man. Having passed the sandwiches, he would have returned to her with full glasses of Pims or champagne, they would have drained them laughingly together. Then as night closed around them and the guests departed or disappeared indoors, 'he quietly took her hand in his. Both fell silent. Their eyes met, and then their lips, she felt his erection on her thigh through her filmy dress...'

★

'Mrs. Dewar! You're dripping. You can't have slept through all this!

Why didn't you ring? You knew I was here. My God, what a state you're in! This is the last straw! We're going to have to insist that you wear a dressing at night. Now I'll have to put you in your chair while I change the sheets, and you know what that means. I have to go all the way down to the basement for Mr. Burns because I'm not allowed to lift you myself. You are the *limit*, Mrs. Dewar, the absolute *limit!* Here's your tea.'

'He embraced her,' said Helena Burnside, 'She fell into his arms. Or would have if there hadn't been a bomb on the table which needed to be disposed of.'

'What on earth are you talking about?' Esther was on her knees, mopping the floor with a cloth.

'I wasn't on earth. At least, not this earth. I was happy. There are other planets, other times.' Crossly, she shook off her trance. 'You don't have to clean up, Esther. I was waiting for Sue. I don't want you. I don't like you.'

'I don't like you much either,' said Esther, making for the basin with the sopping cloth,' but we have to face reality, don't we? Look, I'm sorry. I'm going to wash my hands and then I'm going down for Mr. Burns. It's not seven yet. Sue won't be here 'till after breakfast. So please, Mrs. Dewar, try to cooperate. Do you want the radio on, or the TV? Shall I sit you up for your tea?'

'No, thank you. I only want my life back, my nice new life. The life I should have had and deserve to have, except that people like you keep taking it away from me!'

'What? Mrs. Dewar, you're crazy as a coot, you know that?'

'William,' said Helena Burnside. 'Henry, not Bruce.' But she wouldn't let any of her suitors see her in this temporary state of degradation. She would arrange to follow Harry de Caux to Venice. He would be playing the violin in Vivaldi's white, classical church, – what was the name of it? – and there she would surprise him after the concert. Imagine it, a moonlit summer night, the city a miracle of water and misty twilight. First they would drink gallons of that lovely Prosecco at Florio's in the Piazza, and then they would hire a gondola. The Lagoon would be mass of starry, floating lights, and smells of caulking tar and brine would be mingled with rare perfumes, honeysuckle, roses. He would be playing his Amati violin for her alone, the concerto by Mendelssohn, the gondolier listening, amazed; and afterward the gondolier would serenade them as they lay, body to body, stretched out under a canopy of galaxies. Santa Lucia. The music floated through her head.

But first of all she had to dispose of the little bomb wrapped in silver foil that lay on the carpet between them, a fire in its flint-like base. Quick. Henry mustn't see. Grab it, toss it into the Lagoon! And now in her hand, it burst into flame as the tea leapt from the cup onto the counterpane, scalding the rucked, transparent skin of her knuckles and the liver spots on the loose casing that hung like a badly furled sail from the crumbling bone of her forearm.

The Day I Brought Water

Sinéad Morrissey

It's nearly night-time and it's summer so the sky is red and animal clouds are in it and moving quickly. Summer means fires on the estate, houses and mattresses and cardboard boxes. I'll find them on my way home through the back path, the whole sky full of smoke and boys running and when I go inside for my tea I'll talk about the new fire. Summer means Mum sunbathing out where the bins are, and earwigs all over our house, in key holes and towels and beds, and the whole street skipping with one big rope singing On the Hillside Stands a Lady until bed-time. Parents coming out in twos and fours then to bring us in and the last one tying up the big orange rope and going away somewhere else because he's lonely.

Nearly bed-time now but I want to watch the news, all by myself, so I'm taking my TV that rolls ducks and boats and the Tower of London across the front of it to Row Row Row Your Boat Gently Down the Stream out to the playground in the middle of the back path. I am setting it on a wall and winding it up and sitting down on one of the round stone seats by the round stone table in the living-room part of the playground. The big girls with tall black shoes are nearby and some of them come over to me.

'Can I brush your hair?'

They are sitting round me in a circle and when they've finished I get up onto her lap and I brush hers. I remember her. She was the baby-sitter once and we watched a film with pirates and ships and canons and she laughed when Dad asked her if she wanted something to drink, laughed about it with her friend who came later, just before we went to bed. I'm telling her again how she looks like the woman I saw singing on TV.

'Who, Suzy Quatro?'

The girls are laughing. They are leaving together now, back down to the big road at the front. The sky is dark red now and the clouds are black. Boys are here in the part that's lower down than everywhere else. They're jumping on top of a blanket they've set on fire. They come up to the wall and knock over my TV. I'm running behind the wall to pick it up. I'm running home.

All sun. My brother leads us through bushes opposite our house and inside there's a space. Somebody's made chairs from planks and tyres and boxes and everyone is here already, the whole street, but we've missed it. It's stopping. So we come back out again. The bushes have the white squish berries all over them that kill you if you eat them. The whole street goes off together and leaves me and by brother and Richard. And now the three of us are far away from the back path and we've been walking for a long time. All sun. We see a dog with one eye.

Four men are lying on the grass under a bridge. We go over to where they are because they told us to. We're standing now, watching them. Mostly they do nothing but sometimes they spit. They're looking at their shoes. They only have vests on top and their faces are dirty.

'Will you do something for us?'

He's talking to my brother. They don't have shoes. They have big black boots, scraped away and white around the toes.

'What?'

He's not smiling. He's not promising things.

'Will you bring us something?'

Before they promised sweets and I went with them. I saw chocolate bars and chews and rock so I followed.

'What?'

He's not smiling. He's not giving us anything.

'Will you bring us water?'

The last time was nearly night-time and the sky was red. Red for ages and ages. Now it's after lunch. All sun. They lie and spit and stare up at us, into the sun.

'Water?'

Only one of them is talking. Every time he speaks the other three laugh and roll about, pulling at the grass.

'Yeah, water. Four big pint glasses of water. From your house. Is your house close? Can you get there and back in ten minutes?'

They're all sun-tanned. Their hair looks wet. They push their fingers through it and it stays where they leave it.

'No. It's further than that. About twenty minutes there and back.'

The one speaking has curly hair. It's light. The colour of skin in pictures.

'Twenty? Well lads, is it worth waitin' for?'

They laugh, far back in their mouths, as though they don't want to laugh at all.

'Jesus, Mick. Lay off it.'

He's looking up at my brother and his voice is a different voice now.

'We're thirsty. It's that simple. And we want four big pint glasses of water from your house, that's twenty minutes from here, there and back. So you and your two wee friends are going to go back to your house, get the glasses, fill them up with water, and bring them back to us, and you won't be any later than twenty minutes, and you won't spill any along the way. Ok?'

He's looking like someone else now. The tall one. The one with the I-Know voice.

'Do we get something?'

Sweets. Clove rock and lemon bons–bons and twirly whirly bars, on the top shelf of a wardrobe inside a bricked–up house.

'No you don't. You get to do us a *favour*, ok? Christ. Kids today. Runnin' fuckin' *businesses*.'

He spits. The others roll away. They lie with their feet towards us and they look up at the bridge. He's staring at my brother. And we've whirled around and we're running into the sun.

They didn't move but we're moving now. We're running. My brother shouts out that we're running to beat the clock. I don't know the bridge where the men are lying but now we're in a street. I can remember it. I asked a big girl to tie my laces here and she did, but into a hundred knots instead of just one and they wobbled in a pile on top of each foot. I had to put my feet up one by one onto Dad's lap when I got in and I watched them all come undone under his fingers. And we're into another street now and from here I know the way. We come to the big road my brother sang Finders Keepers on, the road I always think of when I hear a Why Did The Chicken joke, the road me and my Mum and my brother stuck our thumbs out on to try and make cars stop when we missed the bus from town, though no car did and we walked all the way along the road until we got home. The men didn't move but we're moving now, so quickly I'm tired and I want to stop running but my brother is shouting how we've got to keep running to beat the clock. Past the school and the shop where I got the pink pretend jewellery set for my birthday. I watched it behind the glass every day until my birthday came and then I bought it and when Dad lifted up the earrings they dropped and smashed on the bathroom floor, so he bought me a whole new pretend jewellery set in blue. Down the back path and past the playground with the low part in the middle and the living-room where the two boys saw me sitting on the wall watching the big girls smoke cigarettes in their tall black shoes. The men under the bridge didn't move but the two boys did and I followed them. I walked behind them and they turned round to me very often and smiled. They promised and I went but when we got there there was nothing there. And the one who was tall and thin told me the whole time where we were going, where it all was, the things they promised, and he turned around as he walked and smiled at me the whole time. And it was nearly night-time and the sky was red. Past the playground and down the back path to the big wooden gates showing the way to the houses. And I'm tired of running but my brother and Richard are home already, so I keep running, right up to the back doorstep, and then I stop. I'm sitting and putting my head on my arms on my knees. I'm breathing quickly. My heart is loud.

Glasses of water appear beside me in the biggest glasses we've got. They come one by one and stand beside my thighs. I watch them from under my elbow. They're dancing in the sun. The sunlight goes right inside the water, and dances there, and I watch it through the glass. I think about the big shadow my brother and Richard run into in the hall every time they come out of the kitchen, holding another glass of water in both hands. When the shadow goes out into the back yard and moves across it in a line until all the squares are covered, the sky's already gone red. I sat on the back step one time and watched it move across. It was straight, like a ruler, and slow, and the sky was red and the clouds not turning black, just redder and redder. I sat there for a long time. Mum and Dad standing in the yard had no shadows. They talked in low voices I couldn't understand and then they just stood and didn't speak. Just looking at the two boys who came and stood in our yard. The two boys stood by the gate and didn't speak. It was quiet and the sky was red and I could hear my heart, still banging inside me. I felt the metal edge of the step hurt the skin under my leg and I watched the big shadow move across the yard, slowly, like the tide coming in in straight lines instead of in waves.

❧

'I'll take two glasses 'cause I'm the biggest.'

My brother has stepped over the glasses into the yard. He's shaking my arm. I look up and the sun goes into my eyes. He's handing Richard one of the glasses. Richard is still standing behind me in the big shadow. One glass is still standing beside my thigh.

'Come on, you've got to take one too.'

I'm standing up and turning to the shadow and bending down to pick up the last tall glass with the sun inside its water. It's heavy and full. Richard steps past me into the sun and when I turn round we're standing together and all of the glasses are in our hands.

'We can't run this time, but we'll walk fast. If we run, it'll spill. Let's go.'

My brother and Richard are moving up and down in front of me, getting more and more ahead, like they're on boats. Their heads are down, looking at the glasses. Their heads go up quickly sometimes as they look at the path but then they go back down again. They're faster than me. I'm looking at them and I should be taking care over my glass, but I watch their heads instead and when they go round the corner at the end of the back path they're gone and I can't watch their heads anymore. The sky is blue. There's no-one else right to the end of the back path and I'm beginning to hear my heart. I pass the last of the tall wooden gates and now I'm at the playground. I can't see their heads but the sky is blue. The sky was red and no-one was there and I was in a wardrobe. I pushed against it and it opened and I ran to the window. Instead of glass there were boards and bars but part of the wood was broken. I saw so much red I thought new fires on the estate, new fires everywhere, and I was crying but nobody was there. I can't walk anymore because I can't see their heads so I'm putting my glass down on the ground. I'm sitting on the ground and bringing my knees up to my forehead. I put my hands around my knees because no-one is here. I watch the colours that come when I push my knees into my eyes.

Someone is touching my arm now. He touched my arm and when I turned round there was a boy standing in the room and he was carrying my trousers. He helped me to put them on, held them out and I stepped into them, one, two, that's a good girl, and he took my hand and we found the front door and we walked out together. He held my hand the whole time and we walked along a long street and in every front yard boys were playing. I saw the tall thin one right away and the other was bouncing a ball against a wall and he said No but I said Yes and then he kept holding my hand and he brought me down a hundred steps and at the bottom there was the back path. My parents stood at the back door and he talked to them. Then he went away and he came back with the two boys and then he went away again.

'Come on. I'll take your glass too. You're too small.'

I look up and the back path and Richard's face have a purple colour that's changing to blue because I pushed my knees against my eyes. He's bending down to pick up the glass and I'm standing up and watching the blue go away from the ground until it's normal.

'But you've got to keep up this time or we won't beat the clock, ok?'

We're walking. I can walk with Richard easily this time and I watch the glasses as he moves up and down as well as forward and hardly any is spilling.

There are long dark shapes under the bridge so the men are still there. The one with the curly hair is looking at his watch. We're standing right in front of him now but he doesn't look up. One of the others is sleeping. The other two are slapping cards on top of other cards that sit in a pile between them. They don't look up or stop playing, even though we've come back with the water.

'Thirty-four minutes children.'

'I know, I'm sorry. My sister fell behind and sat down, so Richard had to go back for her.'

He's looking at me now. I want to sit down again. Put my knees against my eyes and watch the colours. I don't.

'Your sister?'

'I'm sorry. She's only four.'

'Are you only four?'

I'm looking at my brother. His hands are full. I look back at the man and he's still staring at me. I don't speak. His voice is different again.

'Some cat took that child's tongue out.'

He spits. He drops the spit slowly to the side of his feet. Then he lifts one boot and stamps on the spit with his heel. He looks back at my brother.

'Did you spill any?'

'No.'

'Lads! Room service has arrived! Get your fuckin' act together! Sit up, you! There's a lady in front of you!'

He kicks the man who's asleep on his side, but he sits up so quickly I know he wasn't really asleep. The other two put down their cards slowly and turn their heads to us.

'Are we going to get those glasses, or are you just going to stand there holding them all day?''

My brother and Richard hand over the four glasses to the

four men. They take them. Now they're all standing up. Looking down at the water in the glasses in their hands.

'Thanks very much.'

And then he looks up, looks at my brother the whole time, and he empties the water with the sun in it into the grass at the side of him, where he spat, looking at my brother. They all do it, one after the other, looking at my brother, four taps turned on and spilling into the grass, until the last glass is emptied and the sun's gone with the water into the ground. They're handing back the glasses. We stare. Richard and my brother take them, still staring, and the four men pick up their cards and walk away.

Where the Real Trains Run From

Sheenagh Pugh

I was lonely that summer. We'd moved house, away from the city I'd always lived in, to the outskirts of a small country town. School was out till autumn, and there were no kids my age nearby, so I had no-one to hang out with. Well, I had a brother and sister, but they were four years younger. Besides, being twins, they never took much notice of anyone else.

Our garden backed onto fields. I wasn't impressed. When we lived in the city, I'd see fields from a train sometimes and think how it would feel to walk on cool, smooth grass, like a huge lawn. But fields aren't like that at all. They're hummocky, full of prickly weeds and cowpats. Talk about the view, you can't see it because you're too busy watching your feet.

That day, I soon had enough of nettles and instead of crossing the stile I went through a gap in the hedge. Very anti-Country Code. I came out in a narrow lane. It was hedged on both sides and in the still air the smell of wild garlic was overpowering. It was very quiet, too. No farm machines, just a whistling, a little way off. I wondered what bird it was.

The sun burned the back of my neck and I had half a mind to turn round and go home to my computer. But there was a bend ahead and I wanted to see around it. It was where the whistling came from. I listened again and realised it wasn't a bird at all, not unless birds in those parts could whistle 'You'll Never

Walk Alone'. I thought about birds with red and white scarves being Liverpool supporters, and got the giggles.

I turned the bend and saw a low wooden gate with green paint peeling off it. Beyond, there was a ridge with a flattened top and then a deep ditch. I climbed the gate (it was too stiff to open) and walked up a smooth slope to the top of the ridge. Then I knew where I was.

It was a railway station. A little country halt, but it must have been long disused. The ridge was a platform, all grassed over, and the ditch, of course, was where the rails had been. They were gone now; you could see in the gaps between the tall weeds that came nearly up to the platform. I remember a flower with big purple bells, and another with wide white heads.

There were no buildings on the platform, but I could see poles where a sign had been. At the end was a signal, rusty and leaning. And halfway down the platform stood a person.

I thought at first it was a boy, because it had on a T-shirt, jeans and trainers. Then I thought, but my little sister dresses like that. The figure had its back to me; it was neither short nor tall. The hair maybe a bit short for a girl – but then again a bit long for a boy. I called 'Hello,' and it turned. But the face was no help, though it was sort of nice – thin, clever, dark eyes, a bit of a smile around the mouth. So I asked "What's your name?'

'Ally,' came the answer, which was a lot of good. Alistair, Alison? I thought of asking what it was short for, but it seemed too obvious. Anyway it was so long since I'd seen anyone my own age that I didn't care; all I wanted was for us to do something together. So I said 'You doing anything particular?'

'Just waiting for a train.'

I laughed. Ally looked at me, eyebrows raised. 'I don't see

what's funny.'

'Oh, come on. I mean, you can see no train's run here in years; there's no track, even.'

Ally picked a grass stalk and chewed it. 'This is where the real trains run from.'

I didn't know what this was about; maybe I'd met a head case, but it was still better than nobody. I tried again to tell what Ally was. I could see one plain earring, but anyone can wear them. I thought of the twins; how did I tell them apart? Not that I could, always.

Then, behind me, way down the line, I heard an unbelievable sound. I turned, and there it was, coming towards us round the bend, down a track that wasn't there.

It wasn't even just a train. It was a steam train, like I'd seen on holiday sometimes, a gleaming green engine with the sun glinting off its brasswork and its golden dome. It was hauling a couple of little red wooden coaches, like something come alive off a Hornby set, and white smoke puffed clouds from its funnel as it whistled.

I was stunned. I turned to Ally and shouted 'What the hell is that thing running on?'

'Whatever you think'. Perfectly calm, no surprise at all.

'What sort of answer is that?' Enough, Ally seemed to think.

It eased up at the platform, with much chugging and puffing. I thought it was the most beautiful thing I'd ever seen. Ally opened a carriage door and stepped in. So I did, too.

Inside it smelled of leather and wood polish. It had leather straps for opening the windows. Ally did.

'You have to watch that, on a steam train,' I said, maybe showing off a bit, 'the smuts might get in.'

'Not on this one.' They didn't, either. The white smoke curled in sometimes, but there was nothing gritty in it. I leaned back in the seat – it was deep, with faded red-green upholstery like the ones in the observation car I'd been in once – and looked out. I had no idea where we were. I remember passing fields with lambs, which was odd because even I knew August was too late for lambs. They were fun though, playing king-of-the-castle on a hillock while the ewes munched away looking bored. I think they're my favourite animals.

Ally was whistling again. Did that make him a boy, I wondered? But my aunt was always whistling. I looked at the face. Boy or girl, it was how I'd always imagined my friend looking. I mean the ideal friend, the one you dream of having, who never gets embarrassing or ratty or too busy. None of my friends had ever been that. I don't suppose I was, either.

I liked the way we didn't have to say much. With some people, you can't just say nothing; one of you has to be talking all the time or you feel awkward. With Ally, it didn't seem to matter what we said, or whether we said anything. I felt very relaxed, considering I was in a train on a track that didn't exist.

Ally touched my arm and pointed out of the window. I saw we were on a viaduct, passing a city below. Then I cried out, because it was my city, the one I used to live in.

'It can't be!' I shouted, as if Ally had said it was. 'In the first place, it's about two hundred miles away, and there was never a viaduct.'

The more I looked, the more I saw of my old home, only not quite. The layout was the same, and the park, and the landmarks I knew. But there were trees lining the streets, and fountains in the square, where I'd always thought there should be fountains, and what looked like a new leisure centre. We'd only been gone a few months; I couldn't believe they'd made all these changes in such a short time.

'I wish they hadn't waited till we left to do all this. Look, there's no litter, even, and they've torn down the derelict factory at last. It's perfect.'

Ally smiled and said nothing. But something *I'd* said was prickling at the back of my thoughts. The city, and the lambs, and the train....

'Why doesn't it need tracks to run on, Ally?'

'Because it's the real train, the one you see in your head when you say *train*. Like the city is the one you see when you say *city*. The others, the copies, all have something wrong with them, but the real train is everything a train ought to be. And of course it only goes through real places.'

'Where does it go *to*?'

'Oh, come on, think!' As soon as Ally spoke, I knew: it could only go to the sea. And it did.

And it wasn't the chips-and-rides place that the twins would have adored, nor the prom with fancy shops where my parents would have bored me rigid. It was my kind, which no longer surprised me. A wide, white beach backed by grassy dunes, cliffs each side and waves coming in fast and strong, throwing surf in the air. There were wind-surfers in the sea, their sails as bright and transparent as butterflies, but not a soul on the beach except me and Ally.

'You should have a swim,' said Ally. Even before I said 'I haven't got my gear, and I don't think I'm a strong enough swimmer for this,' I knew that I had and I was. It was scary, and breathtaking and joyful, all at once. I remember singing at the top of my voice while the surf broke over my head, which probably isn't possible.

By the way, if you're waiting for me to say 'and then I woke up and it was all a dream,' I may as well say that I shan't. You can't dream real places before you see them. Until that day, I'd never seen the lane, or the disused station. But I found them plenty of times afterwards, and stood for hours on that platform, waiting for something to happen.

I don't recall when we decided we had to go back. But we crossed a meadow to get to the train. It was studded with flowers: red, blue, yellow, white, every colour but orange – I've never liked orange. And the springy grass felt just like a lawn, not a hump or nettle anywhere.

'I wish I knew the names of these flowers.'

'Scabious,' said Ally, 'red campion, tormentil, sea-pink, snow-in-summer. You don't normally see them all out together.'

In the train back, I spent a lot of time looking at Ally's smile, listening to Ally's lazy, pleasant voice, wondering how to hold on to it. I'd begun to suspect what Ally was, you see, and I don't mean boy or girl but something deeper. I think I had a feeling, even then, that however often I found that station again, there would never be anyone but me on the platform.

I wanted the journey to go on forever, and it did seem to last a long time. But it ended with us standing on the grassy ridge, watching the train vanish round the bend in the track. After it was out of sight I could still see its smoke, and hear the hoot that sounds like escape and loss and adventure. And when I turned,

Ally was already walking away.

'Hey,' I called, more because I wanted Ally to turn round than for any other reason, 'are you a boy or a girl?'

Ally, walking into the sun, almost lost in light, half-turned. 'Why, does it matter? Anyway, what are you?'

And walked on, laughing.

—

Six Departures

Helen Clare

For centuries no-one came, or coming turned back at the valley's entrance. Only when the cities had left no place for them and the river ran their debris to the sea, did they track to its clean source, to the place where the landscape opened to reveal the secret the ice had left.

Few at first, they scooped their homes from the faulted rock, their sheep snivelling at grass roots in the too thin soil. In winter the river slowed, became brittle, paused at its falls. The valley entrance sealed, sure as stone. They learnt to judge the seasons - the level of fog on the valley's rim, the precise purple of the snow of the hills' bare ribs, the pale smell that signalled the thaw.

When the babies came they were smaller than expected, but thrived. The next generation were smaller still. These children crouched in the crannies of the hillside, ran bent up its slopes, tumbled like pebbles.

Soon there were more people than sheep, more sheep than grass. They learned to spin, to weave. Each spring they packed horses and made a path out, traded for food, leather. They stitched and built lasts for cruder feet than their own.

It wasn't enough. The land was gouged for stone and coal. The water turned bad; a shift in the wind brought unfamiliar smells. But there was food, shelter and church. Children stooped for hours beneath factory roofs and spent Sundays on their knees.

Leaves strewn on the valley floor covered the dark stain of

soot-blackened rock. The children kicked up the shale on the valley floor, warned away from falling stones and glass. A new kind of silence. Schools and a firm road out.

Thaw by thaw the sons and daughter of the valley leave to make their mark on softer ground. Only the old remain tending their graves, waiting for the river to run clear.

They take little with them, the sons and daughters of this place. The names of their forbears, their bibles, the stories their parents told them. Much of these they will drop along the way.

In the expanding cities there are tall buildings, wide roads. They learn to walk upright, believing they have grown taller, that the place they have left is too small, as if the valley were doored like its houses and they could not stoop to get through.

No more the thin soil and the solid rock. Now they walk over tunnels and culverted rivers. There's a new tension in their ankles. If they do not fall they feel they must leap.

They fall in love with the sound of their own footsteps. They can not stay. All that is gone. They move on and in time they slough each place like a skin as their bodies grow beyond it.

Having discovered the horizon, the expanse of the sky, which shocked them at first, draws their eye each morning. They feel they must find what is beyond the buildings, beyond the trees, beyond the mountains, over the sea.

They are journeying still, or so I hear, through landscapes outside of my knowledge and beyond my imagination.

- - - - - - -

Damn sure you wouldn't like me here. Snooping. But it's still my house. I still have my keys. I check the wardrobes. How easily you've spread your clothes across the two. There's a blouse of hers, not much more. My wedding dress is where I left it – on the shelf wrapped in a black bin-liner. My tampons are still on the bedside table, recognisable by the buy-one-get-one-free sticker. Does she ever think about where you've been?

I expected to find something of myself reflected here. Little has changed. The curtains you I bought and you chose. The ones I always opened too soon or too late. The bedspread transferred from your flat. The pictures you brought back from our holiday. That holiday.

Officially I'm here to pick up my mail. It's in the spare room. Along with the things you've decided are mine. Mostly junk. I sort it without opening the envelopes. My initial. Your name.

You've already asked me to have my mail forwarded. I'm not sure why I won't. You say the reminder hurts too much. A year on. I don't believe you. No hurt in your voice, or your face. I only came to make sure you hadn't changed the locks.

This room was to have been the nursery. Through the window the climbing roses bloom pink and yellow, twenty foot up the elder tree. Your veg are growing again. Will she steam and freeze your veg. Pickle your chillies, chutney your tomatoes. Make jam?

Sometimes I dream we're still married. There's a pile of washing, growing like an onion from somewhere in its centre. Your clothes. I'm trying to separate the clean from the dirty. But I can't tell. I can't bear to put them to my nose the way I used to do. Downstairs the cleaner has neatly folded your ironing.

I see she's put pots of candles by the fireplace. I'm surprised you let her. Still she knows enough to keep her cleansing lotion on the shelf at the back of the bathroom and not disturb your display on the shelf above the sink.

I'd planned to take some stuff back. Remove myself slowly from that room. But I'm less sure than you are what's mine. The mirror you bought me because you wanted it. Pottery dragons. The book my mother bought you. But I'm sure as I can be that everything outside that room is yours. Even the things I paid for.

Maybe even the wedding dress was someone's fantasy of me. Yours or mine, husband. Yours or mine.

All that was ever of me, the initial before your name on the envelopes that plopped down on the mat, I'll take - a letter from an old friend, a programme for the Oval.

I shut the door behind me, letting the Yale lock drop, not needing to use my keys, remembering that other time, both of us weeping on either side of the door. Stumbling to the tube station. Watching the mice on the tracks, trying to measure the forces that held me to the platform. Emerging an hour away, turning to look back only on Wandsworth High Road, to see a train pass across the streaky sky above Sainsbury's bright sign, holding my breath, recognising beauty. Breathing.

– – – – – – –

He was waiting for it to happen, waiting to snap. For some time he'd been wondering when it would come. Sometimes he would think it had happened and then wake up in the morning still in one piece. Once he broke down and cried in the record section of the library. Another time he hit all the keys on the piano, fisting them down in clumps that made loud flabby sounds. Afterwards he was still there.

Lately he'd been only able to play Chopin; and that too fast and too loud, and the rhythm gradually escaping from his control, becoming untidy. He hated sloppiness. Crossings out and wiggly lines, sticky liquid paper ploughed up by cheap biros. Bad haircuts and tatty ties. Shiny patches on the blackboard and other teachers pinching his chalk.

It crept up on him unexpectedly. He missed his exit on the way to school and carried on driving. He drifted left on to the M61 and found himself delivered onto the M6. Some where on the edges of Cumbria, with the controlled fury over the Queen of the Night thrusting from the speakers, he ran out of petrol. He left his car on the hard shoulder and walked.

Up the next slip road, he went, over the roundabout, treading steady up the grassy hump, running down with short, tight steps, the hands in his pockets splaying his jacket, then down a narrow road with fields and sandbagged cottages, their doors opening straight onto the pavement.

He heard the unevenness of his own tread. The left foot slightly the heavier, the heel more worn, probably. A tune began to form. Not so much a tune as a series of chords, shifting from G to C, from the dominant seventh to the second inversion, a fourth note creeping in somewhere, a resounding G tapped by his left heel.

Bach. Somewhere on the last half-page of the first prelude. A throbbing G, the constantly surprising shifts, the relentless move to the home chord. The nearest thing to orgasm possible to in a public place. He closed his eyes for a second, caught his breath and began on the fugue.

Bach. He was playing Bach. Not with the keys. The notes rise from his feet, through his spine, the broken scales stretching across his shoulders. Bach. In all its precision, purity and passion.

The full 48 stretched in front of him, known and as new.

It seemed that by walking through them he might form a plan. Something along the lines of resigning, selling up, releasing capital, buying time.

Something along those lines. But no hurry. You could trust a moment to last for ever, trust music to take you through combinations of notes you could never dream of, to make sequences so beautiful you thought you couldn't bear them, and then at the end to bring a resolution.

The second prelude. E flat. His pace quickened. His face screwed for the forte, the accents, the two parts interlocked as his teeth ground together. He clenched his fists until he felt the nails he'd left untrimmed of late dig into his palms. He could walk through it. Wait to be released into arpeggio.

–   –   –   –   –   –   –

This is the house that sickness built. Come in. Please. It's not often there's people in here. But what's a story without an invitation?

With most houses people leave and come back all the time. This one comes with you. Like a tortoise. Tuck in your head and limbs when things get difficult. Can you imagine that? Did you know that Armadillo armour is made of hair? It's more like that. Of the body. A womb maybe, but not hers.

You needn't worry about pain. Pain is not a problem. You cut your finger, it's not the pain that makes you cry out. It's shock, fear. Damage. There is pain you've known forever. It's as familiar as the salt of your own sweat. You can float on it like a sea that's the temperature, the salinity of your body. You can rock in it like a cradle. It is all the stories your mother told you.

You could stay here for years. Alone. Let be. No-one will follow you here. Why would they? Everyone fears sickness.

It's easy. You tend to your needs. Care for the body that is your house. The house that is your body. Like coral snug in its own case of chalk, that leaves its own body only to reproduce. Becomes like a jellyfish, floating on the tide, its filaments trailing and tangling, its soft body collapsing on the shore. How can that be borne?

You're here now. That changes everything. I invited you. You came in. You can leave of course. End your place in the story. I'm locked into this. The telling of a story is a journey. It is the leaving of a shore with another in sight. There is no going back. There is only arriving or drifting forever.

Or you could stay. Join me here until you're ready to make your own. Be like me; make me less of an oddity. How cosy we might be, living like this together. I can make it work for you. Give you everything you need, so you never want to leave. Maybe this is that kind of story – the gingerbread house. You come to eat. I eat you. One body one home.

You should try and talk your self out of this. Convince me its better out there. Tell me you've been there and survived. Hold a hand to steady me as I step over the threshold. Show me how to live beyond this house.

Let me be you. Stay here. If I can persuade you, trick you to come in and take my place I can leave. Someone has to hold the fort, as it were. We all know those stories.

Tempted? You have to be. Resist and you blow this whole thing open. Turn the page and you show this to be a fiction.

It's not a real house, after all. It's one of those dreams that fall apart when the light comes on. That's why you're here. Your seeing it unravels the vision. That's the kind of story it is.

– – – – – – –

How is this possible? she thinks to herself, sometime in between her second and third orgasm.

What she'd mostly been thinking to herself, until quite close to the moment of her first orgasm was, *Is this OK?*

It had been the question she'd asked to herself on coming up from the underground station into the sunshine and the wide streets that looked suspiciously like the suburbs. It was the question she asked on getting into the car and scrutinizing the face that she'd figured she liked when they'd met.

When she'd stretched herself out, fingers on the jamb of the kitchen doorway and he'd paused in the cooking and drew a finger from the tip to the base of her spine and then reached round and pulled her buttocks to his groin, she'd checked again.

And for sure when she'd kneeled on his bed half-naked and he'd spanked her, she'd asked it then.

It seemed to her this was coming pretty close to not being OK. But she kept checking with herself, every second, every sting, even as she giggled at the exposure, the sheer silliness of it, alert to that moment where sensation became pain and at last she'd have to take control. Clever how he managed to keep just the right side of it. She thought that probably he'd done this before – more than once, and that perhaps he was listening, quite carefully, to the noises she made, watching her shift into and away from the strokes.

After the third orgasm, just before he rolled them both over, and sat her astride him, tucking her calves under her thighs, it seemed she'd got beyond thinking at all.

But she found her head above his. Found herself looking

down on his face. *Bastard!* she thought, and forced his arms behind his head, her teeth in his scalp. *Spank me would you!*

'I'll show you,' she hisses through his hair, 'I'll screw you now,' thinking, *I'll screw you like you don't count, like you don't matter. Like there's a part of me I can push into you like I can take pleasure from you and not care,* closing her eyes not wanting to see how much he's loving all this.

She's screaming towards a fourth orgasm, which strangely, cursedly she can't seem to reach without his. So she's screaming at him, 'Now! Do it! Go on! Give it to me!' and pretty soon she's twitching, panting, biting back the tears, watching as his face tightens as if in pain, and then empties of everything but himself. She strokes his cheek as if she might feel love.

He brings ice cream, holding a dish in each hand. How fragile, how unthreatening, his naked body, his flaccid cock. As she sits up and takes the dish in both hands, he reaches behind her and places a pillow behind her head.

In another time, her head knocks against stony ground and fingers hook open her mouth.

How is this possible? She thinks to herself as she stirs the caramel sauce with her spoon, and picks out the pieces of chocolate with her fingers.

– – – – – – –

When the pictures from Sally Fisher's fifth birthday party are dropped off I believe myself to be the child standing alone at the end of the sofa, one leg wrapped round the other, mouth slack, eyes focussed somewhere in the distance to the left of the camera. My mother points to another child, upright, tight-kneed and placid just left of centre and I recognise the dress, knitted with pleated skirt and bobbles, but not the face.

I learn to pick out my clothes in photographs and shop fronts as I pass, though sometimes it takes a moment or two – in a mirrored bar there'll be a red-haired woman holding a note between two fingers waiting for service just as I do likewise.

I imagine my face as a void, or perhaps like the puppets my mother made from brown paper bags, as if any hand might reach out and crumple in features, or mark a wink or a smile in felt tip pen. Once, at a museum the speaking face of Isaac Newton turns out to be a film projected onto a large polystyrene egg. This I understand.

People I think are my friends walk past me in the street, fooled by a tone's shift in shade of make-up, an inch trim of the hair, the morning's split-second choice between gel and mousse. I'm mercurial they say.

On the tube a man is so convinced he recognises me, he speaks to me in Spanish and won't stop – waving a magazine at me, so that I try to find my face there, or on the hand he holds out as if bearing a platter or a velvet cushion. An old man believes I am his childhood sweetheart from down the road in County Kerry. He draws the map of his life on my blank face.

I decide that my thoughts are so far away they are not in my face at all.

The gift of my reflection was perhaps a consequence of good company and good gin. Or perhaps that's reason people put mirrors in the bathroom.

Whatever. It's true that in that moment, pants round my ankles, bladder releasing itself after the long wait, lifting my face from my hands I sees myself in the mirror. There's no mistaking it. It's the face in the photograph from Sally Fisher's party, and the face on every bus pass and library card since that I've kept stacked in a drawer.

I watch my bottom lip stretch almost to square, and the

tendons in my neck tense, and I think I am going to cry. But I don't. I twist my head to catch my face in a few different angles, touch the bridge of my nose, eye sockets, cheekbones, cheeks, lips, chin checking all the time that I can feel my fingers with the skin of my face as well as my face with my fingers.

They are getting restless behind the door. Jiggling and hissing. I leave my reflection and return to my friend.

I look at him, unsure what the tension in my check muscles the stretched skin of my chin mean. Look into his face for a clue. He smiles back.

—

Singing a Man to Death

Matthew Francis

I keep hearing the tune. Not out loud, of course. It's just that some mornings, usually when I've had too much to drink the night before, I wake up at first light and find it running through my head: *Mete üöbik oo tänabu.* It's been more than twenty-five years. And I only heard it once, or at the most twice. In any case nobody died of it, as far as I know. The music probably isn't fatal, no more than any other of those things that stay with you, the smell of toast, say, or the mauve fluttering the gasfire used to make when you lit it, or the scrape of a stylus across the shiny black grooves of a vinyl record. Remember how the silence before the track started used to be amplified, too? You could probably kill someone using memories if you kept at it long enough.

I used to keep all the essentials of life on a rug in front of the fire: a jar of coffee, a jar of Coffee-Mate, an electric kettle, bread, butter, honey, a toasting-fork improvised out of a wire coathanger, books and papers, a scattered trail of LPs that led to the stereo. The records mostly belonged to Luke, who had thrown out my *Simon and Garfunkel's Greatest Hits* and my *Crime of the Century* and my *Tubular Bells*, and was taking charge of my musical education. After an evening in the pub, we would end up in my room, which was bigger than Tobias's on the other side of the passage and more conveniently situated than Luke's attic-room. I would sit by the gasfire and make coffee while Luke hung over the stereo, so he could take off a record halfway through a track when he decided he'd grown out of it, and Tobias, as usual after a few pints, thrashed about heavily on the bed, claiming to be possessed.

'What is this place? How do I come here?'

'Who are you, man?' Luke would ask.

'I am not man. My name is Eliza Wilmot. I was born in the year of our Lord 1746. I am eighteen years old.'

'Yeah? Who's the king?'

'I know naught of kings and princes. I am a simple woman.'

'You are a simple arsehole.'

'Abuse me not, reprobate. I bring news of the life beyond, and of this life.'

'You're full of shit.'

'Not so. I have left this corporeal world and all its feculent matter. Now listen. LISTEN.'

'If you're a woman, how come you don't sound like one?'

'Listen to me, fools. The spirit is within thee. Harken to its voice. Its word is DO WHAT THOU WILT. DO WHAT THOU WILT shall be the whole of the law. I have spoken.'

Then there would be a long pause, while he seemed to have fallen asleep, until I brought the mug of coffee close to his face. 'What? What? Where am I? What happened?'

Mete üöbik. Remember landladies? How they didn't like you flushing the toilet at night, or using Blutack on the walls, how the worst fear they had in the world was that you would go to bed with someone in their house? Jessie never knocked, she would just appear out of the shadows into the light of the anglepoise, wrinkled and froglike with a helmet of dyed black hair, a cryptic smile on her face. The three of us were in the same room; that constituted a party, and parties would wear out the house, just as surely as posters wore out the wallpaper and sex, if any of us ever managed to get any, would take all the bounce out of the bedsprings.

Jessie didn't shout. The worst she would ever say was 'You are not a worker,' in her peculiar voice which sounded foreign even though its accent was pre-war upper-class English. 'At least Philip is a worker. Even Tobias is a worker. But Luke is *not* a worker!' She would throw her arms round Luke or me, smiling all the time in that unreadable way.

'Ah, good evening, my good woman!' Tobias would shout from the bed.

But she never seemed to hear him. 'Is he tired? He shouldn't be lying on the bed with his shoes on.'

'I expect she's from the Carpathians,' Tobias said one evening after Jessie had left. 'A lot of landladies are.'

'You are so full of shit,' Luke told him. 'You know that?'

Tobias twiddled the ends of his beard. 'There was a Carpathian landlady in Mill Road,' he said, 'who sang one of her tenants to death. Caught him in bed with someone, and after that she would stand outside his door every night and sing to him. As they do in the Carpathians.'

Apparently there was a musical phrase called the Devil's Interval which was considered unlucky in all musical traditions. But in the Carpathians, the Devil's Interval was just one element of an ancient murdersong, somehow kept back from the notebooks and taperecorders of the folklorists. It could never be written down properly in any case, with its quartertones and nasal trills and the occasional noise generated deep inside the skull by an organ that most people don't possess in working order. It was passed on by the village bard-shaman-healer who would whisper-sing it on his deathbed to the chosen apprentice. Or *her* deathbed? Tobias wasn't sure.

'You'd have to have a good memory, in any case. You can only hear the song so many times before you die. It's one of the Numbers of Power. Seventy-seven, I believe. Or seven hundred and seventy-seven.'

'Seven hundred and seventy-seven what?'

'Reprises. Singings.'

'So let me get this straight – you just sing to someone and it kills them?'

'With your fingers in your ears, obviously,' Tobias said. 'Otherwise you would drop dead yourself.'

'That is so cool,' Luke said.

Luke used to break into my room through the window in the

early morning and put a record on the stereo at full volume. 'How about this?' he would ask as I sprang up waving my arms.

'What? Oh God. Fuck off.'

'No, man, I'm serious. What do you think?'

'Turn it down.'

'All right, all right, cool. I made you a cup of coffee. Now what do you think?'

'Oh God. Yes, I quite like it. Yes, it's OK, great. What is it?'

'You have no fucking taste at all, have you?'

He was right. I had no natural taste in his kind of music, and had to work it all out for myself. It had nothing to do with being contemporary. The word he always used about a record he liked was 'authentic', and I gradually came to realize it meant dead. His heroes were Jimi Hendrix and Jim Morrison, Janis Joplin and Nick Drake, all suicides or as good as, all dead before they were thirty. I got to be able to recognize the suicide singers. There was a graveyard hollowness in the voice, as if the singer was already dead when recording it. The effect was even creepier on my record-player, which used to pick up radio messages from the local taxi-drivers, and occasionally let off a deafening rat-tat-tat like a machine-gun firing out of the speakers. Luke would grab the record off the turntable and ask me when I last had my fucking stylus checked.

'It isn't the stylus,' I told him. 'It's just the speakers. It doesn't damage the record.'

'Haven't even got an anti-static cloth,' he mumbled.

'I use that sock. It's quite clean.'

'I'm fucking wasted on you, you realize that?'

Luke saw himself as a rock star *manqué*. He had the looks for it, supposedly, though I couldn't see it myself. His shoulders were so broad he looked slightly deformed, or as if there was a coathanger stuck in the back of his shirt, and his head, with its flouncy greying curls, was also exaggeratedly large. But he would study himself in the hall mirror on his way out to the front door for minutes at a time, and sometimes in the middle of a conversation, he would say, *à propos* of nothing, 'I'm Luke?' like that, with a question mark on the end of it, as if he couldn't believe how lucky he was. And this girl I knew, Yasmin, who had a boyfriend in Kettering, used to refer to him as 'your gorgeous friend', purely theoretically, in the same way she would talk about other women's eyes or figures.

I went up to his room one afternoon and found him lying on his floor, surrounded by naked LPs and tattered sleeves bearing black and white pictures of snowy pine forests, fat women in flouncy dresses and small men clutching zithers. 'How do you feel, man?' he shouted. 'Does this one make you feel kind of anaemic?'

'It's terrible.'

'That is the whole fucking point.'

'Put it off. I can't hear myself think.'

'Isn't it great?' Luke got up slowly, and put the record off. 'You want coffee?' he said as usual, but when I accepted he just stood there, shaking his head slightly, as if testing it for something. 'What do you want to hear yourself think for?' he said finally. 'Aren't you so fucking fed up with hearing yourself think?'

I knew what he meant, then. At least I was fed up with hearing myself think about Yasmin, and the boyfriend she stayed with in Kettering most weekends. She showed me his picture once: solid-looking with a Beatle haircut and the points of his collar sticking out of a blue Marks and Spencer's sweater with a silver diamond-pattern on the front. They'd been going out for five years and were practically married. I found it hard to imagine life in Kettering, where people started going out at the age of fourteen. And I found it hard to imagine Yasmin, whose skin was golden even in the winter, and whose eyebrows looked like Chinese calligraphy, in Kettering at all. I asked Luke once if he knew where it was, and he said it was so unthere it didn't even exist.

I used to wake up at night and hear myself telling her how I'd always loved her, how I had so much more to offer than David because I was an intellectual, and intellectuals made the best lovers. Then telling her that I was an intellectual, and intellectuals could only make themselves and other people miserable, so she must go back to Kettering where she really belonged. Telling her that I knew we were only friends, but why shouldn't friends have sex? She was lonely away from David, I was lonely away from, well, nobody much, and there was such a lot we could teach each other before going back to our respective lives. And then, sooner or later, telling her that even though she didn't love me and I didn't love her, I needed her to please, please, sleep with me just this once and I would never bother her again.

At this point I used to get out of bed. The time was always somewhere between three and four-thirty, the brief period after the last drunk and before the milkfloat. The thoughts stopped at once, to be replaced by a raw, chafing feeling. Then I would sit in my knobbly blue armchair beside the gasfire and listen to records through the headphones. The ones Luke had lent me or made me buy, death music: Nick Drake and Janis Joplin, Jimi Hendrix and The Doors. The only ones that worked in the small hours of the morning beside the gasfire.

But this stuff? You couldn't even understand the words.

He rubbed his face with his fingers as if trying to remove a blush. 'All right,' he admitted.

'All right what?'

'It is crap, most of it. Well, all of it. I just wanted to find the right song. *The* song.'

He had somehow got it into his head that if the murdersong existed you must be able to buy it somewhere, in the record stall at the market, or one of those backstreet shops that sold bootleg albums in plain sleeves. All his life, he'd been looking for a kind of music that nobody else knew about, a musical Holy Grail, except that it had to be a dark one, a death grail. Now he had almost found it.

'You really believe it, don't you?' I said.

'Yeah. No. Well, look, I don't want to kill myself, if that's what you think. Not now, anyway – I'm not even twenty yet, for fuck's sake. Give it a few years, and maybe. Don't you get it?'

'No.'

'Aren't you even a bit curious? About what it would

sound like, a song that was so powerful it could end your life? I mean, listen, man - ' Luke started to pick up the albums and put them back in their sleeves. 'Would it hurt? Or would it be more like a drug, so that every time you listened to it you got higher and higher, until the last time, seventy-seventh or whatever, you just floated away into the other world? Or maybe it would be very subtle, so you didn't even know it was doing anything. It would be like you play it seventy-six times, and nothing happens. And then you put the record away and you'll always know that whatever happens to you in life, if you get cancer, or if some fucking bastard in the White House decides it's time for the Third World War, you can just get out your record and that's it.'

'If it works,' I said, but he wasn't listening.

'Or get this, right? You go through the rest of your life knowing that one day you might hear that song. Like you have kids, and one of them thinks, oh I'll just put that funny old record on, and you walk in at that moment and say oh God, not that one! But it's too late. Amazing, eh?'

'Yes, and the kid doesn't know that it was the record that made you drop dead, so he plays it another seventy-six times and dies himself.'

'Now you're getting it.'

'But that's crazy. Why should you want to kill your own child?'

'I don't, man, I don't even have a fucking child. This is a hypothetical child, right? If he can get himself born, he can look after himself from then on. OK, maybe I throw away the record for the sake of the kid. I still know that one day I might walk into a party and find they're playing my tune.'

'They wouldn't. It's crap.'

'So what? I'll be middle-aged by then. I'll be a chartered accountant, living in a semi-detached, mowing the lawn on Saturdays. I'll be going to parties where everybody wears ties and the music is just automatically crap. Except that in my case the crap would be like heroin, or russian roulette or something, it would have an edge to it.'

'Look,' I said. 'First of all, you don't even know this song exists. It's just some stupid legend. Second, even if it's true, who on earth would make a record of a thing like that? It would be illegal, if it existed, which it doesn't. And thirdly, even if it exists, and it is on record, how the fuck are you going to know when you hear it? You said yourself there might not be any symptoms.'

'That's what I like about you,' Luke said. 'You're a wanker, but you're a really logical wanker.'

One day he broke into my room while I was out, made himself a cup of coffee and went away again, leaving a dozen of his Eastern European bargain albums behind. The note said, 'You're right, except maybe for one of these which has been giving me strange thoughts. I don't want to hear ANY of them EVER again! Your turn now. Which is the mindfuck one?!'

The records reminded me of the ancient ones we used to have in my childhood, piled up in a compartment of a pseudo-mahogany cabinet called the radiogram. Mono, all of them. I slipped one of them out – actually it fell out, having no inner sleeve, and wheeled across the carpet. The picture on the cover showed a large grey city, all pillars and pediments; the album appeared to be by someone called Walmar Udmurt.

To my surprise, it had no scratches, just a couple of dull areas that might be a bit fuzzy, or might play perfectly well. I carried it over to the stereo. Maybe I'd play a track, if only to prove that it couldn't do anything to me.

It was a marching band with city noises in the background, even a bit of birdsong, I thought, but no singing yet. The track had only been on a minute when the machine-gun went off through the speakers, and in my slightly nervous state, I thought my head would explode. I took the needle off, and put the record back.

I didn't recognize at first what was wrong with Yasmin's face. Then I realized she had been crying, and it had made her blurry, as if I was viewing her out of focus. This was one of the fantasies that kept me awake at night, Yasmin in tears, asking for an arm round her shoulders, a hug. I almost reached for her shoulders there and then, on the threshold, but thought better of it.

'What's the matter?' It was Sunday evening – she shouldn't even be here. Something must have happened in Kettering to make her come back early.

'It's nothing. David and I had a bit of a barney, that's all.'

I got the impression she'd been practising the phrase, trying to make it sound emotionally neutral, insignificant, even a bit of a joke. What would Luke have made of the word she used? *Barney*, what the fuck? That is such a nonword, man. I instinctively looked along the passage to the stairs before ushering her inside. No sign of him.

She didn't want coffee, she said. She'd been drinking tea for three hours already. So I offered her whisky, a bottle I'd had for my birthday and hardly touched.

'I don't like it.'

'Nor do I, much, but it'll make you feel better.'

'All right.'

We sat together on the rug in front of the gasfire, drinking whisky, while she cried. I'd never been this close to her before, not for so long, anyway. She was wearing a fluffy black cardigan that made her look like a kitten, and I kept thinking how strange it was to cover all that smoothness with something so hairy, those thin shoulders with all that padding. I could smell her tears.

'I always thought I was going to marry him, you see. Ever since I met him. And then suddenly, all at once, I'm on my own again. Do you know what it's like to be on your own?'

I felt wiser than I'd ever been in my life, as if I had lived everything that human beings were capable of. 'Everybody goes through that,' I said. 'But you're not alone. I'm here.'

'You're really sweet, Philip. Thank you.'

After a couple of whiskies, her mood started to change. She dried her tears and became recklessly cheerful. 'Sod him,' she kept saying, 'sod him, sod him. There are plenty more fish in the sea. And I've always got you, haven't I, Philip?'

'Of course you have.'

'Do you feel like dancing? I want to dance.' She kicked off her shoes and stood unsteadily on her black-stockinged feet in front of my gasfire. 'What music have you got?'

The trouble was, I didn't have anything suitable. She went through my record collection with an expression of growing impatience. 'They're not mine,' I said. 'Most of them belong to Luke.'

'Haven't you got anything like, oh, Doctor Hook? And what are all these foreign things?'

'They're Luke's.'

'Luke must be really weird. Don't you have any music of your own?'

'Luke threw it all out.'

'Oh, look at her. Isn't she beautiful?'

It was one of the East European records, with a picture of a woman on the cover. *Mete Üöbik,* it said, and underneath, Jezamin Rääkima. Presumably the name of the singer – rather like Yasmin, which seemed an omen. And yes, she was quite good-looking in a black-and-white, pearls-and-hairspray sort of way. I'd noticed her before when flicking through the records, but that was all.

'What's this one like, Philip?'

'Oh, it's... you wouldn't like it.'

'Let's try it. Come on, we could dance.'

'It's very old-fashioned. I don't think you could dance to it.'

'Oh go on. We could smooch anyway, you can smooch to anything. Don't you want to smooch with me, Philip?'

She was full of these words this evening. I looked at her standing by the record-player in her black fuzz, and wanted desperately to smooch with her. My mind was working fast now, as if it had known all my life what to do in this situation. From the smooch in front of the gasfire to the gentle capsize on to the bed by the wall was only three and a half paces, and I knew exactly how I was going to get there.

When you put on a record, assuming you do it right and

don't jab your stylus down in the middle of a track, there is first
no sound at all and then the sound of amplified silence. That can
last as long as thirty seconds, rather pleasurable ones usually, in
which you prepare yourself to listen. You find out also at this stage
whether the recording is old and likely to be scratchy or not. This
time it was not too bad, just a bit wheezy. But the silence seemed
to last longer than usual, long enough to let me get back to the
rug, hastily push the coffee things out of the way and wrap my
arms round Yasmin's furry exterior, which collapsed in on itself as
if I'd knocked all the air out of her. She was very small now. I'd
got right inside, to the kernel of her. I could feel her body, naked
under all those clothes, squeezing me back. Then the music
started.

For hours after all this was over, I still thought that sound
was bells, huge churchbells of a kind I'd never heard. White-
sounding was the phrase I used to myself, picturing bells made of
some milk-coloured metal. They were playing a tune, but it was
so overpowering that it seemed to be in my bones rather just than
my ears. Then, over the top of it came an unnaturally deep voice,
a flat guttural bass like someone vomiting in slow motion. The
strange thing was that I somehow recognized the voice as
belonging to that elegant woman on the album sleeve. It was a
ghost voice, a voice that had ceased to be human.

Yasmin froze in my arms. 'Take it off.'

I ran to the record player and lifted up the needle. 'It's all
right,' I told her when I'd got my breath back. 'It was on at the
wrong speed, that's all. This record is a 78.'

'It was horrible.'

'Don't worry, it isn't meant to sound like that. It's just that
my stereo doesn't play 78s. I'll put something else on for you.'

'No,' she said. 'That's all right. I'd better be going anyway.'

At about five in the morning, the first traffic noises started outside
my window, and I gave up trying to sleep. I got out of bed and
crouched over the fire for a while. Then it occurred to me that the
record that had ruined everything was still on the turntable. I took
it off and put it back in its sleeve. That was when I realized what

those milk-white churchbells had been – of course, a piano. Probably at a normal speed it was a sweet little song about shepherdesses and babbling brooks. Good enough for smooching to, assuming Yasmin was right and you could smooch to anything. But she wasn't right, was she? There were some things you couldn't smooch to.

I gathered all the records together. They were mine, now, and I could do what I liked with them. Luke had probably never paid more than 50p each for them, in any case. If I'd had a real fire I would have thrown them on it and watched them burn or melt, probably both at once. As it was, I had an idea. I took the pearls-and-hairspray record out again, inserted the hook of my home-made toasting-fork through the hole in the middle, and sat down in front of the fire.

Mete üöbik oo tänabu. Me õitselind on tänavu. How delicate they were, records. You had to hold them by the edges, keep them out of the sun. Just breathing in their vicinity seemed risky. They played not only music, but every knock and scrape and slip and shake that had happened to them since they left the studio. Jessie probably looked on her house as a sort of record, one that endlessly replayed to her all the mess and clumsiness that was lived in it. Even the smell of toast, she claimed, could keep her awake at night. I wondered if the smell of scorched vinyl would disturb her. It was getting pretty smoky in the room by now, so I thought I'd better stop. In any case, the half-melted records weren't exactly disposed of. I put my clothes on and went for a walk. There were still very few people about, and I was able to throw them in the river without being seen. To my relief, they sank.

And since nobody died as far as I know, I probably didn't hear the song again, that morning months later, just before we left for the summer. We were all going to be back in College next year, which didn't bother me much. Luke and I hadn't got on so well since I melted his records, which he claimed he'd only lent me and wanted back. Then there was the thing between him and Yasmin after Christmas, but at least that didn't last after the calamitous evening when Jessie walked in on them in bed. We ended up being polite to each other, Jessie and Luke, Luke and me, Yasmin and me, Luke and Yasmin probably. I had the feeling that maybe she had really got to him, the way she got to me. Except that he had the memories out of it, I suppose. All I kept were the fantasies, memories of fantasies.

So, tricked awake by the early dawn, I probably never did hear a voice floating down from the top of the house, a very high soprano, rather beautiful in a cracked sort of way:

> *Mete üöbik oo tänabu maeal läin*
> *Meie üöbik on tänävu muuale mend.*
> *Kord oli ühel vanal ausal mehel*
> *Me õitselind on tänavu maale läind.*

But I still remember it, somehow or other. And every time I think of it I have this vision of Jessie, her helmet of dyed black hair, her froglike face, standing on the dim stairs with a finger jammed into each ear, singing and singing.

Best for Value, Best for Choice

Joanne Limburg

'Ooh, let me! Let me!'

Dan passed Sarah his car key and watched her click the remote central locking button, which she did in the style of a Charlie's Angel picking off an evil henchman. She had never been out with a man who could afford a car with this feature before, and it always made her laugh to hear the surprised little 'ooip!' noise it made when Dan pressed the button.

'You know you just kill me,' said Dan. 'It takes so little to get you excited.'

Sarah handed the key back. 'Are you complaining?'

'Nope,' he replied. 'Shall we go?'

He put his arm round her shoulders and they sauntered into the supermarket together, passing under the banner that expressed approval of their union:
BEST FOR VALUE, BEST FOR CHOICE.

'I've never been to a place this big,' she said, as the doors swished open, 'I mean, not being a driver myself.'

'Oh it's just brilliant,' he said. 'I do virtually all my shopping here now - it's like, you can get your whole life under one roof.'

She could easily believe it: the place was the size of an airport terminal, but without the sense of space. Everywhere she looked there were goods, goods, goods, piled and stacked, hung and displayed, lined up and gleaming along the uncountable aisles.

Moving among them were people in overwhelming numbers, jostling each other with enormous trolleys. Mostly they looked as if they knew exactly what they had come here for and where to find it. Sarah supposed that this must be because of the signs hanging from the vast ceiling, which organised all the goods and people under sensible headings: WOMENSWEAR, GARDEN FURNITURE, ELECTRICAL GOODS, they said; PHARMACY, CAFÉ, PLAY AREA.

'So where's the actual food?' she asked, but Dan was already marching ahead, pushing a trolley towards a sign that said FRESH PRODUCE. Of course he knew his way round here. It was all part of the grown-up and efficient behaviour that so impressed her. He had a responsible job; he lived in a flat which he owned and kept in good order himself; he could be up and dressed on a Saturday morning in time to do a big shop before lunch. It was a revelation to see so many people, such a multitude of good people, beginning their weekends elbow-deep in healthy salad leaves. She felt repentant as she pictured Saturday mornings back in the flat where she and two other postgraduates lived together like well-lettered pigs, with newspapers all over the floor, and instant coffee served in nearly-rinsed mugs.

When she caught up with Dan, he was choosing onions.

'Oh here you are,' he said. 'What do you think about shallots? Are shallots overdoing it? If I served you shallots would you think I was overdoing it?'

Even though they'd only been going out for a few weeks, Sarah knew better than to underestimate the importance of this question. Dan's cooking was sacred. Already she had spent hours in his kitchen, watching as he cooked meal after delicious meal. All he seemed to expect of her in return was evidence of her enjoyment, which was easy to provide. Today he was gathering ingredients for a dinner party the following evening, a major performance for his colleagues, their partners, his boss. Sarah had listened to him agonising about it for days and supposed that it would be girlfriendly of her to come and help. She also liked the idea of the two of them walking behind the one trolley, like a proper, established couple. She had nothing to say about shallots.

She really had nothing to say, but as there seemed to be a lot riding on her answer, she thought for a moment and then tried:

'Overdoing it? Well wouldn't that depend on what else you were serving?'

This turned out to be a very successful strategy. Dan nodded vigorously.

'That is *so* completely true. I'll hang onto them, improvise around them, make it up as I go, you know, build up a sort of carefully balanced – you know, scope for creativity, sometimes it's better with these things not to be too controlled, because then you can really release the potential of...' His voice died away. '....lemongrass?' he finished, looking suddenly quite pathetically at sea. 'Ye-hess! With the fresh herbs – that way!'

He left Sarah minding the trolley. She looked down it, noticing the toddler's seat folded flat and unused at the handle-end. It reminded her of her family's weekly trips to the local Sainsbury's all those years ago, when the trolley seat had always been full of her little brother, one podgy leg sticking out on either side. That had been the last time a supermarket had seemed as vast as this, and it had long since become a branch of Blockbuster's. She could remember some even smaller places, like the Co-op down the road, where once she had gone in proudly, a seven-year-old sent in all by herself to help her mother, to buy two tins of Whiskas and a packet jelly. The woman stacking the shelves next to the till had smiled at her, saying she was a 'proper little shopper'.

'I'M A PROPER LITTLE SHOPPER' said a flag in the here-and-now as it went past Sarah's nose. It was attached by a perpendicular wire to a miniature trolley which a little girl was pushing in the wake of her parents' grown-up one. Her little sister had a tinier trolley, also with a flag. They had a baby brother, squidged into the seat just as hers had been. The whole family, Mum, Dad and kids, were clearly united in their determination to shop properly and were making a great success of blocking the potato aisle.

Dan returned, with lemongrass, fresh herbs and a bunch of assorted chillis. He threw them into the trolley and then surveyed its contents.

'Looking *good*!' he decided. 'OK …' Now he was looking around again and muttering to himself. 'Need some leaves…' Sarah wondered suddenly if he still knew she was there, and thought she had better remind him.

'Can I get anything?' she asked.

'Sorry what?'

'I know I'm minding the trolley but –'

'Are you? That's cute, you don't have to do that. If you want to help you could get some – yeah, could you grab some sweet potatoes?'

This turned out to be difficult, as the sweet potatoes were not with the usual potatoes, where they should have been. For several minutes she went round in circles, obstructing decent families in the course of their shopping, before she managed to find them, grouped with other gnarled and expensive items, under EXOTIC. And when she went to find Dan, neither he nor the trolley were where she had left them. Was he always going to wander off in supermarkets? She heard herself let out a sharp breath through clenched teeth.

'Husband wandered off, dear?' asked a voice at her left shoulder. She looked round and saw an elderly woman, supporting herself on a sort of high, wheeled basket.

'Oh he's not my husband,' she replied, then added, without knowing why: 'It's the first time we've come here together.'

'It is, is it?' The woman threw a sceptical glance at the sweet potatoes. 'What are these, then? Something special for a special dinner?'

'I guess - yes.'

'I see. Now I always cook a cauliflower on a Saturday. I do feel sorry for you young girls, with all your choices. In my day you just did what was expected. Well, good luck.' And with that she trundled away.

She heard Dan before she saw him, and followed his voice to FRESH FISH:

'…I mean with salmon you need to keep it simple, right? You could so easily ruin it when it just speaks for itself, if you see what I mean?'

'I wouldn't worry, sir. It's hard to ruin good salmon like this,' said the assistant. 'How much would you like?'

Dan was clearly put out by the suggestion that salmon might worry him.

'Now hang on a moment…' he said. 'I've got a feeling my guests might be sick of salmon actually. Maybe I'll take some tuna instead? Now for a dinner party I could sear it – really *flash fry* it, or…'

Sarah was relieved that he did not ask for her opinion on the fish. If he had asked her she might have had to admit that she had avoided all kinds ever since the discovery of a bone in her fish finger one school lunchtime. That would have been awkward, given that he was so set on cooking it. She supposed that on the night she would just have to swallow her disgust along with whichever sort of fish he served.

For now, she was content to lean on Dan's trolley while he told the fish counter assistant everything he knew about cooking tuna. Dan liked to tell people things, but that was forgivable, she thought, in a person who knew so much. Since she met him she had learned quite a lot: about food, obviously, but also about cars, property prices in different parts of London, Premier League football, which were the best fake goods to buy in the Far East and where were the best places in Britain to go rock-climbing. As it happened, Sarah knew quite a few things herself, but rightly suspecting that Dan had little or no interest in them, she let him chunter on. She had had enough of polysyllabic, all-night break-ups with other people who read too much. In any case, she had plenty of friends to talk to, and hoped for different things from Dan.

SAUCE, said the sign, cheekily. OIL, it nudged. Dan had plumped for the salmon after all and now he wanted some soy sauce. Sarah followed him past winking rows of chutneys and marinades until he stopped in front of a group of shelves stacked with bottles of brown stuff, all identical-looking but for their prices and labels.

'Now, I'm gonna have to think about this,' he said.

He picked up a couple of bottles. One had a blue and white label, while the other's was red.

'You see, these are both great,' he began, 'but it all depends on whether you're looking for subtlety, or more of a *kick*...' There was a lot more to think about, but nothing that Sarah could do beyond agreeing that it would be a bad thing to overwhelm the fish, so she was free to watch an older couple in the same aisle. They were performing a kind of resentful pas de deux: she would select a bottle of olive oil, a bottle of balsamic vinegar, a jar of pesto; the moment she placed the item in the trolley, he would remove it and replace it with an alternative brand, another kind of vinegar, a different-sized bottle; sometimes it was the other way round, *her* turn to undermine *him*. They did not make eye contact at any time; neither did they speak.

Sarah could find nothing to say on the subject of olive oil, nothing to say about artichoke hearts, nothing to say at the cheese counter.

On the way to the drinks aisle, Dan made his disappointment clear.

'You know, you should really widen your horizons: people expect a woman of your education to know more about food.'

'Well, you can teach me,' she tried.

'I shouldn't need to,' he retorted.

She held her tongue, accepting that a woman such as herself – an overgrown student who lived in rented squalor and could barely boil an egg – stood in dire need of correction. Dan had been appalled by her flat. He had said that the kitchen made him feel sick to his stomach and the bathroom was a health hazard. He wondered how she could bear to sleep on such a rumpled sheet, how she could even think straight when her desk was so disorganised. She could not persuade him to spend a single night at her place, and for the last few weeks had rarely slept there herself. As they shot past CONVENIENCE, she realised two things: first, that her laundry was building up and second, that she was desperate for a Pot Noodle.

They hit WINE BEER SPIRITS in silence.

'You'll be looking for white wine? For the fish?' she suggested, hoping to redeem herself.

Dan laughed. 'Well even an idiot knows *that*, for God's sake!'

'Thanks ever so.'

'Sorry,' said Dan, 'Sorry, I don't mean to laugh at you, it's just hard not to sometimes when – sorry. So you're into wine then, yeah?'

'Well I drink it.'

'Cool. So, what shall I go for then? We could go for German or French or New Zealand, playing it safe, you know, but I was thinking maybe something more radical, like Bulgarian – or even English – most people don't realise it but there are some great English wines, could be a talking point, what do you think?'

'Up to you,' she said curtly, but he didn't seem to register either her answer or the curtness of it. He was already scrutinising the first of many bottles, perhaps to see whether or not it said 'Talking Point' on the label. Sarah's gaze wandered to the SPIRITS end of the aisle, where a man was deliberating over the malt whiskeys. He had exactly the same intense, thoughtful look on his face as Dan had on his. After some time he selected one of the square bottles, slipped it under the lapel of his jacket, and ambled away. He reminded Sarah of a magnificent delinquent from her undergraduate days, who had introduced himself by sidling up to her in a bar, pointing at her then boyfriend who was ordering drinks, and muttering, 'Now that man has what I would call a punchable face.' She had decided to chuck the boyfriend then and there, without much regret.

She turned back to Dan, who was now making space in the trolley for three bottles of safe New Zealand and three of daring English. How handsome he looked. Handsome and well-dressed. Handsome, well-dressed and − *scrubbed*. All at once she felt unbearably sorry for him. There he was, blamelessly arranging wine, quite unaware that the new girlfriend who stood by his side usually just pretended to listen, and thought him scrubbed. She was ashamed of herself; she would atone by being helpful.

'And some dessert wine, maybe?' she suggested.

He gurned irritably.

'No, there's no need for that. Anyway I haven't got time to fart about choosing more wine − let's go.'

Dan was in a hurry all of a sudden. He propelled his trolley with an air of strained patience, as if it were a whining child he was itching to smack, and the look on his face showed clearly that he had too much on his mind, what with the shallots and the fish and the contrasting wines. Sarah had noticed this look before, when he had had a bad day at work, when she had annoyed him in some way, or, worst of all, when something had put him in mind of his ex-girlfriend. Already, she knew better than to ask what was up.

The signs and banners were getting tetchy as well. LAST DAY OF SAVINGS, they warned. MIND YOU DON'T MISS OUT. Every shopper Sarah saw looked fed up or even angry, and she was convinced that several of them were pushing trolleys straight at her. It all came to a head under LAVATORY PAPER, when Dan stopped abruptly and someone's trolley hit her straight in the back. She turned round and saw the mother of the Proper Shopping Family, scowling at her. The woman made no attempt to apologise and as she manoeuvred past them Sarah heard her muttering something to her husband about silly girls getting in the way.

'I need to get some cleaning stuff,' said Dan. 'I've let the flat go to pot lately, it's not fit for guests. Wait here will you.' He vanished into HOUSEHOLD CLEANING, leaving Sarah standing by the bog roll.

He had abandoned the trolley in the most awkward place, jutting out halfway into PET PRODUCTS. A hail of tuts and sighs made it obvious that it and she were very much in everyone's way. She pushed the trolley forward a little. A greyish, pinched-looking man trying to get to the Four Rolls for Two promotion snapped 'Excuse *me*,' in a pointed fashion, so she pulled the trolley back again. Then she decided to haul it round through 90 degrees so that it blocked less of the aisle, but this only made her the sworn enemy of another young woman, who needed to get to the cat litter. She gave up then and concentrated on trying not to look as if she and the trolley had anything to do with each other.

At once she heard a thud. She looked up and saw Cat Litter Girl sprawled out on the floor. Someone was barking 'One down!' into a walkie-talkie. A few moments later, two women in blue uniforms came surging round a corner and rushed to the girl's side. One propped her up while the other opened the bottle of Lucozade she was carrying and thrust it into her hands.

'Don't worry, love' she said, 'happens all the time at this end of the store. People don't realise what a long slog it is, going round. Have a proper breakfast next time, OK?'

'Still here?' asked a voice at Sarah's shoulder. It was the Cauliflower Lady.

'Reminds me of my second husband,' she said. 'I came home and there he was on the kitchen floor: dropped dead, just like that.' She peeked inside Dan's trolley. 'Nearly done, then?'. Sarah nodded. 'Just as well. You're looking a bit off-colour yourself, dear.'

Dan reappeared, his arms full of serious germicidal weaponry. The message was clear: no stray particles in my flat. Any body, large or small, wishing to retain the option of staying there, would need to make appropriate and careful efforts to fit in.

'Dan?' Sarah asked.

'Uh-huh?' he replied absently, as he rearranged his trolley again.

'So what should I wear to this dinner?'

Dan started at this. 'Sorry? What?'

'I said what should I wear to this dinner? Is it supposed to be a formal thing, or what?'

'Ah...' Dan pulled a face and rubbed the back of his neck. 'Oh shit this is awkward. You see, the thing is, this dinner –'

'Yes?'

'Well the thing is – did you just assume you were gonna be there?'

'*Sorry?*'

Dan's face did its best to look abject.

'Believe me I did *consider* it but – well it's a bit early to show you to my colleagues really, and a dinner like this – I arranged it weeks ago by the way, before we even met – it would sort of make you my official girlfriend, and – don't get me wrong, that is – I only broke up with Lucy three months ago, and that was three years, we were even engaged – I mean don't get me wrong I really really like you but – under the circumstances it could hardly be appropriate to serve up someone I only picked up at a party a few weeks ago, you see my problem, don't you?'

Sarah said nothing.

'I said I do *like* you,' he pleaded. 'Tell you what, I'll squeeze you in for a quick lunch -my treat - before I have to start preparing. OK?'

Sarah took a deep breath.

'Dan,' she said at last, 'I hope you get all the best stuff in life: great offers, great choice, great value. Mind you don't miss out now.'

She headed straight for GOODBYE, not even seeming to notice the shoppers and trolleys parting in front of her, as the waters of the Red Sea must part before the valued and the chosen.

■

Gunpowder and Vanilla

Sophie Hannah

'Listen to this,' I say to my husband. He looks up hopefully. At this stage he is willing to give me the benefit of the doubt; he believes I might have something interesting to say about a mountain or a big lizard. '"Dear Briony",' I begin to read aloud.

My husband frowns. His eyes dart left and right, looking for an escape route. By now he will have noticed that I have a letter in my hand, not a newspaper. He is more interested in the activities of people we don't know than those we do. 'Get on with it,' he says.

'"Dear Briony,"' I begin again. '"Thank you so much for the wonderful book. What a lovely Christmas present!"'

'Christmas present? It's bloody March!'

I sigh. 'Please just listen. "I can only apologise that it has taken me so long to acknowledge receipt of and thank you for this kind gift. Beatrix Potter is one of my favourite authors. I have an excellent bath book that features Mr Jeremy Fisher – I strongly recommend it."'

'Who?'

'Jeremy Fisher. He's a Beatrix Potter character. A frog.'

My husband seems suddenly to realise that the letter is odder than it is boring. 'What's going on?' he demands. 'Briony hasn't bought any books for anyone. She's four months old. Who's it from?'

'That depends on your point of view,' I say.

'Anna, I haven't got time for games.'

'It's signed "With a whole lot of warm regards, Gunila".' I wait for this information to sink in.

'Gunila. Gunila…' He's trying to place the name. He

knows he's heard it before.

I give him a clue. 'When she was born, you said it was a bloody awful name, and why would anyone want to call their child something that sounded like a mixture of gunpowder and vanilla.'

'Oh – Thing and Thing's baby.'

When we were expecting Briony, we attended private ante-natal classes, along with four 'Thing-and-Things'. My husband is not normally able to remember the name of anyone who hasn't led a polar expedition or chaired a House of Commons enquiry.

'Natasha and Milo's baby,' I say.

'Well, the letter's not from her, is it? She's also only about four months old. Natasha must have written it.'

'Yes, which means I was right,' I tell him, wondering if I enjoy being right a bit too much. 'When Gunila was born and we sent her that hat and bootees set, instead of getting a thank-you card from Natasha and Milo, Briony got a thank-you card from Gunila. Remember, I said it was odd at the time and you denied it. And then at Christmas, we got a card from Natasha and Milo, and Briony got a separate one from Gunila. Again, you denied that was weird.'

'I don't remember any of that,' says my husband, 'but I'll take your word for it. And before you try to demolish my case with your ruthless logic, as I know you like to do at least once before lunch, there's no need. Obviously I underestimated the lunacy of Natasha and…'

'Milo.'

'Yes. That…' – he nods at the letter – '…sounds insane.'

I hear a faint cooing noise from upstairs. Briony is awake after a long morning nap. In a few minutes she'll start to cry as she realises she's hungry. I am in a rush to present the rest of my evidence before I have to go and attend to her. 'Insane is right. Listen to the rest of it: "I don't know about you, but I feel that a lot of the board books that we babies are given are more than a little patronising. Often they have only one word on each page, beside a substandard drawing of the object in question. No story, no characters – I'm sure you will agree this is pitiful. Whereas what Beatrix Potter does so well is create a whole world that springs to life, full of likeable characters and interesting stories. If she can do it, why can't other writers make the effort? Anyway, thanks again for the enjoyable volume. I hope you liked your Christmas present from me. Your mummy wrote and thanked my mummy, but it would have been nice to hear from you too. With a whole lot of warm regards, Gunila." Well?'

'Psychos,' my husband mutters.

'Exactly! And do you remember what they got Briony for Christmas? That awful bodysuit with 'Love Child' written on it.'

My husband had thrown this straight in the bin, a fact that I did not include in my thank-you note to Natasha and Milo. I couldn't even persuade him that we ought to donate it to charity. 'Why not just cut the platitudes and have a T-shirt that says "My parents shagged"?' he'd grumbled. My objection to the bodysuit had been different; I don't like the idea of making children wear words. It seems exploitative, since they can't choose the words themselves.

'So what are we going to do?' I ask.

'Do? Nothing. Avoid them.'

'Maybe we need to do more than that.'

'Well, that's all I feel *I* need to do,' says my husband firmly.

'Seriously, though, don't you think it's sinister? I mean, a Christmas card from Gunila to Briony, that's one thing, but putting the words of an entire letter – a fairly opinionated one at that – into a baby's mouth… And that bit about "your mummy thanked my mummy, but it would have been nice to hear from you" – I mean, that's a criticism of me, isn't it?'

'She obviously wants you to join in the game of pretending the babies are writing to each other. Maybe she thinks you're a spoilsport. Ignore it – she's clearly a nutter. I'll get Briony.'

And that is the end of the discussion for the time being;

for ever, as far as my husband is concerned. I wonder if he's right.
Should I just ignore it? Am I a spoilsport?

I find the phone. One by one, I ring the other Thing-and-
Things from the ante-natal group. Becky and her husband aren't
in. I don't leave a message, since what I have to say would sound
too odd, recorded. Caroline and Liz are both in, though their
husbands are out. They tell me that Felix and Molly have both also
received thank-you letters from Gunila this morning. Did
Felix/Molly get a bodysuit with 'Love Child' written on it for
Christmas? I ask Caroline/Liz. No, they got different slogans:
'When I grow up I want to be just like my mummy' and 'Made
with 100% love' respectively. Did both babies write to thank
Gunila personally, rather than using their mummies as a conduit?
Yes, both did.

I read first Caroline and then Liz the ominous line from
Gunila's letter to Briony, and ask them what they think. In doing
this, I am breaching one of the unspoken rules of our group. We
never bitch about one another; we are quite strict about this. It is
almost as if we fear that, being a group of women with babies that
meets every week for lunch, the danger of a two-faced, back-
biting atmosphere breaking out is so great that we must have a
clear system in place if we are to avoid it.

'Natasha's teasing you,' says Caroline. 'She wants you to
enter into the spirit of the game.'

'And you think that's all it is?' I ask. 'You don't think she's
seriously cross with me?' Caroline does not. Neither does Liz,
who says that Natasha doesn't intend her comment as a dig, but
rather as a guide. 'She thinks you're being slow on the uptake,' says
Liz. 'You haven't realised that it's Gunila and Briony who are
writing to each other, not you and Natasha - she probably thinks
you're too busy to notice, so she's giving you a gentle nudge in the
right direction.' Neither Liz nor Caroline, I realise, has mentioned
Milo as a possible agent of action. Husbands rarely feature in our
conversation; when they do, their place in a sentence is beside a
comic expletive and nowhere near a verb.

'But it isn't the right direction, for me,' I explain. 'I really don't like the idea of…impersonating Briony, in a letter. It seems a bit sinister. I mean, Briony and Gunila are real people, not ventriloquists' dummies.' That last part came out a little too vehemently.

I realise I have overstepped the mark when Liz says, coolly, 'I'd better go - I'm in the middle of puréeing a butternut squash.'

Later that evening, I get hold of Becky, and am not at all surprised to discover that Callum too has been engaged in correspondence of a first-hand nature with the prolific Gunila. I wonder why it bothers me so much, when it doesn't seem to bother any of the other mothers.

At the next mothers-and-babies lunch (at Liz's house - it is her turn), I make a point of cornering Natasha for a private chat. 'Listen, I hope you don't think I'm a killjoy,' I say brightly. 'I know I'm probably a bit odd, but I just can't bring myself to write letters as if from Briony - I feel a bit funny about it. I hope you don't mind.'

Natasha gives me a wide-eyed stare. 'What are you talking about?' she says.

'Well…your…Gunila's letter to Briony.'

'What about it?'

'The bit that said…'

Natasha puts out a hand to stop me. 'I'm not interested in what it said.' She gives me a pointed stare. 'It's rude to pry into other people's correspondence. What sort of example would I be setting Gunila if I did that?'

Natasha flounces off. I am so shocked by her response that I cannot move. Is this some elaborate joke, I wonder, or is she truly mad? I can hear her in Liz's lounge, saying 'I've brought some fondant fancies - not home-made this time, I'm afraid!'. I hear Liz, Becky and Caroline cooing over the cakes. I know that I won't be able to phone any of them later and tell them about this latest instalment of Natasha's lunacy; Liz has perhaps already redefined me as an over-sensitive trouble-maker and I don't want Becky and Caroline to do the same.

'Why not?' demands my husband later, when I tell him what Natasha said to me. 'Tell them all she's a freak. Say you want her and Gunila kicked out.'

I laugh, so absurd is his suggestion. Bad-mouthing one mother to the others in the group is a serious enough breach of our code, and one I have almost committed. Bad-mouthing one of the babies is the absolute worst sin of all. We all know this, even though we have never discussed it. If I committed major fraud and went to jail, I would be viewed less harshly by Liz, Becky and Caroline, and certainly Natasha, than if I suggested the eviction of Gunila from our weekly get-togethers.

'I can't do that,' I say. My husband wouldn't understand about the mums' code of ethics, so I give him another reason: 'If you try to convince someone about the unsavouriness of someone else, it's you who ends up looking unsavoury.'

'Yeah, right,' he mumbles sarcastically. 'Like at Harold Shipman's trial, when no-one thought any the worse of Shipman but everyone really hated that bitchy prosecuting lawyer!'

'But I haven't got hundreds of dead bodies in the way of proof,' I explain. 'I've only got a few weird comments.'

'Well, then, you've said it yourself. No proof. Natasha may be bonkers but she's not a monster. So stop worrying.'

'Okay,' I lie. I fear that Natasha is, indeed, a monster, all the more terrifying for being one who makes excellent chocolate brownies.

A week later, we are invited to an 'at home', to celebrate Gunila's christening. My husband and I are invited by Natasha and Milo, and Briony gets her own invitation card from Gunila. They arrive on the same day, in two separate envelopes. 'This is my last chance,' I tell my husband grimly. 'If Briony doesn't RSVP in person, separately from ours, Natasha will write me off.'

'I'm fed up with this!' he says. 'Just send a reply from Briony and get the madwoman off your back.'

'What, allow myself to be emotionally blackmailed? Give in?'

'Anna, this isn't the American civil war. What does it

matter? Just send a reply from Briony. I'll bloody do it myself if it'll…'

'You will not! Promise that you won't!'

My husband shakes his head, bemused and disapproving at the same time, and wanders off into another room. 'Leave me out of it,' he says.

The next day I write a friendly – perhaps overly friendly – card. 'Dear Natasha, Milo and Gunila,' it says. 'Yes, thank you, we'd love to come to Gunila's christening party. We're looking forward to it.' I sign it from myself, my husband and Briony. This is, I feel, a reasonable compromise. I don't mind including Briony in this way, since it is customary, on Christmas cards for example, to sign on behalf of the whole family.

I show it to my husband. 'So you caved,' he teases me. He is trying to watch a televised debate about the war in Iraq, which started yesterday, and I am distracting him. 'You signed it from Briony.' I try to explain to him the difference between a family signature which includes a baby, and a separate letter from a baby only in which strong views are expressed that the baby cannot possibly hold.

My husband shakes his head impatiently. 'It'll keep Nutasha happy, anyway,' he says. His comment reveals to me how little he understands. I send the card, after adding a PS: 'Let me know if I can bring anything', since another rule of our organisation is that one must do as much cooking when one is not the host as one does when one is.

At the next mothers-and-babies lunch, Natasha ignores me completely. She refuses even to make eye contact. Becky, Liz and Caroline don't notice; they are too busy eating her summer fruit muffins. I am grimly happy with the situation. I now loathe Natasha (and, if I am honest, Gunila as well, since it is difficult to like a baby whose parents you detest). Nothing need change, I tell myself. I will speak only to Caroline, Liz and Becky from now on. Natasha will do the same. Our lunches needn't be disrupted.

As Natasha and I are not on speaking terms, Milo telephones my husband three days before Gunila's christening party and apologetically tells him that it would be great if he could make a goat's cheese, tomato and caramelised onion tart and bring it to the party. My husband is confused; he doesn't know about the equal-cooking-and-inconvenience rule and thinks that Milo has a bloody cheek. I consider refusing to make the tart, but decide to keep the moral highground by fulfilling my culinary responsibilities.

At the party, the husbands stand in one corner of the garden and drink whisky and beer and talk about whisky and beer and the war in Iraq. All are against, apart from mine, but the discussion is amicable. The wives talk about weaning and sleep. Again Natasha and I completely ignore each other and again nobody notices.

Two days later, Briony and I are at my parents' house. I phone home to remind my husband to make up Briony's bottles for the night. 'Another letter's arrived,' he tells me. I am surprised. I had assumed that Gunila would have dropped Briony when her mother dropped me. 'Read it to me,' I say, worried it will be hate mail.

I hear the tearing of paper, a silence, then a disgusted snort. 'Fucking fucks!' my husband bellows.

'What?' I ask, my heart lurching. For the first time since this whole business began, my husband sounds as if he cares. Therefore it must be serious.

'"Dear Briony, I'm sure you are as distressed as I am by the behaviour of George Bush and our own leader Tony Blair.'"

'What?' I gasp.

'What?' says my mother, who is standing behind me. 'Doesn't he know how to make up her bottles?'

'"Not content with wreaking havoc in Kosovo and Afghanistan, they are now waging war on Iraq for totally selfish reasons. They want control of all the world's oil reserves, and Bush wants to tie up his father's loose ends by defeating Saddam Hussein. America has already murdered too many Iraqi babies, with their callous sanctions, and now they will murder more in this imperialist war. Innocent babies will die, and we, as babies, need to make our voices heard in protest. There is going to be a demonstration in Leeds city centre next Saturday, in Millennium Square, and I urge you to get your parents to bring you along. Down with Bush! Down with Blair! See you Sat, Millennium Square! With a whole lot of warm regards, Gunila." Anna? Can you believe it? This is fucking outrageous! What are we going to do about it?'

My husband's take on events in Iraq differs from Gunila's in several crucial respects. I tell him we'll discuss it when I get home.

This turns out to have been a mistake. When I raise the subject later, he says, 'I've already dealt with it.' I am alarmed; my husband has never already dealt with anything, apart from his own work and matters concerning the upkeep of the outside of our house.

'How?' I ask.

'I wrote back. Or rather, Briony did.' He grins mischievously.

'*What?*'

'Don't worry, I knew you'd want to be in on it.'

'Oh, thank God! You haven't posted it yet.'

'No, I have. But I've kept a copy to show you.' He produces a folded piece of paper from his pocket. I grab it.

'Dear Gunila,' it says, 'I will not be attending the anti-war protest in Millennium Square on Saturday, and I object to your pernicious letter. You say "Down with Bush" and "Down with Blair", but there is no mention of Saddam Hussein and his barbaric regime. Why doesn't he deserve a "Down with"? You talk about saving the lives of babies, but it is Saddam Hussein, not George Bush or Tony Blair, who buries children in mass graves along with their dolls. It is Saddam Hussein, not George Bush or Tony Blair, who tortures children in front of their parents, and who puts children into plastic shredders. Oh, sorry, didn't you know about any of that? Well, you should stop reading *the Guardian*, with its blinkered, one-sided opionion pieces, and read some reports from human rights organisations instead. Ten thousand people a year are murdered by the Ba'athist regime in Iraq. What do you suggest we do about that? Ignore it? It is one thing to say that you do not support the war for the reason that war is a barbaric and brutal thing – nobody would deny that. But it is quite another actively to oppose it, and portray Bush and Blair as the only villains involved. True, their motives may not be entirely pure and honourable, but if you were living in a human-rights-abusing dictatorship, if your loved ones were reguarly being disappeared and tortured and murdered, how would you feel? Would you only want to be liberated by the entirely virtuous, or would you just be desperate to be freed, even by the morally compromised Americans? You probably can't even imagine such a situation, can you, because you live in leafy Roundhay, enjoying all the benefits of a democratic way of life. The worst thing that's ever likely to happen to you is that some minion won't get your caramelised goat tart ready on time. Please don't send me any more of your foul outpourings on this matter. You might want to lend your support to Saddam Hussein and the Ba'ath party next Saturday; I do not. Yours sincerely, Briony.'

My husband grins proudly. 'Pretty good, hey?'

'Oh my God,' is all I can say. I want to run to the phone and ring Becky, Liz and Caroline, but I know there is no point. I'm finished. I'm out of the group. But I don't care about that; the only thing that bothers me is that he signed it from Briony. He wrote about war and torture and murder and he signed it from our baby daughter. I do not speak to him for two days.

On Wednesday morning I get a phonecall from Becky. Her voice sounds strange. She tells me the lunch this week is cancelled. I know she's lying. The others will meet and discuss what to do. Natasha will bring my husband's letter along, and everyone will gape at it in horror.

Five days later, Briony gets another letter. This time it is not merely from Gunila. All the babies have signed it. 'Dear Briony,' it says. 'We have all read your letter to Gunila and were extremely upset by it. How could you write such nasty things? We are, however, willing to give you the benefit of the doubt. We suspect that that letter actually had nothing to do with you. We think your daddy wrote it. He said almost those exact same things to our daddies quite recently. We are deeply shocked that he could put such violent sentiments into the mouth of a baby. If we are right, and if you can assure us that this wicked letter is the handiwork of your daddy and your daddy alone, we will let bygones be bygones and of course we will be happy to see you and your mummy at our lunches as usual. But if you stand by the letter, we are afraid that we can no longer be friends with you. It's up to you. Regretfully, Gunila, Felix, Callum and Molly'. I can picture the four of them, in their parents' arms, at the anti-war demonstration. Dancing to Gunila's tune, as always. I hate Gunila with a passion.

My husband is contrite. 'I shouldn't have signed it from Briony. I got carried away. Maybe I should write to those four babies and admit responsibility, you know, and sign it from me.' I can tell he feels bad for ruining my mother-and-baby lunches. I am past caring. I get a piece of notepaper and write a letter to the whole group, to Becky, Liz, Caroline and their husbands, to Callum, Felix, Molly and Gunila, and to Natasha and Milo. I write 'Dear', then all their names, and then I just write, in large capital letters 'FUCK YOU ALL'. I don't sign it from anybody. I consider making twelve copies and sending each one separately, but decide that would be mad. I must extricate myself from the madness, not sink deeper into it. I make only one copy and send it to Natasha. She will make sure everyone sees it.

My husband says that when we have another baby, we can go to ante-natal classes again and meet a new lot of families, and I can join a new mother-and-baby lunch set.

No way, I tell him. Nobody bothers with ante-natal classes the second time round. Once you've had your first baby, you realise that those classes don't prepare you for the reality of parenthood. You spend hours fixating on matters that will not apply to you, like what to do if you notice that a bit of the umbilical cord is hanging out of you before the baby is born (stick your bum in the air and stay in that position all the way to hospital), but you never learn anything that will be of actual, practical use (like, says my husband, what to do if your baby is ostracised by apologists for the Ba'athist regime). He is quite right. None of the text-books, none of the classes, prepare you for that.

—

A Tray of Ice Cubes

Gerard Woodward

1

Daphne and Colin were spending Friday evening as they spent most Friday evenings – in front of the telly with a microwaved dinner and a bottle of sweet German wine, watching their favourite programme; *a camcorder compilation of matrimonial mishaps and wedding-day disasters* called 'The World's Worst Weddings'.

Each programme treated its viewers to a parade of doomed brides tumbling down church steps, or skidding backwards and landing legs-in-the-air on dance floors. Beautifully crafted, four-tiered wedding cakes toppled slowly sideways like Pisan towers and then collapsed into rubbly heaps of icing. Horses bolted with their empty landaus from the church gates. The weather outside the churches was always turbulent, lifting the brides' dresses up over their heads to reveal saucy bridal lingerie, or whipping the top hats off the heads of the men who chased them through churchyards like farmers after troupes of grey hens.

This anthology of crookedly shot, poorly focused visions of minor catastrophes had Daphne and Colin in stitches. They laughed until they hurt. They winced at painful bits (drunken sword-dancing, marquees bulging with stored rain), drew in their breath, gave each other mock-horrified looks, groaned, giggled, shook their heads pityingly and put their hands over their mouths.

By the end of the programme, as the credits rolled quickly over a reprise of the choicest clips, Colin and Daphne felt exhausted. Their jaws ached and their voices were hoarse. But at the same time they felt refreshed and reassured by the sense they had that other people's lives were a train of small calamities, and that while their own lives might not be everything they'd wished for, at least they were ordered havens of static objects and common sense people. The World's Worst Weddings renewed for them each week their sense of their own worth as people while fortifying them for the routine struggles of the week ahead.

Daphne was manager of the Erith branch of BurgerWorld where she supervised a crew of twenty surly teenagers and two shift managers. She could handle (though rarely needed to) one hundred and fifty customers an hour. She was a good branch manager. She had, in the words of Dale, her area executive, 'ketchup in her blood'. She was blonde, wide, buxom and clever. She was forty-seven.

Colin her coeval, childhood sweetheart and husband of thirty years was a bus driver. He had power-steered red double-deckers from Trafalgar Square through the suburbs of South East London for almost as long as they'd been married. In the early days he had sat alone in the forward cab of a Routemaster, obeying the bells, buzzers and knocks of his conductor. Then, at the beginning of the Seventies, he was asked to merge two people into his one body and become both driver and conductor of the new pay-as-you-enter buses. It had been difficult at first, and he felt bad about the conductors who lost their jobs, but he managed the transition with some panache. He has twice been a finalist in the South East Bus Driver of the Year Awards. He genuinely cared about his human cargo. He took corners carefully. When he stopped he stopped gently and his passengers all nodded in unison. His sedentary life and fondness for the odd pint had given him a roly-poly figure and a thickening of fat around the neck. His hair was dark but thinning on top, combed back and out of the way behind his ears, half an inch short of unkempt. His teeth were sharp, symmetrical, stained with cigar tobacco.

He was stretched out on the couch, still in his bus drivers' uniform which, with its wine-coloured blazer and striped tie, made him look like a ridiculous schoolboy. This added to the shock Daphne felt when he turned his brick-red face, still damp with laughing, towards her and said, in a voice quiet with excitement,

'Love, I think I'm pregnant.'

2

Daphne was busy with tomatoes, slicing them in a machine called a tomato shark.

India, one of her shift managers, was preparing burger cartons. There was a lull in trade at BurgerWorld, as there usually was mid-afternoon. India hated these lulls as they made the time drag, although she found a simple satisfaction in the clever origami of her burger cartons. A flat card envelope is extracted from the packet which, with a deft twist of the thumbs, flips into a three-dimensional box with hinged lid, catch and steam vents.

Of all the crew India was closest to Daphne. They did not meet outside the workplace (apart from the Christmas do) but in BurgerWorld they regarded each other as friends. India liked Daphne's boldness, her sturdiness. She admired her. She thought if Daphne was a building she would be a provincial town hall – solid, sensible, yet not without ornamentation and humour. India would be one of those little striped tents workmen erect over manholes. So she reacted at first with disbelief and bewilderment when she noticed Daphne was crying.

She left her teetering tower of yet-to-be-filled cartons and walked hesitantly towards Daphne as if to a statue that had moved. Closer she could see it was true – Daphne, good old blonde-haired, piss-taking, dependable Daphne was crying. The water was spilling out of her eyes, falling off the end of her nose and salting her tomatoes.

'Are you crying, Daph?' India uselessly asked.

Daphne, whose head was hanging, suddenly drew her face back, as if to make the tears withdraw into her eyes. It was as though she hadn't known she was crying. She fumbled in her pocket for a hanky, couldn't find one. India gave her a serviette.

'Stupid,' said Daphne, holding the paper to her eyes like a

blindfold, still with her other hand on the lever of the tomato shark.

'Anything I can do?' Said India.

Daphne took a deep breath, held it for what seemed like a dangerous length of time, then exhaled loudly. She took the paper away from her eyes, looked at India with a half smile that was meant to say 'I'm fine now', then collapsed into uncontrollable sobs. Some of the other staff noticed. Baseball-capped heads peered round the sides of broilers, or beneath frier hoods. India took hold of Daphne's shaking frame (the first time, she realised, that she'd touched her manager) and guided her into the cramped space of telephones, files, lists and memos that served as an office.

'What's up Daph? What's going on?'

'I can't say. Nothing. Sod it.'

'Don't you think you should talk about it?'

Daphne gave a choked laugh.

'I wouldn't know where to begin.'

'Try the beginning.'

Daphne compressed her lips, shook her head so slightly it was like trembling.

'Is it your old man? Is there something wrong with Colin?'

This was an educated guess. Colin's health was a regular topic of conversation between Daphne and India – his latest digestive problem or heart attack scare, his creeping arthritis, even his occasional lack of libido. India had never met Colin but she thought she must know more about his body than his own doctor.

India could tell by Daphne's stillness that she'd hit the mark.

'What is it? Is he ill?'

'It sounds so stupid, India love. I don't know how to say it. I haven't told anyone, not even my Mum.'

'You can tell me.'

'Well I've got to tell someone…' Daphne was whispering now, even though there was no one within earshot, '…a few months ago – about six months ago – Colin got this idea into his head – I mean he really believes it, that he's...'

'Yes?' India's eyes were round and expectant.

'He thinks he's pregnant.'

Silence.

Then India let out a giggle, quickly put her hand to her mouth as if to catch it, but she carried on giggling into her hand, muffled.

'Don't India, please love.'

'I'm sorry, but this has got to be a joke, yeah?'

'That's what I thought at first. A joke. A sick joke. We gave up trying to have kids ten years ago. I've told you all about that. There isn't a day goes by, even now, when I don't think about the kids we could have had if things had worked out. I could have been a gran by now. But I thought Colin had forgotten all about it. You know he never was that bothered, not really, even when we were going up to the clinic every week. He was doing it for me really. But now it looks like something's got to him... He's started converting our spare room back into a nursery. We had it as a nursery when we were going for the treatment. Just hoping we could put a baby in it. Just to have the chance to muck around with baby things. When we finally called it a day we gutted the room. It broke my heart. We didn't throw anything away, it was funny, but suddenly everyone we knew needed baby stuff. Most of it went to my sister – the clothes, the cot, the majority of the toys. We painted over the Tiggers with oatmeal, then I used the room for my china painting. You know me and my china. We never miss a craft fair. I had a little kiln in there and everything. But now he's gone and painted new Tiggers on the walls. He's splashed out on a posh cot with brass bits on. He says we have to have everything ready in time. It's due in November.'

'Daphne, you've got to get him to a doctor. Get his head sorted out...'

'I know. The trouble is, in every other way he's completely normal, you know, so Colinish, so bloody boringly Colinish. He's still driving his buses, though he reckons he won't fit behind the wheel for much longer. He's given up the pipe and cigars. He doesn't even have a drink now. He says he's got to take care of himself. But what really frightens me is that I'm starting to believe him. It's like I'm going mad as well. I find myself looking at his beer gut to see if it's getting bigger…'

'And is it?'

Daphne allowed herself a brief, sneezy laugh.

'I keep thinking it *is* getting bigger. And he's off the beer. When he's asleep I put my hand on it and feel for movements. Maybe I do feel something kick, or is it just a bubble of wind? Then I'll listen for a heartbeat. I can hear something, but is it just Colin's heart? I don't know…'

'But Daph, you've got to hold on to the true facts. You've got to remember he can't be pregnant.'

'But why not?' Daphne's voice had acquired a haughtiness that was new to India. India tried to match the tone,

'He's a bloke isn't he?'

Daphne closed her eyes dismissively.

'Colin spun me this long story about how he went to a clinic where they're testing out a new type of fertility treatment, which means the man carrying the embryo instead of the woman.'

India is dismissive now.

'It's true,' Daphne continued, 'I've read up about it. There are people doing work on it right now. They say they don't need any wombs, just a place in the body with a good blood supply. They've planted fertilised eggs on the outer wall of the large intestine of a male mouse and it's gone on to give birth. I know they need one of my eggs but Colin says they kept some from when we were going for the treatment. He reckons they've got a whole dish of them up there. I know it's rubbish but I can't help thinking sometimes. And then I look at that huge tummy of his and it moves…'

'Daphne, I don't want to know. Of course he hasn't been to any clinic. He's flipped his lid. He's got to that age, all men get to it.'

Daphne laughed inwardly at the confidence with which eighteen-year-old India talked about men.

'His tomatoes have gone to pot. The whole crop. Every year he grows these wonderful tomatoes. They've got the best spot in the garden, sunny all day long. He even goes down the stables with a shovel so he can mulch the horseshit into them. They're ready by late August. Well, this year he's just left them. He'd lost interest by June. They were still green in August. He says he's gone right off tomatoes now, because of his condition. We used to have such lovely salads,' Daphne looked across at the bowl of heaped tomato slices, like opened hearts. 'I had to pick them myself. Still green. He wasn't going to bother. I put them in brown paper bags and kept them under the stairs. They're only just beginning to go yellow now. He has cravings for potatoes.'

India didn't know what to say. She noticed a poster on the back of the door which reminded staff of the importance of 'add-ons', and provided a script which specified the exact phrasing to be used. If a customer wants a hamburger, staff must say 'would you like fries with that?' If a customer wants a hamburger with fries, staff must say 'would you like a drink with that?' BurgerWorld provides staff with a script for almost every possible interaction with a customer, from the cheery greetings to the cheery goodbyes. Staff are expected to follow these scripts to the letter. India found it very helpful at first, in dealing with customers, to have her words written for her in advance, but after a while she found that it damaged her ability to talk spontaneously outside the workplace. She wanted scripts for every social encounter, and had to work hard at relearning her ability to converse. Now, with Daphne, she longed again for guidance from head office.

'I'm out of my Depth, Daph.'

'I'm alright, India love. Get back to your prep. I'll sort my old man out somehow.'

India went back to her prep, magicking cartons out of nothing. Daphne went back to slicing her tomatoes. They never, for the rest of their lives, say anything to each other on this subject again.

3

The World's Worst Weddings is on. Daphne is watching it alone. Colin is having a lie-down upstairs.

Daphne isn't finding the programme funny this week. She is watching it but the laughter isn't coming. Those toppling wedding cakes just look sad now. The windy wedding days, flooded marquees, runaway carriages. One clip in particular makes her wince – when a groom faints during the ceremony, falls into his wife-to-be and knocks her to the floor.

But she watches the programme anyway, even though she hasn't found it funny for weeks. It is November now. Last year this programme saw them into winter, took them up to Christmas. But Daphne wonders if she'll watch it again.

Colin is watching it on the portable upstairs, which produces a stereophonic effect. The laughter from the programme is thus given a strangely haunting quality, as though it is not coming from the television, but from the house itself.

Daphne, as the programme finishes with a curious note of triumphalism, barely notices the call coming from upstairs. Colin's weak voice comes down to her

'Daph, love.'

'What is it?' She calls back, slightly impatiently. For the last two weeks Colin has been off work and has spent most of the time in bed.

'Can you come up, love?'

She leaves it for a few minutes, clears away her mostly uneaten pizza, puts a half-empty coffee mug into the sink, wipes the worktop and then goes wearily upstairs. Six months of worrying have exhausted her.

She walks into the bedroom. Colin is lying on his back on top of the bedclothes. His abdomen looks huge to her, suddenly, a great dome, all blubber, she is sure, but it has grown anyway over the last six months. He has the tv remote in his hand and is gripping it so hard his knuckles are creamy white. The portable set on the dressing table is a babble of advertising.

'What's up?' She was going to say, but on seeing Colin's

face realises. He is red, his breath is short and his face is loose with fear, the eyes helpless.

'It's starting, love.'

Daphne sits beside him. His whole body seems to clench and unclench like a fist. She puts her hand on his clammy forehead.

'Take it easy, love,' she says, 'Just stay calm.'

'I feel funny in my tummy, Daph,' he says, 'Love, I can feel it coming out. I think my waters have broken.'

She notices a dark stain on the bed spreading out from between Colin's legs.

'I'm scared, Daph, all this stuff's coming out.'

'Don't worry.'

'Can you stop it coming out, Love, get a towel or something.'

She goes to the bathroom, returns with a bath towel they were still paying the catalogue for.

'Open your legs, Love.'

He opens them. An unpleasant odour rises. Daphne presses the towel up against him.

'Shall I get the doctor, Colin?'

'No,' he says urgently, 'No, please.'

'A midwife?'

'I think it's too late, Love.'

The bed is warm and wet. Suddenly Colin clasps his swollen belly, shouts to Daphne,

'It's coming, Daph. Get something to catch it. Quickly, Love, a bucket, anything.'

She rushes to the bathroom again. There is nothing suitable. She has to go downstairs to the kitchen. The only thing she can find is their non-stick wok. Daphne has only used it once in five years.

Colin is moaning when she returns. She puts the lips of the wok up against his perineum. Thin, cloudy liquid dribbles into it. The bedroom reeks. Colin is crying, tears running sideways down his face, his lips wide, his tongue like a plump little plum in his mouth.

Later Daphne clears up. She yanks the sheets off the bed, piles them into the already overloaded washing basket, then wonders what to do with the mattress. Colin is downstairs on the couch in a dressing gown. She has given him a bath and he smells nice. After she has sorted the bedding out Daphne comes downstairs into the tv room and kisses Colin on the crown of the head, where his hair is thinnest, taking in the fragrance of his scalp.

'How about a drink?' She says.

Colin thinks for a moment, then nods, almost apologetically.

'A nice gin and tonic?'

Colin nods again.

Daphne goes to the kitchen, takes a tray of ice cubes out of the fridge. A dozen nuggets of frozen water. As usual she has trouble extracting them. She bends the tray as much as its metal will allow, and there is a tired, creaking sound. Then something snaps and an ice cube pops out and clatters on the worktop. She has to use a knife to get the rest out, levering dangerously at the chipped edges of each cube. There must be an easier way of making ice, she thinks as she divides her four cubes between two tumblers, splashes some gin and tonic water on top of them and listens to the wheezes and cracks as they expand into the warmth of the alcohol.

She takes the drinks into the tv room and sits with Colin for the rest of the evening, then they go to bed. Daphne leaves the tray of ice cubes out on the worktop. She forgets to put them back in the fridge.

In the morning, when she comes down into the kitchen, yawning and almost happy, her heart falters when she sees the tray of ice cubes on the worktop; it is a trembling, lively, blood-warm tray of water.

-

The Man Who Moved Boulders

Joe Sheerin

It was her idea

'Darling, I've been thinking a lot.' He hated anybody thinking a lot. It meant problems, and problems which started off as insubstantial ideas became in time heavy as boulders. They break the uneventful cadence of life and leave one unsure. He waited. The room held its breath. A minute earlier neither he nor anyone else in the world was thinking. Now a thought like a giant boulder hung on the precipice of the hill ready to roll down with thunderous force threatening the fragile two day shelter that he had constructed for himself at weekends after a dull, tiring and unadventurous week. And he knew why thoughts were like boulders. Because, as in the story, they tumbled with irresistible force down into the valley and lost momentum. There they had to be picked up, usually by him, and humped back – a great round armful of limestone rock up the hill again until he neared the top where it broke free from his embrace and bounced its erratic way down again to the valley floor where he repeated the task. Rock down. Man down. Man and rock up. Rock down. Man down. Rock and man back up. And so on and so on.

'We've had eighteen years of marriage. I know we've had our problems, what with the overhanging pear tree which cost us a bit in the end and that lump I had, which seems to have gone its way, thank God. But on the whole things have been very good for us'

He waited.

'Let's have a party. A particular party. We can renew our marriage vows. A proper ceremony in church. I know you don't believe but it would give the whole thing weight and dignity. We could invite loads of the people that were at our wedding. The girls would love it'

He switched on the bedside lamp and waited. She sat up and moved the second pillow to the bed head. She trailed her hand on his hair. The two things that caused the most problems were parties and ceremonies. This was a combination of the two. A giant stone. More than that a primordial rift in the earth's crust. It was probably an idea like this that made the Grand Canyon. Maybe one god said to another god 'I see miles of flat prairie land here and buffalos grazing.' The other god saw nothing of the sort. He saw miles and miles of rocky sierras. 'Fuckin hell!' And earth tore itself apart and poured out its bile of molten lava on the head of the second god. The first god as we now know had his way.

'Let's plan it. I've worked it out in my mind but I want you to be part of it.'

'It's Sunday night. We'll discuss it tomorrow.' It was a feeble response but it was easier to go along with the idea especially at 11:30. At 6:30 the alarm clock would rock the room like the after shock of an earthquake and he would have to mind himself to face the week's stone carrying. The morning ritual was always the same, get up, urinate, shave, shower. breakfast, bowel duty. The latter was the daily event which he enjoyed most, the only autonomous act he carried out all day. Alone and isolated from the world he relished that three or four minutes of peace. It had some Freudian significance he was once told. Then the briefcase, the car, the M25, the dreaded Building. All day spent travelling from the computer room on the ground floor to his office on the second. Back to the computer room. Back to his office. Ideas varying in size from pebbles to boulders. The others didn't seem to mind. He'd pass them on the stairs. Young balding men would skip past carrying huge chunks of limestone on their neck and shoulders like Atlas. Or fragile girls just out of university, already the mistresses of pebble-carrying, lugged handbags pregnant with stones from the machine room to the print room down to the post room and back to the machine room again.

When he complained they just pouted in disbelief or one or the other of the balding young men would tut and, balancing the boulder on one broad shoulder by one long arm, would wink or goose a pebble carrier as she passed.

On Monday night the idea hadn't died. Instead it had grown huge and rugged and threatening, like Goya's giant, an immensity of stone ready to fall on the feckless imagination and crush its namby-pamby bones in the dust. After dinner they sat down. This was a big one. He thought of events in terms of boulders. Christmas was a ten boulder job. Birthdays six or seven. This was a fifty boulder at least.

'Your mum. My parents, Trevor and Cynthia, John and Simon.' She had a pen. As she made suggestions he thought of good reasons why he didn't want any of them there. For each one he carried a heavy stone of expectations. For his mother the stone of son, for his mother-in-law the double stone of son-in-law and husband. For Trevor, John and Simon and the rest the stones of friendships which he didn't always reciprocate until he sometimes felt himself trapped inside a collapsed cairn. They all carried an agony of responsibility about them, each one different but equal in their own way. But at times like this it's easier to go with the flow. The list finally closed at over thirty people.

'We'll have another honeymoon.' Her enthusiasm stopped the scream rising in his throat where it hung in the sub velar region. A stone near the top of the hill broke free.

'Where shall we go? Portugal or France?'

'Mogadishu,' he suggested.

And he wondered where it was. Somewhere in Africa for sure but where? He imagined an ex-French colonial town with houses the colour of sand and streets made of sand with thin Lowry-like women, but colourful, carrying loads of washing or vegetables on their heads gliding up the main sand street.

Excusez moi. Pouvez vous nous diregez a l'hotel de miel de lune.

'Be sensible. You choose.'

France. It was nearer. Some small hotel in Brittany where

the menhirs were visible from the bedroom window and while she was having a bath he could walk down and sit or lean against one of them and smoke a fag and close his eyes. Perhaps the thing would never happen.

Three months later he was wearing a new suit and she was wearing a pale blue dress with lace trimmings about the hem and on the cuffs and collar and a garland of flowers in her hair. She was carrying a rather large bouquet of myrtle and philadelphus, which maybe wasn't a wise thing to do considering the hay fever season was in full bloom and her asthma was aggravated by it. To be on the safe side he carried her inhaler in his inside pocket. They were both standing in front of the altar of the parish church and behind them to his left on the groom's side two or three people and to his right well over twenty if you included the children.

The priest, his striped trousers visible under his chasuble, held up his hand when the first hymn had finished to announce that the ceremony proper was about to begin. He gave a little cough.

'We are here today for Frank and Sarah to renew their marriage vows. Renewing marriage vows is not a sign that things have gone wrong in the past. Far from it. It is a sign that things have gone good because if things were bad they wouldn't have come here today to renew their badness.'

Frank tried to follow the reasoning but his mind wasn't up to it.

'This ceremony,' the priest continued, 'will be similar to the original ceremony, minus of course the ring which I see Sarah proudly wearing at this moment. But there are a few emendations, which Frank and Sarah have themselves written and wish to be included.'

He turned to Frank and at that moment the sun broke through the stained glass window to the priest's right covering all three of them in what looked like psychedelic clingfilm.

'Frank do you take this woman (sotto voce) for the

second time, to be your lawful and wedded wife?'

'I do.'

'Not yet, you don't. I'll give you a signal when you do.' And he mumbled on to 'until death do you part?'

I fucking do, mate.

'And do you, Frank, promise to give thanks to God each and every day you rise for the great gift of life.'

I won't miss a fucking day, squire

In all Frank had to say 'I do,' at least three times. Each time he answered he was actually looking at the roof of the church and seemed to be accepting the cornice as his lawful and wedded wife for the second time.

In the middle of Frank's renewal a sound not dissimilar to a short sneeze broke out on the groom's side. Someone was crying, probably his mother. It was shortly returned from the bride's side by a similar sound. A sporadic ping-pong of emotion continued throughout the ceremony.

Now it was Sarah's turn. Frank looked at her. Her eyes were closed gently, the ball of the eye socket swelling out the eyelid. She had her fingertips joined at the front of her bouquet. Her first 'I do' had a slight wheeze about it. The second was laboured while the third was inaudible. Frank reached her the inhaler from his jacket pocket but because both of her hands were engaged with the bouquet he moved in front of her and put the inhaler gently between her lips cradling the back of her head with his other hand. Her eyes were streaming but she sucked in deeply a few times, shook her head to show she was finished and said a final 'I do' in a clear high voice.

'The bride and groom may now sit with the congregation,' said the priest and went to the lectern and leaned his elbows on it interlocking his fingers. 'Jesus as we know never married but we do know that He attended a wedding feast. It's no coincidence that that wedding feast was the occasion of His first public miracle…'

Frank was looking at the church tower built in the twelfth century. He wondered how much stone had to be lugged up the rickety beechwood scaffolding. Perhaps one hundred and fifty tons. Maybe more. Four men carrying a three hundredweight cut block up a rickety ladder on to the landing, on to another rickety ladder. Another landing. Another ladder. And so on to the top. Of course there were accidents. Stones fell and men fell under them. The very spot where a minute before Sarah and he stood was probably where a labourer fell, only the man's head and his hands and feet visible. His ribcage and his heart and his guts mixing into the dark wet mud like crushed blackberries.

> *Did you hear to-day up in the new church a stone fell on Ethelred.*

> *Is he dead?*

> *Dead as a pig's arse. He was crushed into paste.*

> *Poor Elfrida. She'll be a loose hoof in the village now and that's for sure.*

> *She's one for the kerls I hear , a right kerl's girl. It's the Norman blood in her.*

> *Give her a month or two and she'll be gagging for it.*

Everybody was getting up and leaving the church. He joined them and took Sarah's arm in case she could read what he had been thinking. At least twenty of the fifty boulders were in place and set securely on the rim of the hill.

Outside the church porch they were besieged. By hands and voices. 'It was a beautiful service.' 'I could have cried my heart out.' 'Sarah you look stunning. You've lost so much.' 'Two stone since January. I thought I'll get into this or I'll die. It was an effort.' And she patted her slightly obvious waist. He fielded the language. Roger, who was best man at their wedding and now an established head teacher, shook his hand warmly and spoke of how beautiful the ritual was. So did Maud, the original bridesmaid. He thanked them effusively, perhaps too effusively. Another two or three boulders in place.

The children and a few of the more adventurous adults had already crossed the road and entered the gardens of the community centre where the reception was being held. Frank drifted away and followed them. The grounds were beautiful in the clear warm sunlight. The lawns undulating and close-cropped green and beyond the lawn a hedge of rhododendrons spread its excess of pink and mauve blossoms like delicate paper flowers strewn prodigally over the branches. It drew him to them and he stood before them in a kind of adoration. They didn't belong here. They should have shut up shop and not produced a single flower, just green leaves and a few aborted buds like the English laurel. They should be repatriated to their home in the Himalayan foothills, like the Grecian marbles and the Assyrian freezes and the Egyptian stuff. Take them all back to their homes. Return everything to how it once exactly was.

The hungry had by now all gone to the reception. Even the priest was scurrying across the lawn like a man ready to eat his share of free food. Frank made his way to the hall. The outside caterers had done a good job. The tables sagged with food and drink, cans for the kids and bottles of red and white, each with a ribbon around the neck. Pink and blue balloons and silver streamers hung from the ceilings and garlanded the tables. He took his named place beside the bride for the day. The waitresses glided in and out serving across the right shoulder as one should. Everybody tucked in. More boulders in place. Before they had nearly finished the meal, Roger tapped a spoon on a wine glass and called for a speech. He meant that he wanted to make a speech but everyone looked at Frank and Frank looked at the table. This was a heavy one. He got up.

'It's better to marry than to burn, said St Paul.' He looked to where the priest sat intently stripping a drumstick of its meat. 'It's much better than burning and the second time round it's even better.' What a stupid thing to say. He should have prepared something just in case. 'Let's drink to the bride. She has a daily beauty in her life and today is all of our days but her day more than the rest of us.' He sat down and got more applause than he deserved.

'And the bride herself,' said Roger noting that Sarah was already in a half standing posture.

Sarah spoke. 'I would like to thank everyone who travelled here to join us on this blissfully sunny day. In particular my mum and dad and Frank's mum, I know the sacrifice she made to be here. I would like to thank our many friends all going back eighteen years and beyond for their loyalty and goodwill. I thank all of you especially the Father who married us all those years ago and who is with us now. Finally I would like to thank my wonderful husband who has been a tower of strength for all of us and who has made the last eighteen years so precious and our two beautiful daughters who are on the threshold of such an exciting life. Because life is good and people make it so.' At this she received genuine applause and Frank felt the inadequacy of his own presentation beside her dignified words. Still a few more boulders were back on the hill. A five or six boulder holiday and everything was sorted. She didn't sit down as people expected but trailed her hand on Frank's head and motioned for the inhaler. 'This is not only a blissful day for all of us but also an occasion for telling you a secret which has been welling up inside me for the past weeks. Nobody, not even Frank who is my rock and my fortress, knows what I'm about to divulge. Well, the doctor does.' And she paused. A tremor of terror ran from Frank's head down to his arse. This could only be bad news. Sarah had been ill recently. Was the lump back? She was never one to complain, a real trooper but she had obviously been unwell. He would be devastated without her. The girls would be wrecked. What a time with Phoebe just about to start her A levels. He looked sharply and apprehensively at his wife. She however looked calm even radiant and bent down and kissed his head where the hair was thinning at the crown. Two full moist lips pressing against his scalp. Everybody except the priest and the children had stopped eating. Jaws held in mid-munch. Wine glasses frozen in mid air between table and lips.

'I'm…… well I'm pregnant.' There was triumph in her voice. 'Seven weeks to be exact.' And she took Frank's hand and held it to her tummy for the remainder of the speech. 'I know at forty two I should have tests. But I won't. It would be like throwing this precious gift back in God's face. This new life, this living happiness has come to us so unexpectedly that we are lost in the miracle of it all. It will be a December baby and December babies are full of hope and joy.' At this there was such a cacophony of voices. People left their places and hurried round the bride and groom. There was such congratulations and hugs and Frank was kissed again and again sometimes on one cheek and sometimes on both French style. Even the waitress in her smart black and white pinafore kissed him and held her breasts against his beating heart.

Frank barely took it in. He looked at the hill above him and watched the boulders, which a moment ago were as settled as those abandoned by the last ice age, begin to move. The started slowly and gathered momentum bouncing down the slope, through the roof of the hall and on to the table. One as light as polystyrene and as ominous as granite landed and bounced over the priest's head who was now holding a drum stick in each hand. Others landed amongst the food scattering the remains of salad nicoise, crushing chicken portions to smithereens, smashing wine bottles and wine glasses and only barely avoiding the cake with its delicate pink and pale blue icing. All of them unerringly took a final bounce and landed smack on Frank's recently kissed head. He got up from his seat in a dream and headed in the direction of the toilets.

'Uncle Trevor, Uncle Trevor, you know that man. You know that man,' the boy was breathless, 'you know that man that just got married.'

'Mr Perry. And it's not *that* got married. It's *who* got married.'

'Whatever. Well I just saw him in that rhododendron bush and he was, he was defecating.'

It was a big word for a six year old boy to use but he used it correctly and accurately.

Trevor and Maud ran to the bush but when they reached it Mr Perry had pulled up his trousers and had covered his activities with a large flat stone.

'In heaven's name Mr Perry, what are you doing in there?' screeched Maud. 'Your wife is frantic. We're all frantic. Somebody must cut the cake and start the dancing and you're the man to do it.'

'I'm your man,' said Frank. He looked at a rhododendron flower the colour of crushed blackberries and he took one petal and pushed it against his nose. He inhaled as deeply as his smoker's lungs would allow. And it was a light and ascending scent like the old Bisto adverts he remembered as a child. And how he wished it could pick him up by the nose and carry him over the rooftops and across the motorway and out into the land.

—

Nowhere Man

Cliff Yates

'Look love, are you sure about this?'

'Absolutely.'

'No, really?'

'Really.'

'They'll never let you back.'

'What do I care.'

'What about the printing job you wanted.'

'They've no intention. I've been there *four* months.'

'Seriously. Think about it. You've always wanted that – blank paper…'

'…one end, full colour the other. Jude I *have* thought about it. They'll never let me.'

I was shaving, Jude was watching me, leaning against the radiator. I'd already shaved that morning but it was a big night. People are often surprised when they find out I shave – *What's the point when you're invisible? I'd grow a beard down to my knees.* No they wouldn't.

Jude was doing her best but it was really too late. And I'd had enough of time and motion. All I wanted was a printing apprenticeship but *Think of your potential*, they said. Their profits, more like. An invisible time and motion person – the printers wouldn't have stood a chance. Then I did the deal with the union rep and started faking the figures. As I said to Jude, I was the first double-agent in the history of time and motion.

'Can I borrow your lipstick, love?'

'Which one?'

'The one with glitter.'

'Frosted. Here, let me. Where's your lips?'

She stood back, admired her handiwork. And there I was: a mouth in the bathroom mirror. Jagger. Watch my lips: *You can't always get what you want.* Brilliant. Then I put on Dad's old watch. Nineteen-fifties, brown leather strap. It was always fast, but I wasn't wearing it to tell the time.

'What about the union?'

'I can't stay just for them. Besides, it can't last much longer.'

'I just think you should tell them.'

'They'll survive.'

She knew I was right. The union rep had guessed things were coming to a head, had tried to talk me round. But I had to do something. Before getting slung out. Time was running out, especially after the graffiti. And I didn't want to go quietly. I'd been quiet for too long, lurking around: *Careful not to knock into anyone or knock anything over. Don't sneeze, whistle, and stay out of the toilets if anybody's in there.* Go quietly? No chance. I was going out in style.

The taxi-driver spent more time gawping at us through his rear-view mirror than looking at the road. He was staring at my head – where my head would be. Alison touched up the lipstick. The driver nearly missed the red light on Corporation Street, he was that distracted. Didn't do more than twenty the whole journey. At least I wasn't eating.

The strange thing was, even though the taxi couldn't have been hotter, I was shivering. Jude put her coat round my shoulders, took my hands between hers and rubbed them, but it made no difference. I wasn't exactly sure what I was going to do, that was the problem. I was going along to the dinner dance in lipstick and a watch, intending to expose the bosses and their devious ways, and have a good laugh doing it. But I still wasn't sure exactly how. I thought at first that I'd go along dressed up as Father Christmas with bandages around my face – jump up on the table, unwind the bandages, strip off (like I did at school) and make an amazing speech. But I'd never have got in, not even in fancy dress. I hadn't got an invitation, remember. I didn't exist.

So I sneaked in. First off was the standing around. Cocktails. Trying to make yourself heard above the music. Jude looked gorgeous in a black number, tottering about on heels. Sure, a couple of her friends guessed what was going on but they were already tanked up, so big deal. *If she doesn't mind getting touched up by that freak, so what?* Jude reckoned they were jealous.

Then the dinner. I just stood around, nicking the odd bit of food. The watch and lipstick, frankly, were a dead loss. Nobody noticed. It's like people only see what they expect to see. I dropped the watch into Jude's handbag.

It's weird, but Jude knew where I was the whole time. She says that the air moves when I walk around, and things go quiet when I come into a room. *Like when an owl or a kestrel's flying over.* No, I don't know what she means either. But she looked for all the world as if she was watching me, narrowing her eyes, trying to make out what I was up to.

The last dance of the night: Ferguson, the managing director, a pair of reindeer antlers on his slicked back, immaculate hair, was doing a slow waltz with Joyce Jones, the personnel manager's wife. Cheeky sod. It's that kind of place. You wouldn't believe it. Ferguson's a cunning bastard. Eyes cold as glass, tiny pupils that stay that way, as if he's stoned, which he isn't. And he's got this funny smell.

I came up behind him, put my arms around him, lifted him clear of the ground, and dropped him. Joyce shrieked, put her hands up to her mouth. It seemed to knock the wind out of Ferguson because he stayed still. I thought he'd had a stroke or something. The band had stopped playing; the drummer carried on a bit longer, tapping the snare, until he realised. It was that quiet. Everybody was just stood there, staring at Ferguson. Then he sat up, slowly, holding his arm.

And looked straight at me.

How did he do that? I have no idea. But you should have

seen his face. He was a bit shocked but he didn't look particularly
angry. He looked as if if he understood something that he'd
suspected for a long time, and that he was going to do something
about it. He glanced round for Jones, who started vaguely towards
me. You could tell what *he* was thinking. I'd had this coming a
long time.

I was shivering again and, almost without realising, I'd
picked up a knife from the table behind me. For the second time
that night, a Stones song came into my head: *Please allow me to
introduce myself…* The knife clattered on the ground – I heard it
before I realised that I'd dropped it.

That's when I should have jumped up on the table and set
to with the speech. But at that moment – with Ferguson on the
floor staring up at me, I worked it out. Until then, I simply didn't
realise how many people knew about me. It was like a light being
switched on: a massive fluorescent light. Because it was obvious
that virtually everyone in the room knew that I was there. And,
apart from Jude, I didn't have a friend in the building.

The lipstick – I wiped my mouth with the back of my
hand, turned, grabbed the tablecloth and pulled it, heading for the
door. There was a clatter as cutlery and plates hit the floor, and
someone called out. I don't know what they said. It was like
everything had slowed down, right on cue, and was coming from
a long way off, distorted. I let go the tablecloth. A couple of
waiters came towards me, but they didn't know what was going
on. How could they? What they should have done was shut the
door, but they didn't think of that. I ran past the cloakroom,
grabbing a coat and I was outside.

I ran down a couple of streets, put on the coat and
walked. All the shops were lit up, decked out in Christmas lights.
I'd stopped shaking and felt pretty good. There was no going back
and that's exactly what I wanted. What was I going to do? You're
probably thinking that MI5 would want me, like the CIA in that
film – Memoir of An Invisible Man. But seriously – I'd be more
trouble than I was worth. They probably hadn't even heard of me,
and I wasn't going to advertise. I was fed up with being a shadow.

Know what the union rep called me? 'Nowhere Man'. Says it all, really. And there's a weird truth in it, because it's as if I have no sense of place. For instance, we're in a café and I go to the toilet... next thing I'm checking out the kitchens, testing the soup, or sitting around in the staff social area listening in on the gossip. I have no sense of ownership. I go where I want, when I want.

I let myself into Jude's, put *Spotlight Kid* on the stereo, and ran a bath. She came home eventually, climbed in with me. We talked for ages, in front of the fire, wrapped in towels. She knew what was coming and made it as easy as she could. She fell asleep, and a couple of hours before daylight I let myself out.

The Archive

Grevel Lindop

You need to realise that none of it is guaranteed to stay secret. No
letter, no diary, no private note. Once someone dies or becomes
famous, that's it. People read everything, go through it like carrion
crows with a dead sheep, a bone here an eye there. Executors,
librarians, collectors, auction houses. Anything can turn up at any
moment, and the copyright laws won't help you. Intellectual
property? That's a joke. These people have no respect for property
of any kind. It's a voyeurs' paradise.

The archivist is just heading this way with another boxful, the
usual cardboard slab tied up with linen tape. This is the third and
last for today and it shouldn't take long to check. Her handwriting
never changed much even over the nineteen years and three
months. I'm polite to the archivist, a touch of geniality in the
smile, make her feel comfortable. Thank you *so* much. Nice old
buffer, spectacles on end of nose to heighten the effect. Mustn't
overdo it and fall into caricature, though. A little puff of breath,
get the pencil out. This kind of library doesn't allow ink in the
manuscript room, not even ballpoint. Something might get spilt
on one of the manuscripts. By God it might.

Looks like a new box, not much dust on top. Good sign: contents
probably haven't been listed yet. Not that the name 'Marie' is
going to mean a thing to anyone, not after the job I've done. Just
as well people don't sign love-letters with their surname. And of
course even on the airmail letters she never put a return address.
Wouldn't have done for an undelivered letter to come back for me

to open, after all. Can't help the hands shaking a bit as I untie the box, though. Another little step into hell each time I open one, feel like those fellows defusing UXBs during the war, one false move and you'd be plastered all over the street.

Sometimes think the main risk must be the sweat-marks I leave. The first time I did this it was in the library of the University of Texas at Austin. It was July and stewing, despite the air conditioning. When I saw one of her letters to him – just the edge of the familiar lavender-blue paper, three quarters of the way down the pile – I broke out into such a sweat that I found drops were falling straight off my forehead onto the top sheet and starting to blur the ink on some teenage imbecile's fan letter to the great literary man. I remember wondering afterwards if sweat had DNA in it. Come to think of it, I've still not found out. Not the sort of question you want to ask anyone in the know. Would sound too bloody incriminating.

How I got away with it that time I'll never know. Security in those American libraries not up to much, I suppose. I simply removed the letter (only one, thank God). Didn't have anything to substitute, let alone the right shade of blue. Kicked myself afterwards: drawers full of the bloody stuff back in her study in Leicester, could have brought a ream of it with me and slipped in a sheet, so even if they counted up there'd be no obvious gap.

But I hadn't planned ahead. I wasn't in Austin to look for Lennox correspondence anyway. I was supposed to be doing research for a book on the young D.H.Lawrence and wanted to see the Lawrence papers they'd recently bought. I told myself that getting back to a bit of research would take my mind off the things I'd discovered after Marie died. But while I was looking through the catalogue under 'L' the other name caught my eye, pierced and yanked it like a fishhook in fact, so that I almost yelped with pain, and there it was:

Lennox, R.F.: notes and draft chapter for *Rose in Flames* (1976), also miscellaneous letters to, 1974-7, forty-five sheets.

It hit me like a punch in the stomach. I wasn't interested in his lousy novel - of course now I can see how wrong I was about that - but the main point was obvious. If these were letters *to* Lennox from the 1970s, chances were that they might be part of the other end of the correspondence I'd found stashed in the space at the back of Marie's desk drawer, the day I'd tugged it right out in my frustration and tried to push it back, only to find it blocked by something soft and lumpy which turned out to be a wodge of sixty-three letters from the bastard Lennox written, as I say, over a two-hundred-and-thirty-one-month period. Did she, I wonder, intend me to find them? Were they a little personal archive left for me so I could reinterpret my marriage?

That time at Austin it wasn't much, but still it was plenty. Just a sheet of stiff blue notepaper, folded once across, written in her handwriting and reading:

> Baby,
> We can't this afternoon. He's taking me on the Grantchester trip. Tomorrow? Forget me not
> X

The effect was like some malign magical illusion. It seemed as if someone was running a video in my head. Cambridge Contemporary Writing Conference, 1976. Lennox, as usual, one of the guest writers, along with John Fowles I think it was, staying for half the week and giving an evening reading plus a talk about the plight of the modern British novelist. Modern literature wasn't Marie's thing (so I thought then) and she usually stayed away from the afternoon seminar papers, which were more academic, for a 'rest'. But some afternoons they had outings, and now I could see, as if down the wrong end of a telescope, the trip to Grantchester Meadows, some actor reading Rupert Brooke to the assembled company on the lawn of the Vicarage (since polluted by one Jeffrey Archer) and the tea with, of course, honey.

In particular I remember she seemed to take ages to get onto the coach and stood on the step for a long moment apparently looking back at something. Was he somewhere in sight? Sometimes I feel if I could just get the focus sharp enough in memory I'd be able to see the reflection in her glittering pupils, and it would be a tiny doll-like figure, framed in a miniature college window, waving discreetly and wondering whether the next afternoon's seminar would give him a chance to fuck my wife.

But it was that 'Baby' that hit me hardest. Christ, Marie wasn't some brainless American sophomore, she was a scholarly medievalist, a specialist in Chaucer and fifteenth-century manuscript illumination. Someone who dragged reluctant students through courses in Middle English. That she could demean herself by addressing anyone - let alone Lennox - as 'Baby' opened a shaft into depths of obscenity I'd never known existed.

I saw at once that this sordid scrap of paper couldn't stay in the archive. By dint of moving files and notebooks around on the table, I managed to fold it twice, then slide it up my cuff and into my sleeve. It's a technique that's served me well since, but at that time naturally I wasn't looking out for jackets with loose cuffs as I do now. Still, I got it out of sight, and in due course went to the toilet. By that time I was soaked in sweat as if I'd just swum to the library and if anyone noticed me they must have thought I was having some kind of attack. Which, come to think of it, I was. But I felt better once I'd thrust the paper into the bowl (to soak it so the tearing wouldn't be audible), ripped it into very small pieces almost pulping it in the process, and flushed it with great emphasis down what they like to call the 'john'. I waited a while and flushed again to make quite sure no faint swirls of the ink remained tainting the water. She always used a fountain pen.

But of course the blue touch-paper, as you might call it, had now been lit. Even as I walked back to the reading-room and checked through the rest of the file (no more notes from Marie, thank God) I realised that if this could happen in Austin it could happen anywhere. I would have to reassess things. I spent the afternoon pretending to work. I even asked for some of the D.H.Lawrence papers just to keep up appearances, but my mind was racing. Lennox's reputation had sagged a bit since his death in 1990, and of course problems with the booze had hit his creativity several years before that, truth to tell. He hadn't produced a half-decent novel since 1982.

But he was still a fairly big name and his relatives hadn't hesitated to sell his papers when they could. He was a messy bugger. Personally I like to keep my papers tidy and in alphabetical order, but not Lennox, they were all over the place and completely scrambled. Private letters mixed up with bills and bits of manuscripts of his novels and stories. He'd no children, so his nephews had disposed of his papers in batches to anyone who wanted to buy. I checked the *Index of Literary Manuscripts* and was pretty appalled at what I found. There were bundles of stuff everywhere from the Brotherton Library in Leeds to the Special Collections at Buffalo. The biggest batch had been bought not long before by the British Library. That took several days of work and a lot of care. I'm still not sure they don't have their suspicions. Hopefully I won't have to go back there for a long time, if ever.

I'd gradually lost touch with him around 1980 soon after his drinking took hold and, as I now know, his affair with Marie had finished shortly after. I thought she seemed even more withdrawn than usual about that time. Up to then Lennox and I had been – or rather I used to think we'd been – pretty good friends and there were even notions that I might write a book about his work, which could have boosted my career and done his no harm either. He needed a spot of academic respectability: he already had an *avant-garde* reputation and of course his novels were famously 'explicit' as they would say nowadays. People spoke of *Rose in Flames* in the same breath as *Portnoy's Complaint* and *Last Exit for Brooklyn*. But a solid critical survey comparing him to the likes of Golding and Lawrence would have done him no harm at all, or so I told him.

Of course I now see he was overrated. That florid style. Artificially pumping up the prose to get a fake intensity. I've always felt the sex in Lawrence's novels works because it's purely symbolic. In real life of course a career demands one's best energies. I'm told Lawrence himself was impotent at the end of his life. Probably put it all into his novels, and so much the better. Marie and I weren't that concerned with sex, or so I thought. And of course if one doesn't want children that has its bearing too. But for some years the three of us were really quite close, or I thought so. We all went to Italy together, we met most years at the Cambridge conference, and I now realise Marie's regular 'research trips' to London were the pretext for seeing him in between. Oh, we were all good friends. I've got signed copies of all his novels. It never occurred to me until last year to wonder why he never inscribed them to Marie as well. At the time I thought it was a gesture of respect for me really: acknowledging that as a critic of modern writing I was the natural one to appreciate his work. Not her.

It wasn't until a few weeks after the Texan revelation that the answer hit me. I was back home, looking at the row of spines on the top shelf in my study and wondering whether to carry the whole lot out into the back garden and turn *Rose in Flames* into a reality by making a bonfire of them (I know how tricky it is to burn books, but there was some paraffin in the garage) when I felt quite literally as if the floor had fallen from under me and I was dropping through space with a sensation of cataclysmic vertigo.

I dragged the volumes off the shelf and began scrabbling inside the front covers looking for dates of publication. My hands were shaking so much that I ripped some of the pages, but that was neither here nor there. Most of the dates came within the right period, and of course what I realised was that most of these much-debated sex scenes were likely to represent the clandestine antics of my late wife. The impulse to shred the paper down to a fine dust with my bare hands was overridden solely by a desperate need to establish the truth. I remember getting very drunk later in the evening but the books survived.

After long analysis of these passages I remain uncertain. I cannot conceive of the Marie I knew playing any such part. But then I recall that 'Baby', and certain other details in her letters and, less often, in his, and I wonder. I wonder, in particular, if he failed to dedicate the books to her because she was already inside them. No dedication needed. But did she ever read the novels herself? I simply can't remember. I thought of her as an Iris Murdoch person.

I like to think I'm thorough, not an inspired scholar but a systematic researcher. I've kept up with what's where, and I've worked steadily. Usually it takes at least three days: one to assess the security in a new library, one to find out what they've got - if anything - in the way of Marie's letters, and then one to do the business. I soon realised that the lavender-blue wasn't the only paper she'd used - as indeed you'd expect over a period of nine hundred and eighty-eight weeks. Sometimes there were sheets torn from exercise books, or white typing-paper, or the old Departmental letterhead we used to use. She would embellish the University coat-of-arms with little doodles.

Thought-provoking, that. Made me wonder whether she'd sometimes used the Departmental pigeonholes as an address for him to write to. Maybe he put his letters in brown envelopes and typed the address so they'd look official. Was I imagining it, or did I remember occasions when she was off ill for a week or so and specifically told me *not* to collect her mail from the office because she 'couldn't stand thinking about work again yet'? Was she afraid

I'd look too closely at an envelope?

I knew from the start that simply obliterating things with ink was no good. You'd be caught in thirty seconds. And anyway there's ultra violet and so on, you can read through any deletion these days. And simple destruction was too risky, though I'd got away with it that once in Texas. In some libraries now they count the sheets to make sure you give back what you receive. No, the trick is to remove each sheet and replace it with something similar but harmless. I've collected a pretty complete repertoire now. Getting old paper isn't as hard as you'd think. Dusty old departmental stationery still lurks at the back of cupboards here and there. You can still occasionally find stacks of pre-metric typing paper buried in discount warehouses, or part-used Silvine exercise books in the piles of rubbish at car boot sales and house-clearance shops. You'd be amazed. On occasion I've had to cut blank pages from the ends of oldish art books and trim them to the right sizes. But I reckon I can match most things now. The paper simply fills an extra suitcase when I have to make an overnight trip. Generally I leave it in the back of the car and just find what I need once I've checked the archive.

And of course I've become fairly adept at churning out her handwriting. Mostly, to get the general look, I copy a few meaningless passages from her lecture notes. Just as well I've still got those, they're in her study exactly as she left them the last time she went into hospital. Once I've produced a page or more that looks pretty much the same as the real thing I go back to the reading room and substitute it. I get the original out of the room as soon as I can and bingo. Sometimes I've burned the letters but I prefer the toilet. It seems purgative, and isn't a 'john' what they call a prostitute's customer? Goodbye, dear John. Though I have to remember to check the flush first. A blockage could be disastrous. Sometimes I have irrational fears that there will be a major pipe-obstruction at the British Library and it'll be like a repeat of Dennis Nielson with those body parts. Though actually the sheets were quite thin and I got them into pretty small pieces as I recall.

Private collectors are the real nightmare. I keep an eye on the salerooms now and two years ago I had to bid quite steeply for a batch of Lennox papers against a library and an unnamed collector. Fortunately I'd had the vision to check my overdraft facilities beforehand and I squeaked through. All for a single letter of hers, which was in with a bundle of rough drafts for an unfinished novel and similar twaddle. I had a struggle with my conscience. I could have cleared the overdraft easily by reselling the other material, but felt it wouldn't be right to make money out of a man who had cuckolded me for six thousand nine hundred and eighty-eight days. And moreover, suppose somebody checked what had been in the original bundle, and noticed that it had all come back on the market except a letter from one 'Marie'? Questions might have been asked. In the end I burnt the lot.

Then there's the threat of a biography. So far, surprisingly, there hasn't been one. Lennox is still something of a cult figure, not a mainstream writer, and no one has wanted to invest the time yet. Somebody phoned up about a radio programme a few months ago. They said they'd heard I knew him, and would I be willing to do a short interview as it was twenty-five years since his death? I fobbed them off, said I'd hardly known him, but then wondered if I'd done the right thing. Perhaps a pre-emptive strike would have been more effective: go on the air and say he was homosexual, for example. Impotent, perhaps better still. Like Lawrence. But there are dangers that way, might get into complications. I even toyed with the idea of doing a biography myself. I could write Marie out of the story completely, so her reputation would be safe, and I'd have the perfect excuse to check out every possible holding of Lennox papers. I'm already known to archivists as having a special interest in Lennox, though that's not an idea I encourage.

Now I'd better brace myself to confront this box. It's the poems and the little drawings that I hate most. I never saw her do any such thing during her lifetime. The first time I found one of her poems to Lennox I thought I was going to cry. Then I realised that what I really wanted to do was vomit. I had a job to keep it down. I hope there won't be any poems or drawings this time. But if there are, that's just too bad. You have to be thorough with this kind of thing, and I've promised myself to destroy every trace. I suppose you could say it's become a labour of love. Anyway, here goes.

I Cannot Cross Over

After Antonio Tabucchi

Sean O'Brien

'You don't want to go down there, pet,' she said, pausing in the mouth of the lane. 'Come in here for a nice drink with me.' Beyond her I could see the beer signs through the windows of the bar.

'Sorry but I can't,' I said. 'I'm supposed to be elsewhere.'

'What's that got to do with owt? Come on.'

The bells of the cathedral church began to toll, sending mass flights of starlings racing over the old town. The light was taking on the neon edge it gets at six o'clock in summer. It was the magic hour for freezing lager and pepper vodka.

'Sorry.'

'You won't get a better offer.'

'I know, it's just –'

'Suit yerself. Bloody poets.' And she was gone with a clatter of heels over the cobblestones. I couldn't remember how we'd fallen into conversation. Maybe walking down from the Metro station at Monument. Maybe she asked for a look at my paper. It didn't matter. I liked her with her piled up dyed blonde hair, I liked the frankness of her manner and her cleavage. But I had to be elsewhere. You know how it is, in the middle of things.

I turned off into Pudding Chare. What would her name be? I saw clearly – and maybe it was true – that she was called Lorraine and that by day she worked on a cosmetic counter in Fenwicks, wearing terra cotta make-up. It seemed a strangely romantic life to me at that moment, though doubtless filled with the normal obstructions and sadness.

As I hurried on I looked into the window of a bar round the back of the newspaper offices, a place once used by print workers. There was already half a crowd in there – blonde girls, their heads averted, none of them precisely her.

On the steps of the Lit and Phil Library I met Harry the caretaker sweeping up the glass from a broken sherry bottle. Harry was a naturalized Aberdonian. His expression always indicated that his suspicions were being confirmed.

'You're late the night,' he said.

'But not too late, I hope.'

He studied his watch.

'Well. No. But divvent fuck about. Miss Quine is long away and I want to get a good seat in the Innisfree. For the exotics.' He winked, like a lustful automaton. I imagined his female equivalent in her pinny and headscarf sliding stiffly out of the door behind him on her track, while he was drawn back into the darkness.

'I just need to check something.'

'Aye, well, it's a library,' he said, and turned back to his sweeping.

In the main gallery the three girls at the issue desk sat reading and fiddling with their long fair hair, perched on stools like mermaids on their rocks. None of them looked up as I passed – I could have been anyone – but I heard a faint echoing *tut* as I reached the doors at the far end. Was I a nuisance? I was a member. I went down the stone staircase, past paintings of the nineteenth century magistrates and antiquarians who had nurtured the library towards its present sepia perfection. None of these long-gone gentlemen would meet my eye just now.

The Silence Room is a place I do not care for. It is a brown chamber crowded with stacks of county records from the eighteenth and nineteenth centuries, as well as some impractically narrow tables at which anorexic pedants sometimes crouch to labour. It feels like an abandoned work by M.R. James. Bad enough on a spring evening when the light comes faintly down the crack between the library and the Coroner's Court and through the crusty window. Unthinkable on a foggy winter night.

All I knew was there was meant to be something in there for me to collect, perhaps a message. Where would you hide something in a library? Not among the books, surely. That could lead to misunderstanding: you might mistake a scribbled execration for the message. You could end up standing there, pondering the meaning of *nonsense* or *shite*.

I paced the parquet floor, wondering where to look. Fortunately the pedants had all gone home, leaving only the faintest tremor of disapproval. I felt beneath the tables each in turn, in case there was something stuck there with gum or worse. Nothing. But I couldn't simply leave: where would I go? I cast around, at a loss, then noticed, not for the first time, that the grille covering the radiator beneath the window had been loosened, as if in some incomplete act of maintenance or vandalism. Now I put my hand inside. The sudden heat shocked me. I was feeling awkwardly around when I heard a voice.

'Now then you dorty fucker. Get yer hand oot of its arse man.'

'What?'

'I'm not surprised yer fuckin deef neither.'

It was the poet Ralph Cowan. He was a drunk. In fact he was more of a drunk than a poet, though his real vocation was heckling. His jacket sagged to one side under the weight of a bottle. He brandished a ham and pease pudding sandwich in one hand; in the other he waved a sheet of paper.

'Yer looking fer this, reet.' Ralph was in his pomp.

'What is it?'

'Fucked if I knaa, canny lad.'

Suddenly indifferent, he handed me the paper. On it was typed, 'I cannot cross over.'

'That's a quotation from the great storehouse of local song and story,' he said, examining his sandwich. 'As ye would knaa if ye was from round here.'

'I do know, Ralph.'

'Not properly. Wouldn't be possible that.'

I looked at the line of typing again. The typewriter ribbon was worn, with both the red and black strands showing through.

'Ye gannin fer a drink?'

'Not with you.'

'Ya cunt. Go on.'

'No thanks.'

'Go on, cunt. Call yerself a poet? Howay man, what about the republic of fuckin letters, man?'

'I'm busy. Let me through the door, Ralph. Don't make me knack you.' He stepped aside.

'Busy? Aye, writin more daft radio shite about Collingwood's monument. Aboot which ye knaa fuckin fuck all by the way.' He followed me halfway up the stairs. 'No need to be stand-offish, like.'

Back in the gallery I could hear the drumming of rain on the glass dome above. How quickly the weather had changed. Seeing Ralph's familiar brown hooded mackintosh on the coat stand by the coffee hatch, I slipped it on and left without a second glance.

When I came out on to the street I had a sudden sense of the urgency of my situation. Wherever I was meant to go, and for whatever purpose I was meant to go there, I needed to be making better progress. Now there was torrential rain, with thunder unrolling overhead. Crowds of girls in next to nothing ran shrieking over the road between hydroplaning taxis. A drayman's horse had been struck by lightning and lay smoking and hissing on a zebra crossing while its owner stamped and raved in the flooded gutter and passengers flooding from the railway station rushed past with umbrellas and briefcases raised like the accused on their way into court. A police car nosed slowly through the crush. I thought: I must write it all down when I get chance.

In this town everything gravitates towards the Quayside, so I decided to let physics take its course. But then as I made for the steps beside the ruined castle keep I saw the lights of the bar at the entrance to the high bridge. I didn't want to drink with Ralph Cowan, but I could certainly do with a refreshing beverage. And perhaps, with chance to reflect, my thinking would be clarified. Once through the doors, though, the signs were bad. The place was heaving with lawyers talking at the tops of their voices. I ordered a pint of stout and took a seat in the brown mirrored gloom of a bay as far as possible from the crowd.

What now? I thought. I could simply sit there and smoke cigarettes and drink beer on the off chance that something would happen. Waves of new lawyers came in, loud with triumph and worldly wisdom. Gradually they spilled backwards from the bar area, preening and jabbering until all I could see were their expensive corvine backsides. I looked down in despair. Under my glass was a crudely printed leaflet. I examined it. *Poetry Workshop*, it said. *Upstairs, tonight.*

I couldn't remember how long ago it was since last I climbed the sticky treads of that narrow staircase. The memory was both immediate and remote, like a first visit to the dentist. There was a sweet sick smell of beer and smoke. At the first turning I nearly collided with a woman in a red PVC raincoat. She pushed past me, putting on a pair of sunglasses, weeping, swearing under her breath. It was always a hard school, I thought, but tonight's workshop could barely have got started.

I slipped through the door and peered through the pall of smoke in the Function Room. A dozen participants of all ages sat with bowed heads at the little tables, writing furiously on lined pads. At the front of the group stood Harry Demarest, high priest of the Beginners' Group – a gaunt grey man with an eyepatch and a thermos flask. It was, he gave people to understand, his manifest destiny to issue weekly disappointments to his obedient secular flock. They would thank him in the end. He had a plate in his head.

'You can't come in,' he said. 'You're not a member.' Then, recognizing me, he muttered, 'Got summat for you.' He began to search one of the many carrier bags of manuscripts and magazines and small press publications which surrounded his table. 'Brought it with me, I know that.'

'What is it?'

'In a manila envelope.' He continued ferreting. Everyone had stopped to watch. Some of them took the chance to dab their faces with Kleenex. 'Got it,' Harry said at last. He handed me a stiff seven by five manila envelope. Nothing was written on it. The group waited.

'Open it, then,' said someone.

'How do I know it's for me?'

'She told me it was,' said Harry.

'Who did?'

'Dunno. Some French bird. Blonde.'

Not French, I thought, but Belgian. Zsa Zsa Maeterlinck. At last.

'We haven't got all day,' said Harry. 'We're only booked till eight.'

I opened the envelope. Inside was a single black garter trimmed with red.

'O-ho!' said someone.

'Best be off,' I said.

'Aye,' said Harry. 'Some of us have got poems to write.'

By now a heavy fog had rolled in up the river. The traffic tiptoed off the bridge and the drunks tiptoed under the traffic. I don't know why, but I felt my way along a wall of glazed white brick until I found a gap and skated down a cobbled alleyway into a back court surrounded by stooped and ancient solicitors' offices. Only the stairwells were lit now, their grades of desolation rising to the dim yellow spaces under the roofs, where the lifts turned back and the cares of innumerable forgotten lives lay stacked in manila folders, awaiting the attentions of rot. This was something else I was going to have to get round to writing about, afterwards, whenever that might be.

Melancholy overtook me now. I could taste the fog, as though I were breathing through the woollen scarf my mother had made me wear as a child. It had a stony, watery, acrid taste. It was like something official which everyone had mistakenly assumed was long gone into exile. It was like the first day at school. I felt afraid.

Another entryway led me into a street with flooded gutters, running beneath the viaduct, a place of informal archway garages and erotic assignations conducted on a similar economic basis. The yellow mouth of a pub leered out of the gloom, so I went in. The bar was empty, but there was the loud steady noise of many voices somewhere in the building. Behind the bar a calendar showed Miss September, Zsa Zsa Materlinck wearing a smile and a garter. I noticed that the year she represented contained only nine months. Time was pressing.

'Private party,' said the florid, brilliantined manager, emerging through the smoke, his tooth glinting to match his tiepin. He twirled a gold Albert hanging on a chain from his waistcoat, and nodded towards the hatch. 'Funeral, like. Stout, is it?'

A barmaid with a face like a large red fish in a beehive hairdo leaned through the hatch.

'We need some more crabsticks, Maurice,' she said.

'What do they fockin dee with 'em aal?' the gaffer said. 'Have you ever seen anyone actually eating one?' he asked me.

I tried to look noncommittal. But really I knew where the crabsticks went – down the cracks of the plush benches at funeral buffets.

'Whose do is it?'

'Dennis Foot. Ye knaa him?'

'I know of him.' Dennis Foot was the legendary angling correspondent of the *Argus*. He too had been a poet. And now he was gone to his long home. Or perhaps they would bury him at sea, or burn him like a Viking. I struggled to find anything to add to this thought. Call yourself a poet?

Eventually I asked, 'What did he die of?'

'Seafood poisoning,' said the manager. 'Never touch it meself like.'

The barmaid came through with a new tray of crabsticks.

'Go on, pet, since you're here.'

'I'm a vegan.'

'We're very broadminded. Hang on. You're him. Aren't you?'

'Perhaps I'm not the person you should ask.'

'I've gorra note from your pal.'

I couldn't remember having any pals. I couldn't remember being in this pub, or this pub being here before.

'The skinny one. Wears a coat.' She took a betting slip from her bosom and handed it to the manager. He looked at me carefully, then put on a pair of spectacles and read the note:

'"The river is wide but I cannot."' What's that supposed to mean, like?'

'Hard to say.'

'Sounds bloody daft,' said the barmaid. 'Vegan, right?' She exchanged glances with the manager.

'I could show you me poems if you want, like', he said, shyly.

'Actually I'm a bit pressed now.'

He carefully took off his spectacles and re-pocketed them in his waistcoat.

'Word to the wise,' he said.

'Of course.'

'Yer barred.'

Back in the fogbound night a coal train crawled past, high overhead, adding its rusty black sweat to the fog. Press on, I thought. The viaduct curved away and quiet fell. Now the street was edged with metal fencing topped with razor wire. I had heard of this place but never visited it before. The Cultural Quarter. A gate stood open. I picked my way across the rubble and rags to a low concrete building which felt as if it stood at the edge of a cliff. It was the kind of place the army would have used as a venereal clinic. In fact it was the premises of a publisher. The door swung open. So this was my pal. Harry Maddox.

'Been a while,' he said, extending a cold white hand from the overlong sleeve of his dark overcoat.

'I wasn't expecting you,' I said. 'I thought you were dead.'

'That's rather an emotive term,' said Harry. He offered me his hipflask. I declined. As he tipped his head back there came the faint pang of vodka, not a smell, just a rumour, one for the columns of Intimations in the *Argus*. Harry led me inside. The front office contained nothing but old catalogues. The storeroom held only old ladder-style shelving. Beyond both lay the editor's office. This too was empty, except that in the middle of the floor stood a wooden pallet bearing several stacks of shrink-wrapped calendars. One package had been ripped open. Harry handed me a sample. Zsa Zsa was still smiling. The garter, I now saw, was part of a pre-Christmas theme, matching her hat.

'So what happened? Where's all the poetry?'

'Pulped. Turned into these.' He flicked through the slick pages. The muses addressed their compliant smirks to eternity.

'The culture turned against us, that's what. Or the economy. Or both. Or they're the same. Or something. Anyway, there was no call for these either.'

'All a bit valedictory.' I said.

'You what? We're past all that.'

I looked at the calendar. Miss May in her green scarf reached across the void to Zsa Zsa, her September cousin.

'No chance of any royalties, anyway,' said Harry, looking at his watch. 'It would appear the guvnor's fucked off. Fancy a drink?

'I've got to be somewhere.'

'That's what they all say. Where are you headed?'

'The quayside, I think. That's where I've been trying to get to all night.'

'Ahuh? I'll come down with you.'

It was sleeting through the fog as we picked our way down the steps between the wrecked nineteenth century warehouses beloved of alkies and the producers of costume dramas about the nobility of toil. Fires burned in a few rooms half-open to the air. Dim figures reclined and howled or held out brown bottles which we politely refused.

'You're ready then,' said Harry, as we reached the foot of the steps, where the bass-heavy judder of music could be heard.

'Am I?'

'Why else would you be here?'

'I'm not with you.'

'Then why'd you come?' He shook his head.

'Am I supposed to know?'

At last we came out on the street. It was crowded with the usual drinkers, groups and singletons passing silently through the music along the potholed road, slowing the night traffic along the quays. Faces I knew raised bottles in recognition and moved expressionlessly on. The sleet had turned to snow, the broad slow flakes landing on the men's bald heads and the women's naked shoulders

'I'll leave you here,' said Harry. He hailed a girl who stood in the red doorway of a bar. She waved back and went inside.

'What am I meant to do?' I asked.

He shrugged, shook my hand coldly again, then slipped over the road as the crowd thickened about him.

I let myself be drawn along with the drinkers. An eddy carried me to the river's edge, where I stopped to lean on the railings and looked down into the black waters. They were high tonight. The tide was running swiftly away, parting smoothly at the high bridge-pillars, bearing a mass of branches aloft like antlers. Among the branches, pages from the calendar surfaced – all Zsa Zsa – and were snatched below. Then, slowly, but without slowing, the water grew smooth as a mirror. My face appeared in it, with the moon on one shoulder and another face to balance it. I spoke to the figure in the water.

'You don't live here.'

'I don't live anywhere. That's the trouble, son.' The figure drew deeply on a cigarette and breathed out smoke into his white hair.

'Well, I can't help you now.'

'I know that, son,' my father said. 'Nor I you.'

'Why does it have to be you?'

He smiled bitterly. I saw the handsome devil he had been. 'Perhaps it's an ordeal.'

'Ordeals are normally rewarded,' I said.

'Are they? Are you sure? Then perhaps I'm your reward. Walk with me anyway.' He turned and threw his cigarette into the water. But when I looked up there was no one beside me. The crowds had thinned out, too. The swing bridge was open and stragglers made their way up the approaches. The waters stood still as a sealed pool, in perfect black silence. There was no sound of voices, no breaking glass, no distant traffic in the streets above the quays. The music had ended, and one by one the lights along the quay went out. I looked around for my father, for Harry, for any companion to come with me over the bridge. All gone.

'It can't be as important as this, whatever it is,' I said.

By the time I stepped onto the bridge there was only the moon's cold lamp, with a face I liked to think was Zsa Zsa Maeterlinck's, with the snow falling into the water, and by this light I saw quite clearly that this was a river with only one side.

—

A Four Star Novel

Ian McMillan

CHAPTER ONE starts when he opens the door. Maybe there's a preface where he messes about with the keycard, puts it in the wrong way, tries to get in, little red light blinking at him like a daft kid who's just been pinching his apples and denying it. You could even have a bit before the preface where he's in the lift clutching the keycard. He makes a joke to the other people in the lift. It's always the same joke. There's always a sign in the lift saying Maximum Capacity So Many Persons, and he always says 'I wonder who those So Many persons are?' So he might say 'I wonder who those thirteen people are?' Or 'I wonder who those twenty people are?' And it always gets a laugh from the other people, the two or three people, squashed into the lift. Usually.

CHAPTER ONE starts when he opens the door. Hotel room smell. TV welcoming him, personally, to his room. Biscuits. He always eats the biscuits straight away. Point of honour. Chew them biscuits. Opens the window. Always stuffy, these hotel rooms. Lets go a long fart. Long and loud and proud. Holding it together in the lift. I wonder who those fifteen people are, and I wonder which one's farted?

CHAPTER TWO starts when he goes in the bathroom, sees himself reflected in the mirrors. Infinite him. Who are these infinite people in this bathroom. Opens the soap. Washes his hands. Always the same things: the biscuits. The soap. Now it's his room. Belongs to him. Goes back into his room from his bathroom. Checks the room service menu. Puts the free pen in his briefcase. Puts the free notebook in his briefcase. Back at home his wife will say Not another free pen. But pens are always useful. Pens are for writing with. Always useful. Notebooks. Useful. He takes his trousers off. More comfortable. Puts them in the Corby Trouser Press. Wanders around in his pants. Sees himself in the mirror. Stomach in. In. In.

CHAPTER THREE   starts when he gets back in the lift. Nobody to make a joke to. Pulls faces in the mirror. Biscuit crumbs on his shirt. He's early. Absurdly early. Goes for a walk, out of the hotel and down the road, past other hotels. Hotels. More hotels. The aircraft take off and land, land and take off. He turns a corner and

CHAPTER FOUR   abruptly   he's in a street. An ordinary street. Gardens. Cars parked. Kids coming home from school. Skipping. Aircraft taking off and landing. Lad on a bike delivering the evening paper. Doesn't glance at the sky. Down the street, the ordinary street. Stickers in the window protesting about runways. No more runways. These are the houses you see lit up when your plane comes in in the morning or at night. These houses. Glances into a house. Countdown on. Countdown!

CHAPTER FIVE starts with him running back to his room, breathless. Countdown. DRTJOIUED. Eh? Contestants: seven. A dodgy eight. What's the seven? JODERTI. Ah yes, a kind of tent favoured by Algerians. And the dodgy eight? OIDRTUEJ. Yes, it's in. The last word of George VIth. He screws up his hotel notepaper. ROT. Dodgy three. Lies on the bed. Stands up. Sits down. Walks to the window. Walks from the window. Walks to the bathroom. Walks from the bathroom. Cleans his shoes with the shoecleaner thing. Getting dark. Autumn.

CHAPTER SIX starts with him going out of the hotel again. Past the other hotels. Dark now. Planes landing and taking off. Down the street. The ordinary street. Overwhelming desire to go and knock on a door and walk in. Always having it, this overwhelming desire. Just go in. Don't even bother to knock. Family sitting watching TV. Just walk in. Join them on the settee. Say things like Hello. Say things like Don't you remember we met on holiday and you said to pop in anytime. He turns round. Goes back to the hotel. Back to his room. Then

CHAPTER SEVEN starts with him just a few minutes later,

back on the street. The ordinary street. This time he's going to do it. Down a path. Curtains shut, He can hear the TV. He looks up. A big plane overhead. Coming in from LA or Boston or St. John's or somewhere. Somewhere. Walks in. Into the house. Like when you walk into a hotel room for the first time. Except no name on the TV. Exept no biscuits. Except no Pen. Except no notebook. Picture on the wall: a wedding. Different to the pictures you always get in hotel rooms. Walks in. The room. Not his room. The room. Man and woman on the settee watching TV. A western. Bang. Bang. Young lad at the table, writing. Doing his homework. Good lad. Clever lad. Woman looks up. Hello Frank, she says. He's astonished. Amazed. Frank, come in and sit down, she says. He tries to speak. Tries to say My name's not Frank it's Ray. Can't do it. Like he's watching Countdown. An easy three not a dodgy five. It's Ray not Frank. Consonant Carol. Vowel Carol. Consonant Carol. Ray. Though is Y a consonant? Not Frank. Ray. The man is standing up, smiling. Come and sit down Frank. We told you to come and see us, not stay in those hotels. All the same those hotels. All the same. Ray steps into the light and the boy stands up. I've been writing a poem Uncle Frank he says. Do you want to hear it?

CHAPTER EIGHT is the poem. It's not a long poem. Autumn: Leaves in a blanket/a blanket of leaves/fallen like rain/ from the trees/wind is blowing/soon be snowing.

CHAPTER NINE starts with Ray standing there. Poem hanging in the air. Man and woman pointing at him. You're not Frank! They both say it together. Are you a burglar? They both say it together. Get out! Just the man says this. Get out! Just the woman says this. The western. Bang bang. The poem about Autumn, hanging there. Outside the constant almost-noise, almost-silence of the aircraft. I'm not Frank says Ray. I'm Ray says Ray. Get out before I call the police says the man. The boy is crying. The boy is crying *into his poem*.

CHAPTER TEN starts with Ray back in the hotel room. He has ordered room service. He has taken his trousers off again. He is watching the local news to see if he is on. Of course he never catches a plane. Of course he has never been on a plane. Ray wishes he was Frank. Frank was welcome. Frank had a poem read to him, a very good poem about Autumn. It was a very good poem but Ray can't remember any of it. It was a very good poem. Ray stands in the bathroom. Says My name's Frank. Infinity of Rays looking back at him.

CHAPTER ELEVEN is philosophical. Memory, eh? Identity, eh? Who is ever who they think they are, eh? Eh? Frank? Ray?

Yum

Steven Blyth

For a while I liked him. Admired him. Good luck to him, I thought. He was doing what he wanted. Getting what he wanted. I couldn't blame him. She's a good looking woman. Big some might say, but I prefer curvy. Fat? No, voluptuous. That's the word. Voluptuous. Tight skirt. A slit up one side showing a bit too much leg. Or not enough, depending on your view. Low-cut top. That's tight too. Shows off the curves. Nothing like Mary. Well, nothing like her anymore. She used to look a bit like that but, like every one else, she saw it as fat. She could hardly say that now. She eats like a rabbit and spends her days at the gym. A stick. Slim, she reckons. Skinny.

I don't like him now. He's become too familiar. First name terms. A wink. And jokes when he checks in. Stuff like maybe he should sign is as Smith? Or can he get a discount for not staying the whole night? He usually checks in at the start of my shift. Then, about five or six, he comes back with her. She walks straight past. She looks ashamed. And so she should – meeting up in some hotel room for a sneaky shag with .. with who? Her boss, her neighbour, her brother in law?

But he doesn't look ashamed. At first he always blanked me when they passed reception on the way to the room. Now he gives me that little smile. That little I know you know and you know I know you know smile. Cheeky bastard. Does he get some kick out of making it obvious? Once I listened at their door. Laughter, the bed squeaking. Like bloody Benny Hill. But I was still jealous . as hell. It used to be bearable when I thought he felt bad about it.

Sure, he got to fuck her but he was paying a price. Now he's just fucking her. Guilt free.

***

On TV tonight there's a programme about some American bloke called Chad who feeds up his girlfriend, Gloria. She's so big she can't leave the house. Can't move. Just lies on the bed. He washes her, cooks for her. She's huge. I mean just *huge*. Mary is laughing and saying things about how horrible it is to even imagine fucking that. *Yes, imagine fucking that!*

I'm still hungry as usual after some fat free lasagna. Mary says I need to watch my waistline too. Doesn't want me to turn into a fat biffer when she's gone to the trouble of looking so slim for me. We've had that one, of course, the 'I liked you as you were' argument. I told her countless times she was fine, that she turned me on. She won't have it. She reckons she turns me on far more like this. Men like woman that way. Hasn't she noticed my reluctance in the bedroom? Not tonight, though. Tonight I have thoughts of Gloria.

***

I've arranged to do a late shift on the desk because it's their night. They'll leave around mid-night. Back to their partners, no doubt. They do it once a month. Never fail. What is it? His evening out with the lads, hers with girls?

The sheets are in a twisted mess like some kind of whirlpool that's sucked them down without a trace. Two bottles of wine, two paper cups and a cheap corkscrew. Crisps, some sweet wrappers. A banana skin! Kinky. Mary would never go for something like that. Fat content too high for her. Can't find any clues as to who they really are. What did I expect? They aren't going to leave names and addresses. Well, he does leave one but it isn't going to be his real one.

The name and address he gives is John Benson, 23 Lakelands Drive. The more I think about that address, the more I wonder if he has always used that one. I'm sure he hasn't. I go back to reception and look at the computer. Search on the name. He comes up. Strange. Same name but earlier bookings were a different address. It's 23 Hanover Street. Last three times he's used Lakelands. I didn't notice. Wonder why he's done that? I wonder if he's started using his real address. Perhaps that's part of the kick for him. After all, he likes me to know what he's up to. Maybe it's some kind of living dangerous fantasy he's got. Likes the idea of being caught. A fake address is boring and safe so to increase the thrill he's using his real one. There isn't any such place as Hanover Street as far as I know but there is a Lakelands Drive. Maybe that's it. It's funny what turns people on. That's what Mary used to tell me when I said I liked her better before she lost weight. That's in the days when we actually had conversions

★★★

This morning, I drive over to Lakelands Drive. It's a Monday. Best to have a look when he's likely to be at work. If it is his house, of course. A big place. Very nice. Can understand why he hasn't left his wife for his bit on the side. Would be hard to give up this four bedroom, double garage thing. I'm admiring the garden when I see her drawing the bay window curtains. *Her!* She's at his house! A bit blatant. What if the neighbours see? But then again it could be her house. Does she know he uses her address? Does he want her contacted by the hotel? We send out mail-shots to regular customers. That might give her game away. Maybe he's setting her up to be found out because she won't leave her husband. Turfed out and straight into his arms. Very clever.

Now she's leaving the house, heading towards the car on the drive. Jeans and T-shirt. Denim jacket. Little leather handbag. Nothing like the tarty stuff she wears at the hotel. I think of driving off but that might make her look my way and clock me. Too late. She's clocked me anyway. I sit there as she walks over to my car. I feel like some naughty boy whose been caught scrumping apples or getting his ball from the garden. I could drive off but don't. Maybe it's because I fancy her and wouldn't mind talking to her even if it is under these circumstances. I wind the window down.

'You're the man from the hotel.' She's confident. Nowhere near as shy or ashamed as she seems when she passes me in reception.

'Yes'

'What are you doing around here?'

I smile, embarassed. 'Looking for a friend's house.'

She starts to laugh. 'Really? What's his name? Or is it a her?' She knows full well why I'm here. 'He's been giving our real address, hasn't he?'

'What?'

'He's my husband.' She reaches into her handbag and pulls out a little wedding photo to prove it. Bad hair cut, bad suit. Younger, thinner. But it's him.

'You think we're having an affair. That's what we want you to think. It's part of the game. Once every few weeks we get my mum to babysit and go to the hotel and pretend we are lovers. It keeps the spark alive. You know - a bit of sexual fantasy.'

Well, actually, madam, no I don't bloody know. The spark with the stick insect I live with vanished long ago. Her idea of a sexual fantasy revolves around the amount of calories a shag burns up.

'Oh. Sorry. I didn't mean to...' I don't know what to do now. I feel like a right tit.

'It's ok. I suppose we're doing a good job if we fooled you. Although him giving our real address is rather silly. It's hardly what you'd really do.'

'I suppose not.' I start the engine.

'What were you going to do if you found out he was having a real affair?'

I shrug. Drive off. I was going to make your bastard husband's life a misery by telling him I knew where he lived. I was going to make him start paying a price again for being lucky enough to fuck someone like you . Someone who is voluptuous.

★★★

They don't come to the hotel again. I suppose their game, their sexual fantasy, loses something if they know the man at the desk knows the truth, and may have told the rest of the staff. I suppose they're using somewhere else. Tonight would have been one of their nights. I clock off and go to Tesco. Mary is away overnight on some hen do. Some friend of a friend. It's the second one this month. She has the car so I have to walk.

I fill the basket with crisps, cream cakes, lager. Stuff that makes you fat. Stuff that would cause a row if I took it home because it is is bad for me and it makes her diet so much harder if I am there feeding my face. None of that tonight.

A voice behind me: 'Chocolate eclairs! My favourite!' *Her* voice.

'I was just passing. Needed a few bits. I saw you walk in. No car? Do you want a lift?'

'Sure. Thanks.'

The smell of her perfume. I look down at her knees. Her skirt rides up slightly while she drives. The little slit is showing more leg. Not as big as that in the skirt she wore when she stayed at the hotel but nice all the same

It's hard to know who kissed who first. She offered to help me carry my bags into the house. I didn't need help. I only had two. But I let her. I offered coffee. We were both in the kitchen. It's small. A few accidental touches. I think they were accidental. I don't know. Next thing her tongue's in my mouth. Then we are fucking in the living room. She's like a woman who's not done it in years. So much for their spark. She feels so much better than Mary. Softer, fuller. Gorgeous. Voluptuous? Is that really the word? It doesn't seem good enough now. No word does. And afterwards I'm close to her. Want to be close. Don't want to just roll over and go to sleep.

'Fancy doing this again sometime?' she says.

'Yes. Please. Right now ….'

★★★

I pick her up from the pub in my car. She's got a taxi from her place. A night out with the girls. Will be funny being a guest at a hotel for a change. She gets in. I hand her some chocolates from the back seat. 'For You.' Kiss.

'Again!' she says.

'They're your favourites.'

She opens them as I drive towards the hotel. She tucks in. Coffee cream first, then hazelnut whirl. Always the same. She offers me one.

'No thanks.'

'Are you sure?'

'Oh positive. You have the lot.'

Road Kill

Polly Clark

At the moment when Lara's husband was delivering the news of his imminent exit to live with a painter named Caressa, a pigeon fell down the chimney. There was a horrible scuffling sound, as though a creature was going to burst out of the wall. It landed head first on the coals and gave a piercing, heartbreaking shriek before scrabbling helplessly, smoking, onto the hearth.

Lara's husband, Patrick, put down his briefcase, pulled off his jumper and wrapped it around the bird to staunch the flames. There was a terrible smell of burning feathers and the bird fell into an ungainly silence. When he was sure it was no longer burning, Patrick gingerly unrolled the jumper on the floor. The pigeon sat up, blinking. It eyed Lara and opened its mouth, its spike of a tongue arched, an air of excitement about it.

'I'll put it out,' said Patrick. While he was gone, Lara remained patiently waiting for him to resume the speech that began, 'I'm leaving now.' Before any long journeys she always made her husband sandwiches but on this occasion she was not sure what to do. It would depend of course where he was leaving to. If was within London, then sandwiches would not be necessary. She wondered where the sandwich limit lay. Perhaps Cambridge. She would wait to see where he said he was going.

Their daughter, Rosemary, was asleep. Patrick had decided to make his announcement at 11.30pm after a particularly protracted telephone call. Patrick came back into the house, bringing a burst of cold air with him that shook the flames of the fire.

'What shall I tell Rosemary?' she asked him.

'I'll ring her in the morning.'

'And do you want a photograph?' Lara leapt to her feet, almost tripping over her nightdress. 'Here, take this one of Rosemary. And this one.' She handed him a photo of their daughter and another of a small boy on a tricycle. 'Where are you going?'

'Manchester. Here is the number.'

Lara wavered and sat down heavily on the sofa. Manchester was the sort of distance that required sandwiches, but she did not think she could make them.

★★★

Milana was a florid Canadian whose poetry had been well-regarded about fifteen years ago. She did not write anymore because the sadness, deaths and disappointments which had characterized her early work had mostly come true, and true disappointment without hope of reprieve did not inspire her.

She had met Lara and Patrick during her years in London when she had been living the life she imagined a poet lived: one of passionate affairs and feuds. Along the way, Edward was born, named after the poet she had always been in love with from afar, Ted Hughes. The father, a moderately talented sculptor, had been far too heavy a drinker to change his ways and Milana had decided to return to Canada and to begin again.

Edward had singularly failed to live up to his namesake and had remained steadfastly an Edward. He was a stringy, pale boy, with an unnervingly pretty face, and his mother adored him and spoiled him as far as she could in her new life as once well-regarded poet-turned translator. By the age of ten, expelled from schools, stealing and lying, he had brought both sorrow and the police to Milana's new life.

When she got the almost incoherent call from Lara, on the night that Patrick departed, Milana saw an escape.

'Let's go on the road,' she said, after a transatlantic pause. 'Let's take the kids and have an adventure.'

The silence at the other end was broken only by a sniff.

'OK,' said a tiny voice. 'I'll see you as soon as you can get here.'

★★★

Rosemary looked at Edward. Edward looked at Rosemary. Rosemary saw: a pretty boy, the sort of boy that she had already kissed and had already shared a cigarette with after school, over cans of cider stolen from parents and carried around all day until it was warm and flat. He had mean blue eyes and while she would not have categorized them thus, she recognized them. The boy was slightly smaller than Rosemary and one year older.

Edward saw: a girl who was not pretty, but oddly riveting. She didn't smile. She seemed emotionless. She just nodded at him. In the pocket of her little corduroy jacket a packet of cigarettes peeped out. Her mother stood behind her with her hands on her shoulders, evidently unaware of the stash. Edward said, 'I hate it here. It rains all the time.' And Rosemary, at this, grinned broadly.

Patrick had left Lara the larger of the two cars, an exhausted black Audi whose gearstick had snapped leaving a rather savage point. They packed the boot with clothes and emergency food of various types, including: chocolate, beer, crisps, red wine, Melba toasts, corned beef, vacuum packed cheese slices, dried apricots and figs. Lara was to drive and Milana to navigate. Their destination was

Pembrokeshire, Wales, with its wild coastline and fresh air. They put The Rolling Stones Greatest Hits on in the car and the two women sang along. The children sat silently in the back.

★★★

'I think problem with everything is that I can't drive,' remarked Caressa, half-curled up on the bed like a small, scrubbed and extremely cute pig. It was her cuteness which drove Patrick to distraction. She had an animal quality to her, a non-verbal warmth which made him want to pack her into an extremely small, soft container and take her everywhere with him. Mad, he knew. Especially now when she was working up to a speech that he knew he didn't want to hear.

'Why do you say that?' he asked.

'Because if I had travelled more, if I'd been more adventurous, then I would know what I want.'

'I can teach you to drive.'

'That's not really the point, is it?' Caressa said. Above the bed was one of her paintings: the view of a city road from a skyscraper. The detail was amazing, and though painted entirely in grey, such were the subtle differences in tone that it felt like a vibrant city viewed through smog. Patrick often found himself gazing at the picture, then when his eyes dropped and he saw her beneath it, he thought that he might just explode with hope and happiness. She had gone up Blackpool Tower over thirty times to make the sketches, and yet it was not Blackpool at all. It was a landscape she had entirely invented. Patrick clambered onto the bed, reaching for her, but already her face was heavy with sleep. She slept with the depth of those who can make something out of their fears, and therefore take them away for a time, and of course with the peace of the young.

He waited until her breathing was relaxed and even, then he laid a dressing gown over her curled up form and lay back beside her. He was wide awake, as if it was impossible that he might ever sleep again. At the edge of his vision were the strange elongated colours of a nightmare, one he slipped into every time he managed to sleep. He turned and looked at the painting, lost himself in the tiny figures until he felt calm, until he could remember what it was about himself that ever made him think he could walk out of one life and into another, and somehow carry it off.

★★★

As they reached the Brecon beacons, Lara realized that it was over a year since she had been out of London. No holiday, no clean air, nothing for a whole year. She opened the window and let in a howl of icy air.

'Mum!' shrieked Rosemary. 'It's freezing!'

'But it's so clean!' Lara replied. 'Take a big lungful.'

'What it is, is fucking depressing,' drawled Edward, staring out at the mountains, grey and hunched against the sky.

Milana sighed. 'Don't swear, Edward.'

'You're right,' Rosemary whispered, so close that the corner of the cigarette packet poked his arm. 'It *is* fucking depressing.' She gave him an admiring smile, which he did not return.

'Your country's a shit hole,' he murmured into her ear. She was so close that he could see the shape of his face in the dark centre of her eye.

She bounced back to her side of the car. 'What's Canada like?' she asked.

'At this time of year?' answered Milana, turning round excitedly. 'Oh it has snow ten feet high, and the air is crisp and the sky is clear. It is beautiful, really beautiful. Isn't it, Edward?'

Edward grunted and shifted so that he was looking out of the window. Glancing in the mirror, Lara saw the still-chubby boyishness of his face. She wanted suddenly to stop the car, to run round and drag the boy out, to shake him until he understood something. Understood what? *How much you are loved*, she wanted to tell him, so close to his face that her lips would brush his cheek and her voice would shut out everything that was frightening, and he would be in no doubt. *You are so loved, you stupid, stupid boy.*

The mountains gave way to woods. It was almost dark, and it was beginning to rain. Lara switched on the headlights. The white markings on the road gleamed, and the occasional road sign flashed meaningfully as they pushed on. In the front passenger seat Milana was fumbling with the map.

'When are we stopping? I'm hungry.' Edward whined.

'Not long, darling,' said Milana turning the map round and squinting at it in the fading light. 'I think it's the B1267,' she added to Lara. 'And it should be appearing around now.'

On each side were steep banks and huge empty trees almost touching over the top of them. A sign flashed by, and Milana screamed.

A piece of the bank had broken free and was rolling into the road. The lights and the rain turned it into a spinning mix of white and black as big as a tree trunk.

'It's a badger!' Lara cried.

There was a terrible thud, and the car stopped dead. Edward was thrown against Rosemary. His head drove into her stomach. Milana turned desperately in her seatbelt to see if her son was all right. The headlights went out and there was a sudden silence, broken only by the rain.

'Fucking mental!' said Edward wonderingly, peeling himself from Rosemary and staring outside to see the badger.

'Is it dead?' Rosemary asked.

Steam was hissing from the edges of the bonnet. Lara fiddled with the controls in an attempt to switch the lights on.

'I'm going to have a look,' said Edward eagerly.

Lara scrabbled in the glovebox. 'Here – take this.'

The torch sliced through the darkness, the rain swarming in its beam. Edward seemed taller and older than his years suddenly, his eagerness for the macabre gracing him with a look of heroism.

Back home the raccoons tipped over the trashcans and rummaged noisily like beggars. They were so arrogant that they did not run away when you came out to shoo them off. They perched on the trash and stared with their round eyes, like horrible birds. Edward and a friend had taken to shooting them with airguns. The pellets made them scream and jump in the air, and run off dancing. Edward knew about animals when they were hurt, how they found a strange energy, enough to run faster than they ever had. He had never seen any of the raccoons die, though some of them were so full of pellets that blood drooled from them like rain. They always went off somewhere. They never let you watch them die.

Like a spotlight on a field, the torch beam at first picked out only small circles. The badger's fur was in several layers, the shorter grey fur interspersed with coarse black hairs. Edward moved the torch up and down to try to get a sense of the creature's shape and orientation.

The window wound down behind him. 'Are you okay, Edward?' his mother called. 'Is it alive?'

'Dunno yet.'

The black lump shifted at his feet. It mewed like a kitten, then was silent. Edward suddenly felt the rain coursing down his neck and shivered. He moved the beam of light along the creature's body.

'Mum!'

The badger's eye was wide open and furiously bright in the torch light. Now Edward saw that what seemed like darkness was actually blood, gallons of it, pouring out of the animal from somewhere underneath and onto the wet road. The badger hunched itself trying to drag itself away, but now Edward could see that the back half of it was skewed. He turned away, suddenly dizzy. The creature was snapped in half, its hide the only thing keeping it together. It mewed again.

A car door opened. It was Lara, thin and white in the rain, seeming to absorb whatever light there was. She made her way round the other side of the car gingerly, her hair sticking to her face.

'It's still alive, isn't it?' she whispered. Edward's torchlight trembled across the badger, who now succeeded in hauling itself a few inches.

'Oh dear God, the poor thing.' said Lara. 'We'll have to move it.' She bent over the badger, looking for a place to lift it from. Edward found suddenly that he could not speak, that he was transfixed by the blood that was turning the road to sticky tar.

'Rosemary!' Lara peered towards the car and waved blindly. Rosemary clambered out. 'We need your help with this,' said Lara. 'I think it's a three person job.'

Rosemary hesitated, a black statue in the rain. 'I'll help if I can smoke a cigarette first,' she said.

'What?'

'A cigarette. I haven't had one for hours.'

'What are you talking about? A cigarette? You don't smoke – you're twelve.'

'Oh yes I do.' Rosemary, with a smug glance at Edward took out the packet from her pocket and lit one. She offered the box to Edward, who shook his head.

'We'll talk about this later,' said Lara. 'Right now we have to get this creature out of the way. Edward – can you take this end? I'll carry the biting end.'

'Can't I shine the torch? Someone has to.'

'All right. Rosemary, please can you carry this end?'

The cigarette already half extinguished by the rain, Rosemary gripped the coarse but soft body of the badger. Lara went carefully round to its head. Edward thought he might be sick as the badger yelped horribly. It was incredible that these women seemed to have no squeamishness, as though this bleeding agonized animal was nothing especially alarming. *It's sick*, he thought. *Unfeeling and sick.* He shone the beam of the torch half heartedly where Lara indicated.

'I think,' said Lara, drenched and quiet, 'that we will have to kill it.'

'Fuck,' said Edward under his breath.

In the car, Milana was fiddling with the ignition and the controls in an attempt to get the lights working. Fragments of poems, whose original provenance she could not remember spun in her head. Then suddenly, a quick turn of the ignition sparked the fog lights into life, and weak light bathed her friend and the children in front of the car.

They made an eerie procession to the verge, the body of the badger sagging in their arms. Edward led the way with the torch. Black blood covered them, was smeared even on their faces where it had touched their hands and then been transferred as they tried to keep the rain from their eyes. The blood shone on their clothes. Most striking of all was Lara. She held the body of the badger tenderly, her fingers moving gently through its fur. All the life seemed to have drained from her face: when at one moment she glanced up, she seemed not to know where she was.

Lara's mobile lay on the dashboard. Milana took it and rang Patrick.

★★★

When driving, nightmares are frogmarched out of your head. Thoughts are simplified, shoehorned into the rhythm of mirror, signal, manoeuvre. This is why Patrick loved to drive. He believed, still, that he was an exceptionally alert driver. He was especially careful with his mirrors. If you asked him at any moment what was behind him he would be able to say with impeccable certainty, remembering even certain details, number plates for example, or precise make of car.

The motorway was busy in the darkness, full of lorries on their way down south. Shadowy arms leant against cabin windows; podgy night-faces glared down at him. Patrick had both hands on the steering wheel and noted without really thinking the sign that said London: 200 miles.

After Birmingham, the road quietened. By then it was almost dawn and lorry drivers had pulled into laybys to sleep or into Road Chefs for breakfast. The cat's eyes galloped, glowing under the wheels, signs came and went. Patrick was tired, he moved into the inside lane and slowed down. He knew the dangers of being too tired, how suddenly, just once, one didn't look. He knew exactly how that felt, how the car seemed to flinch as it rolled over something, how the shock of not knowing that turned, knifeishly, into *knowing*.

The object that hits you at speed at speed can kill you: at the very least it writes off the car. No matter how small it does not let you continue without knowing that it was there, leaving the damage for you to find and remember. But what of the stationary object? What of the small immobile object that you just didn't see? That waited for you?

Patrick's right hand slid off the wheel. Sweat was pouring off him, though he was shivering with the cold. He wiped the hand on his soaked shirt and shook and blinked. He wondered if he should stop, but he knew that Lara and Rosemary were on their way home and if he kept going he might be there before them. He did not know what he would do when he got there, perhaps just hang up his shirts again, make himself a cup of strong black coffee, and wait. He knew what he would not do. He would not look at photographs. When Lara came in he would *not* say, *I only survived because you forgave me*. That was a nonsense. He said the words aloud. *I only survived because you forgave me,* and the words stuck in the air, turned the inside of the car to ice. He shivered so much he thought he would lose control of the steering. With one hand he turned up the heating and hot air rushed into the cabin.

Already Caressa seemed a long way away. He thought of her face, the feel of her, the peculiarly possible future they had planned. And it *was* possible, for someone other than him, someone who did not know what he knew, who did not have a secret that only one other person could relieve him of. And when he thought of Lara he was glad of the rhythm of the driving, the way it prevented him from thinking of her properly. The problem with Caressa? He could think of her. Their passion was a real demarcated thing; he knew where it began and ended, he knew what it meant. But Lara, and beside her, Rosemary... none of it ended where it should.

A movement to the side of the car caught his eye. A huge bird, like an owl was coasting beside the window, low down, wings wide and still. Patrick stared: it was impossible. There was no bird that could fly so fast, or at least not one that he knew. He saw the individual feathers of its wings, the round, intent ball of its head. Then it pulled ahead, and to the side and vanished.

Patrick was so tired he feared that his eyes would not stay open. Then he saw the bird again, this time standing in the road, facing him, the size of a small child. Its round face housed two enormous eyes that watched him bear down. It was too close for him to avoid and the car slapped into it. He heard the sound, and cried out. He felt the car bump over the bird's body. Patrick gripped the steering wheel, partly to keep control, partly to stop himself from screaming. He knew he must look in the mirror to see what had happened, but was too afraid. The last time he had looked back like that he saw Joshua, his own child, crushed on a toy bike. His wife had crumpled beside the child. Her eyes had looked up at him in the mirror in disbelief.

But then he saw the shadow of a bird, its wings outstretched, soaring out from under the car, completely unhurt. It was huge and solid and alive and it swept up and into the dawn sky effortlessly. Patrick sped up wildly. The final miles to London flew by. He screeched the car to a halt, fumbled helplessly with his keys, ran into the house and switched on all the lights. When Lara arrived, with his daughter, both of them covered in blood and too shocked and exhausted to speak, he was waiting in the living room. He got to his feet, unsteadily. He wondered why Lara's hands were clasped so tightly together and why his daughter did not smile. He had worked out an explanation for everything, and pressed feverishly on. But his mouth would not open, and he watched in horror as the truth he had come to understand – that there is nothing that a man and his wife cannot overcome – never reached his wife.

Long Division

Roddy Lumsden

In my opinion, this world is an unlikely one and, what's more, it may well be the only one and this is among the reasons why I am picking at a few cold chips which Patti Fleischer has, in her anxiousness, left all but derelict on the side of her side-plate in this café-bar in the East Village.

This is my ninth week in America, my fifth in New York City and my third as an acquaintance, perhaps by now I should say companion, of Patti Fleischer. Moving into an apartment with three girls did at first sound promising on the holiday romance / waving the hankie at the airport front, but then Carmen Caffrey, my friend-of-a-friend contact, turns out to be a die-hard health kicker, Marcie Harb introduces herself as a lesbian even before she gives out her name, and Patti Fleischer is in love.

The object of this emotion, a blue-eyed whistler called Gerry (surname a colour - Brown, Green or White, I forget), is in deepest Nebraska on a three-month field-trip and so Patti has a little time on her hands. She also needs some advice. A lot of advice, a lot of the time. Advice is not good for the complexion, or the bile duct, I tell Patti Fleischer, in the hope that she will herehence ask for less of it, but she's far from ignorant. They want her on the talk-show circuit, after all.

Just about every half-hour or so, Patti takes out a purple lozenge the size and shape of a fifty pence piece and crunches on it. She tells me these are her *shame pills*, carrageen extract multivitamins, that they taste of coconut, that they're among the best-known natural enemies of guilt, regret and associated hang-ups. In moments like this, I still feel as if I'm wearing a Fool's hat or a Kick Me sign which is only visible to Manhattanites. After all, it's good, honest self-loathing I'm more accustomed to at home, not this rollercoastering self-help culture which Patti lives and breathes.

I nod and pick something up from the table, a salt shaker or a napkin, say, and I ask whether there is a New York word for it. This amuses Patti Fleischer. The joke will run and run. Otherwise, if I allow a silence to expand, if the quietness between us reaches a height, she'll ask me what I am thinking and this, as often as not, occasions a white lie.

Six months ago, Patti tells me, she got herself a record deal with Sho-Matic. This is an off-shoot of Penumbra which is in turn a subsidiary of Polygram. This is what she's been planning towards since she was waist-high, and I've played the willing victim, listening to the demo tapes which Patti has been working on in a studio in Queens, in trade for her services as a tour guide. Her songs are not exactly to my taste - too smooth, her lyrics on the wrong side of gushy. But Patti can sing. She has something. I won't question that. Imagine Doris Day, but for the now. I mean, not more than one primary colour in the one outfit. Hair kept to its natural colour (on the very brink between red and brown). Cheekbones (did Doris Day have them?).

Patti's biggest problem remains, as it has always been, that she is the daughter of Adam Fleischer, "the" Adam Fleischer. Last year, Patti says, he was the twenty-fifth highest paid actor in the country. This sounds impressive to me until, when I don't press her to, Patti mentions the sum involved. Then it sounds doubly impressive. At least.

On the evening of my first meeting with Patti and the other girls, she decides to take me under her wing, down to an Italian place on Houston for a meal. On the way there, she stops suddenly and when I turn aside to miss her, she is standing there, staring upwards at a rare skyful of stars over Manhattan. Stars can be relied on, she says, and sighs. I say I'd prefer it if the stars reappeared in different patterns each night, the more that we might feel comfortable with our own small matrix of chaos. Maybe it's hunger talking.

For her starter, Patti chooses something I've never heard of called arugula. This turns out to be nothing more than a plateful of salad leaves which, when she lets me try some (rather intimately, fork direct to my mouth) taste like spinach laced with pastis. Patti says she has never heard of pastis. This makes us even and so we shake on it and her hand feels a little cold in mine. The reason we haven't shaken hands earlier is that Carmen introduces us when we are on opposite sides of the kitchen. Patti waves. She's a waver, so I wave back.

During the Italian meal, the first of maybe ten or twelve we have shared in the past few weeks, ignoring a couple of times when we've grabbed a pizza slice or sat up at a bar to gobble a frank in one of the Papaya places, Patti asks me what my father does. I tell her he's a commercial photographer. Weddings and babies, you know, mostly, family groups, local businesses. She says that's very interesting and informs me that maybe I have probably heard of "her" father. Since the only Fleischer I have heard of is Adam Fleischer, it turns out that Patti is correct in her supposing. I try to reel off some films I have seen starring her father, but find I can come up with just two, apart from his TV series *Wrecker*, so I'm hardly reeling at all. Patti names a few others and I hum in recognition.

Patti says she doesn't much like to talk about this subject, but that it's best to clear it from the agenda smartish when she is getting to know someone new. Nonetheless, she talks about it all through her arugula and well into the pasta with shrimp sauce. It turns out I know her mother too. She played Diane Keaton's best friend (or sister maybe) in that film about the journalist trying to prove she didn't sleep with the Vice President. I feel I should confess that I only saw the film to please a friend who'd promised to buy me a few pints afterwards, but while I'm weighing this up, Patti has moved on to talking about her sister.

And it's this older sister, Ruth, who Patti is again talking about now as I pass time by eating Patti's leftover chips. Ruth has already dealt with the problem of the talk-shows, but then Ruth is five years ahead into the whole game and has already screenplayed two films, one of which, *Ticker Tape*, was largely responsible for filliping her father's career, and slowing his backslide into TV action roles.

When Patti asks for my advice, I parry by asking her what advice her family has given her. She says they're supportive, but that Ruth thinks she should wait until after her first hit record until she goes on the TV guest-shows, although radio stations are probably okay at this stage, as long as they focus on her music and play a song and not just ask, as Patti fears they will, all the usual stuff about being a member of a showbiz family. That's my advice too, I tell Patti, for what it's worth.

But then Patti uses the "antsy" word and starts to talk faster. She asks me, hypothetically she says, to consider whether I would be so ready to sit here with her if several situations, scenarios or whatever things were not so. Before she can start listing, I let Patti know that this sounds a lot like maths, or as she would say, math, and that neither maths nor math was ever my strong point, no more so than advice, and I ask her if she'll take another beer.

When I come back up from the toilets, Patti has been writing on the back of a half-price meal flyer for the Mexican restaurant we've not yet eaten in which is below our apartment on Seventh Avenue South. I thought it must be the same man who was handing them out twenty four hours, but it turns out he's one of triplets, according to Marcie. Patti hands the flyer to me and I read the front side first, hoping she will pursue her talent for changing the subject. I ask her what cilantro is, even though I've had it at 1 Across in a *Times* crossword back home earlier in the year.

On the back, Patti has written this:

> *MATH(S) EXAM*
>
> *Work out the following using addition, subtraction, multiplacation and division:-*
>
> *Would you be here if I were'nt...*
>
> *...Adam Fleischer's daughter / Mary Casey Fleischer's, daughter / Ruth Fleischers' sister??*
>
> *...Sharing an apartment with you??*
>
> *...A Singer with a hot contract??*
>
> *...the way I am???*

I stare at this for a while, deciding no more than to keep it forever as an artefact, until Patti says again, c'mon, how much she needs my advice, how this is such a difficult point in her life, how easily things could all go wrong and tells me how much she appreciates my input, with me being an outsider from another country. She says she feels she might get crazy at any second. Just because. Things happen. Things like that *do* happen. She looks at me and smiles. She is good at that.

The truth is that the first three things don't seem to have too heavy a leaning on any of this. I know I'd still be as happy sitting here with Patti if she were the daughter of a broker or a baker. I'm not exactly an authority on American showbiz. I'm much more impressed that she once shook hands with Aretha Franklin at a party and that one of her guitars used to belong to Steve Cropper of the MGs.

Maybe I should come clean and admit that, though I believe in her potential, in her talent, I won't be buying her records for any reason other than the fact that I know her, except maybe if they put a picture of her on the cover. I can imagine being back in Edinburgh and showing it around my friends, saying hey look, I hung out with this here singer lassie for a while in New York.

First, I semi-chastise Patti for her lax manner of spelling and inconsistent punctuation. I ask her where she went to school. Then I state the obvious: that I wouldn't be here with her if we weren't living in the same place, since more likely than not we would never have met. Speaking mathswise, I say, that one is done by performing some simple addition, just putting two and two together. Next, I say that although I do realise what a big deal it is for her to be a member of a famous family, because I'm essentially a foreigner, they aren't so famous to me.

This is a lie, of course. I'd reckon four out of five Scots have heard of Adam Fleischer. I recall a recent bunch of his films on TV back home, an ITV season, and I've already mentioned this to Patti, and she already knew. However, I allow this one to sneak through, functioning as the subtraction. We can take that one away, I say, because it's all but irrelevant.

Because I've been talking, Patti has raced ahead on the beer and she calls the guy over to bring some more. She says again that it's bad for her voice, so I venture some yarns on Florence Ballard, Janis Joplin and a few other girl singers who were mad-keen on the juice and, praise be, she doesn't get any more jumpy. She winks and taps the exam paper. I'm getting mired in my maths allegory by now. I can't see how Patti's not being a singer would change anything, but I can't realistically tie this in with multiplication in any way. I tell her this and she accepts it. Okay, move on, she says.

What I want at this moment is to leave the café. Anxiety is contagious. What Patti Fleischer wants is to discuss the last remaining variable on her list, the one I'm quailing at, the *way I am* one. She points out that I'm almost finished, just the division left. I buy a little time by saying I need to think about that one. I needn't have bothered. Just then, two guys come in and one makes a beeline for Patti when she waves. It turns out that he is a session bassist who has played on some of Patti's songs and she introduces him as Charlie. To Charlie, she describes me as her spiritual adviser, flown in from Scotland, and as one of the sweetest people she has met in all her life. I start necking my bottle of beer.

As soon as Charlie has gone to join his friend sitting up at the counter, I ask Patti if we can leave. It's a no smoking table we're at and I need a smoke. We walk out into the afternoon, down First Avenue and along St Mark's Place. As usual, it's full of the strangest people. We pass a woman reading tarot with the Crowley pack and a guy selling rock-star figurines he says are made from baked chewing gum. An indie girl says, gee, your hair is cool. Patti asks me if we have to come this way and also why I haven't lit a cigarette, saying she doesn't leave half a Rolling Rock for nothing, record contract or no record contract.

I sit down on a stairway and pluck out a Marlboro Medium. Patti sits below me and unties and re-ties her hair. I find this street fascinating, but I've been down here with Patti the week before and she can't see it. Been here too long. I tell her that if she came to Edinburgh, she would drag me to palaces and castles within the first day or two. She can't believe I have a full-scale ancient castle slap in the middle of my home city and yet I've never been to visit it. I point out that it was hereabouts that Warhol did some of the Velvet Underground stuff, that the Beats used to live in the next street. And look, isn't that the guy from The Cramps? Patti just says that it proves this part of the city was always a weirdo magnet. Maybe she has a point.

It's just then that Patti looks at me for the first time in a certain sort of way which I have to ignore. I'm never sure what I want this life to do. Then she asks if there isn't something I'm supposed to be thinking about. Like division. Okay, okay. I take out the "Math(s) Exam" and ask her exactly what she means by *the way I am*. She moves up to my step and edges a little closer along towards me. Now, we are almost touching, only she sits angled in my direction.

Patti explains that the full question is whether I would be spending so much time with her if she wasn't the way she was. This sounds to me very like what my friend Doug once called the *gentle hammer*, the way some women coerce you into complimenting them, into laying your cards.

I tell Patti that if she wasn't the way she was, she would be someone else and so it's a useless question. She admits to this, but says I'm being no fun. And so I allow myself to be hit. I ask for one more minute, for calculations and last minute revision. She laughs. I wonder then what Gerry, her Missing Man, would say if he were here. I wonder if she once asked him the same question, and where, and what he said, and I suppose that he must have answered correctly.

So I light a second cigarette off the arse-end of the first and consider my time with Patti Fleischer over the past few weeks. How she scolded me at the Met for lingering too long by the Balthus painting of the adolescent girl looking with fear and longing at her body in a mirror. How she hid behind a chair while she played me a demo of a new song called "Calling Out Your Name". How she laughed when I suggested a gig at CBGBs and again when I failed to hit any of the ten pins on my first three bowls. How we talked drunk about lost loves late, late into the night and both said a little too much without being drawn in any direction. How, from inside a record shop, I watched that hair blow across her face one afternoon on Carmine Street as she waited there for me.

And how I come to say the things I do now. For I mistrust the word beauty and tell her she is very attractive. For I am unsure of the concept of uniqueness and tell her she is different. For I am fearful of a good many things in this world and tell her that I kinda like her, she is interesting company. And then I spill my guts. The whole hog.

Patti turns to me and looks at me in that certain way again, as if she were gargling with a mouthful of heaven. She takes my free, non-smoking hand, holds it in between her own and I notice then how she keeps one deep blue fingernail, the right index, longer than the others, for her guitar-playing. She squeezes my hand and she tenses up, shivering slightly. I think she might start to cry, or else lean forward to take my kiss.

Patti Fleischer closes her eyes. Stay calm, I tell her.

I miss him *so much*, is what she says now.

We're So Fab We Said All the Right Things

Ruth Padel

1

It was the shortest, darkest, definitely the coldest day of the year, and Joe the carpenter's last working day before Christmas. Joe was diabetic, bald and kind. His teeth hurt. He'd had them capped a week before.

Ann had given him, and the plumber, and the electrician, each a bottle of Famous Grouse.

'In honour of your Scottish moor,' she said. 'When you all went away and left me. When you went shooting in October.'

Joe, Steve and Martin had worked together twenty-five years. Steve had had a pericardial cyst removed from his lung and his ribs broken for it; the scar from the epidural still ached. He wasn't supposed to lift anything, even a hammer, but he lifted things all the time. The pain wasn't getting better. He walked with his leather jacket hitched on one side, a small, plump, Incredible Hulk.

Martin was bulky as the Taj Mahal, Obelix out of *Asterix* with a head like a close-cropped ginger-grey ball. He was clumsy and painstaking with an exquisite tenor voice. He was moody; but when he was happy Ann heard him singing as he worked. Early Elvis, Verdi, Patsy Cline. He had terrible ears which he stuffed with cotton wool. They bled through delicately, little threaded dribbles under snowy tufts in the cold. He never heard the doorbell when he was alone.

Martin and Steve were round the corner, finishing

another client's kitchen before the Christmas deadline. They'd left their Famous Grouses here with Joe.

'I know you don't drink much Joe, and it's got sugar in it anyway – but it might come in handy round the house, the next ten days.'

'Very kind of you,' said Joe. 'Been nice working here. We've been a team, us three and you.'

'You've made the kitchen glow,' she said.

'Got the yellow right in the end,' said Joe.

'After all that Lemon Chiffon.'

Watery sun glittered on the shoulders of whiskey between them.

'Still a bit to go,' he said. 'These cupboard doors...'

The bell rang. She left Joe getting down on his knees, on the floor he'd tiled in fake terracotta. 'Don't say fake,' said the girl at Criterion Tiles. 'Say ceramic. It sounds better.'

She could see Mark through the glass front door. This was their Christmas. Like all their Christmasses these last five years, it would be mainly given over to his last-minute Christmas shopping.

She'd do hers tomorrow: think about it then. This was crisis time, first time she'd seen Mark in nearly two weeks; not since Lucy found out.

Mark was in panic mode. 'I've only got till three. I've got to be the other side of London at three thirty, I've got a list – stuff for the kids' stockings, camp-bed for my nephews...'

His arms were round her before he'd even closed the door. 'It's getting worse,' he muttered into her jugular. 'She's going to a lawyer.'

Ann gave him a Borough of Brent Visitor's Permit, scratched in for half an hour.

'I'm afraid Zoe is around after all,' she said. Zoe, her thirteen year old, had been booked to visit a friend for lunch and hadn't gone.

'Damn.'

'She's taking the dog out now, but her walks never last long. You can't depend on them.'

'Come in here,' he said, sweeping her into the front room, closing that door, pouring himself into and round her, face, mouth, hands, bra, jeans; as if a mountain stream hit by an avalanche had swollen all over the forest in whirls of giant toffee.

'I'm in hell,' he breathed into her mouth. 'I'm going to lose the children, it's all your fault, I've missed you, I'm having a moral crisis, I'm going to lose the house, I can't promise anything in bed, I adore you beyond anything, I want to buy you these wonderful camp sexy clothes from Camden Lock, you've wrecked my life, I can't forgive you, you're everything I've ever loved... '

Love is the only thing, she thought with his arms round her. This isn't sex, it's all of who we are. She furrowed her fingers in the hollow of his spine, as if it were the secret pit of his strength and weaknesses which only she could hold, and felt the ache and horror of the last two weeks in his whole body, his heldback relief at holding her again, a wave hanging so long it thought it would stay in the air forever but now, at last, crashing down onto and into the shore it's been driving to and longing for; the shore it's going to devastate.

All the way up under his jacket, Ann could feel his terror that there might never be a way to take charge again, and his needy rage: that the only way his body could express anything was scoop itself over her.

She heard Zoe's key in the front door, and the panting scrabble of a spaniel that had just missed a thousand squirrels and was purely delighted with life. Unlike anyone else today except maybe Joe with his consummately trued yellow doors.

'Have a coffee,' she said. 'Come and see what they've done in the kitchen.'

Zoe came in while they were in the hall.

'Look, Mark Blythe is here,' said Ann unnecessarily. Why did whatever she said about Mark to Zoe always sound so false?

'I'm going to show him Camden Lock so he can do some Christmas shopping for his kids.'

'Hello,' said Zoe, and flung the dog-lead down. 'What's for lunch Mum and when is it?'

Her blond fringe with its cow's lick covered her eyes. The

dog's paws printed mudflowers on the tiles.

'Sausages,' said Ann. 'You can cook them yourself. I'll start you off if you like, in a while. Joe's here, finishing our cupboards. Why don't you begin your holiday artwork up in your room?'

Zoe's room was the attic, three floors up. They had painted it all summer, white and orange under the eaves.

'Gotta do the research first,' said Zoe. 'On the computer.'

The computer was next to Ann's bedroom.

'I think you should start on the practical side,' said Ann. 'In your room,' she said again.

Zoe went off upstairs. The spaniel grabbed the grubby kangaroo that was Zoe's comforter when she was two, and followed, ears flapping as she leapt the stairs.

'How long have we got?' said Mark. 'I haven't seen you for two weeks, feels like two years, it's hell, she never leaves me alone, it's like living in a madhouse, every room I'm in she comes into and starts going on about you – in front of the children for God's sake – she never mentions you by name, not even by pronoun – just That mad woman, your ghastly friend, going on about your clothes, your age, your hair, saying she's so sorry for me having such terrible taste, you wouldn't believe – Jesus it's even come down to slanging matches between us as to whose lover is the more celebrity singer, hers or mine...'

'Let's have coffee,' said Ann. 'Want a tea, Joe?' she said as she switched on the kettle. The kitchen was glowing yellow chaos, woodshavings, planks, paint cans, spools of masking tape. Joe was on his tummy in the corner with a spirit level.

'This is Mark.'

'Hullo there,' said Joe from the floor.

The dog, who adored the builders, had come downstairs again and was stalking Joe's sandwiches through soft blond heaps of chippings. The naked apple tree outside wagged its brown lace in the wind, throwing stitchy shadows on the walls. A pigeon perched on a branch, stared in, flew off. The twigs dipped and the shadows dipped and bowed with them like dancers.

'Wonderful,' said Mark, looking round. Ann could feel him calling up rags of heartiness, trying to recognize himself and his trademark at ease-ness with whatever happened. 'What a change! It's all so light.'

He'd been against the conservatory. 'What will you live on, sweetheart?' His income was – what? – seven times hers. He'd hated the year he and Lucy did their own house up, all the mess and Chinese takeaways, and found wall-bashing in Ann's home depressing. There was so much disarray in his own life that he wanted something calmer and more welcoming round here. But during the autumn he'd come round to the idea, as the concrete base and shell of the conservatory sprouted up outside. He never saw the daytime mess, the Albanian labourers barrowing clay through the house, the plaster dust, the mess. The kitchen he knew had been taken apart. Now it was nearly back together.

'You've put photos on the walls already.'

Ann had been living in builders' mess so long, she'd raced to get things vertical again: photos of Zoe in the garden with a friend; Zoe on a pony, her parents on a sofa at their Golden Wedding. No Mark.

She watched him looking round. Even in the middle of whatever he was going through, he was checking out his patch.

'You've put up the mad lady on the tiger again,' he said. 'Der... Annie - I thought she'd gone for good.'

Joe laughed from the floor. 'It's the first thing she put up,' he said, 'on our new paint.'

From a religious stall outside a Goan temple, Ann had bought a poster of the Indian goddess Durgha riding a tiger. It had the bright glossy flatness of a Victorian ikon and did not fit Mark's ideas of what was chic.

'It's lucky,' said Ann. 'She's supposed to look after us.'

'She's skiving at the moment then,' said Mark. He looked at the ceiling he'd so often complained was dark and low. It was white now, with recessed lights which Ann and Martin had struggled a whole morning to put in.

'But I did love it as it was,' said Mark. 'A dark bower. So *intime*. My second home.'

For five years they had made love here on the table as potatoes boiled. He'd spread caviar on her nipples, played her guitar, opened gallons of Beaujolais and claret. She'd held him here the night his mother died and he'd sung the song his mother used to sing, standing by the fridge, tears waterfalling down his cheeks onto her hair. He'd begun his first book here, on the laptop she'd bought him when she signed a new contract, because he would never, ever, get round to buying one himself.

This kitchen and her bed had been the centre of their life together. They'd had rows here, made up, given dinner parties, got over all the unlikeliness and wounds of their two-nights-a-week-plus-the-odd-trip-abroad-and-no-contact-at-weekends setup. Which, despite her loneliness at other times and the strain on him, sustaining deceit on such a scale in his violent, recriminatory, media-driven family life, had filled them both, beyond expectation or propriety, with more happiness than either had ever known.

So they told themselves, and told each other. So his friends told them. 'You're the perfect couple,' said Mark's oldest friend from school and his sister Clare, who lived in a village outside Glasgow and had only met Ann twice.

Ann's friends were more reticent.

Mark looked at the radiant walls. 'Golden Rambler 2,' said Ann. 'It makes it look as if there's a light on in here, even when there isn't'

'Cool as a breeze!' said Mark. 'So modern! So fashionable!'

Ann's stomach thought it was going to the dentist. What was happening to them, what about the turkey at the butcher's, cleaning the house for her mother coming to stay tomorrow, the twenty people for Boxing Day lunch, the shelves, saucepans, casseroles on the floor in the front room gathering dust as they had for the last three months? What about mince pies, wrapping paper, decorations, even the damn tree she still had to get?

It was a new cafetière. The coffee grounds flowed in a sharp pyramid of powder into their plastic well. When she pressed the top down, boiling coffee shot over her hand and up her arm.

'Hold it under the tap,' said Mark though it didn't hurt or if it did didn't feel like hurt. He grabbed her hand and turned on the water.

That exaggerated care: that on-spot looking-after, in small

things she managed perfectly well every day of her life, when he left her alone and unlooked-after for days and long long nights when he was too busy with other people to ring.

But he was in a state. He'd do anything to show, just for a moment, he could look after her.

He held her fingers under the water. 'There now,' he said.

'I'm fine,' she said. She turned back to the coffee, poured out three mugs.

'Sugar? Two?'

'One,' he said, indignant. 'I'm not a workman!'

Had Joe heard? Ann said nothing, gave Joe his sugarless tea and took the coffee mugs up the stairs. Zoe was coming down.

'Mum,' said Zoe.' Can we make the sausages now?'

'Here, pet.'

Ann shoved Mark in the study to unwrap his velvet Paul Smith braces, and came down again. She tipped three boar and apple sausages into the frying pan. Hot fat sprang up, a fine drizzly haze lit by sunlight through the conservatory window.

She looked at her daughter, staring at the pan.

'Spike their skins - look, with this - so they don't explode and hurl fat at you, and stay there: watch them, turn them slowly till they're brown on all side. I'll be back in a moment.'

'I can't promise anything,' said Mark as Ann locked the bedroom door. 'I'm shot to hell, I've lost all my mirth, my libido, my –'

'Sssh,' said Ann, holding him, feeling her body sigh as her hair found its nest on his shoulder, stroking the back of his head over and over like a panther licking its cub. 'Just hold me. Doesn't matter. Nothing matters this minute.'

His tongue was down her throat. She could hear Joe drilling below. Opening her eyes, she realized that now she had what she'd been longing for - a conservatory, the tiniest in the world - if you stood by the window in the bedroom you could be seen upward, full frontal, from the kitchen through the roof.

She saw Joe's bald head bowed - was it embarrassment or concentration? - as he started sawing timber. She pulled the blind half-down, dropped on her knees, stroked the back of Mark's thighs and held her cheek against his stripey shorts. He smelt exactly like warm biscuit.

'Oh God,' he said. 'It feels like home.'

He's always so alone, thought Ann as she pressed her lips against him. All those children at home, people at work, endless flirtations and parties, talking about himself all the time but never being with anyone stilly; except me. So surprised he's always been that he can sleep beside me, think beside me, and be quiet.

She remembered one of their rare weekends away. They'd been at a gig together; he'd woken up before her in the morning. Half asleep, her back to him, she felt him run his hand down her like a violin dealer touching a Stradivarius. 'Oh God,' she heard him whisper to himself. 'Oh, God.'

Worship, he used to call it. 'I worship your body, Annie.'

There was an S-shaped mirror from Ikea on the wall by her bed. She'd asked Joe to hang it there: she'd noticed in hotels how Mark, anxious that 'it would never work,' got turned on by mirrors, as if they were the sexiest truth going. Mirrors made him feel real. Facing a mirror he became a god.

When he was hard she stood up and leaned forwards on the bed. They knew each other so well, like acrobats that had swung from the big top together all their lives. She knew he was most confident, at first, like this. He thought this was how she liked starting off; but she'd begun it to help him.

He pushed into her from behind, staring into her eyes in the mirror as if he'd spotted El Dorado beyond mountains or a herd of golden mustang on the moon.

Ann didn't normally like looking at herself – mirrors were a damage limitation act - but when she was with him the looking changed, turned glorious, and helplessly universal: her massed hair and dark pool eyes looking up at his, breasts shivering under his steering, his arms and hands steadying her, his huge chest and lost rapt face.

The doorbell rang.

'Oh God.'

Ann stayed still, waited, listening, heard Zoe clump through the hall to the door.

'No,' said Zoe downstairs. 'Not today.'

The front door shut but Zoe did not move. Ann felt Mark shrinking.

'It would just put the tin lid on everything,' he whispered, 'if she walked in on us now.'

For a moment they heard nothing; then Zoe trod back slowly to the kitchen.

Mark lay down on the bed.

'It's not hard enough. It'll never work.'

Half joke, half despair. Their bodies were old friends; geese that have mated for life and know each other's wingbeats in the dark.

'You're fine,' said Ann. She rolled onto his chest, gathering up the lost acres of his shoulders, pressing his head against her breastbone. 'It'll be OK.'

He began to shake. He held on, cheek cradled against her as if confiding to her skin that he was drowning. Somewhere in a snowdrift, on a desert out in Mars.

'I'm shaking – Annie, what's happening to me?'

'You're here, you're here, you're safe,' she said. 'Just for a moment, you're letting go.'

The dog scrabbled at the bedroom door. Closed doors, especially hers, were an affront.

'I'm lost, Annie,' Mark muttered in her shoulder. His breath was hot. 'I don't know what I'm doing.'

His voice was a luminous blue snake under her hair, ribboning away into the pillows. You couldn't tell if it was poisonous or not. It was hunted, and terribly afraid.

'Sssh,' she said, pressing closer, all his body down. You could use this rage for tenderness, she thought, as an industrial sealant. Skins annealed like clingfilm. Stormblown cellophane.

She felt the shaking die. His muscles relaxed, as she had felt them the first time she ever breathed beside him as he fell asleep.

'I want to fuck you. I SO want to fuck you,' he said through her hair, teeth clenched. She knew he was screwing up his eyes: a small boy wishing himself in space for Christmas.

'Get up above me,' she said, and slithered down on her back till she was looking up at him between his thighs. He knelt up. He loved what he thought of as fucking her face. It seemed so violent and dirty.

'Oh yes,' he said. 'Oh Annie –'

'Mum!' yelled Zoe, close by. She must be - Jesus – right outside the door, thought Ann.

'Mum I'm *still* not sure they're cooked!'

How do people become so dangerous to each other, thought Ann, tearing on her T-shirt, snagging the lace trim.

'Calm down, calm down,' whispered Mark from the bed.

Zoe was sitting on the stairs outside the bedroom, a plate of perfectly cooked sausages on her knee, fork in hand, and the spaniel, eyes rivetted on the fork, at her elbow.

'Mum, they're gross. I'm sure they're not done. I'm a rotten cook.'

'No you're not darling, you make wonderful cakes, it's just you're not very *used* to sausages. Let's see – look, they're nearly perfect - one minute more.'

Ann took the plate and led her child, followed by dancing dog, downstairs. 'There's just a bit of pale on that side of each of them, a line of pale shadow - look.'

She put the spatula in Zoe's hand and fled upstairs. Mark was putting on his trousers.

'We must go,' he said. 'I absolutely must get the stocking fillers. I've got this huge list Lucy's written… '

Ann knew Lucy's writing all too well. The last trip abroad they'd had together, New Orleans, Lucy had already half found out, and left little torn imperatives folded in Mark's shirts. 'Get on with your work! Put down that drink!' Confetti, fluttering about their flat like poisoned snow.

'Also,' said Mark as he laced his shoes, 'I must show you these sexy velvet outfits, get you one for Christmas. I must see you in them, Annie. You'd look gorgeously decadent. I saw them at the Erotica Show in Olympia. She has a permanent stall, she told me. Camden Lock No. 9.'

'Sounds like a railway platform,' said Ann. 'OK. Lovely. But for fuck's sake get out of the bedroom.'

Outside, they passed Ann's car.

'Still got pink shit on the roof,' she said. When he was writing his memoir they'd taken her car to Mull, and parked it in the village by the kirk under a mulberry tree filled with starlings. Ann spent hours in Hebridean drizzle scraping their cranberry mousse off the roof with wet tissues, while Mark wrote up his impressions of revisiting his childhood home on the laptop in the bar.

They reached his car.

'For God's sake don't move the seat,' he said. 'Lucy's convinced you move the seat.'

'Never dreamed of it,' said Ann. 'I haven't displaced her in anything. I've never taken anything she wanted. She thought any sex you got yourself would be the opposite of love: that you were screwing loads of different people she could despise. She kept you out of her bedroom like a one-woman territorial army. I've never tried to harm her. Unlike her, the time she met Neville's wife.'

Neville was Lucy's lover.

'And I've never, ever moved the seat. That must be what *she* does, in Neville's car.'

'She thinks you do,' said Mark. 'She speaks of you in witchy hisses, as Your North London Life.'

Mark and Lucy lived in Blackheath.

He took Ann's London Borough of Brent Visitors Permit off the windscreen, screwed it up and tossed it in the gutter.

'Destroying the evidence,' he said.

2

'Glow-in-Dark Stars?' said Ann.

'Too expensive,' said Mark. 'Leave it to me, darling, will you?'

He called everyone darling. Waitresses, girls on the phone he'd never met. Ann still liked it though, when he said it to her. She watched him mooch through aisles of white-sheeted trestles, looking for stocking-fillers, stout and plush in his grey wool coat, but also furtive - as if different bits of him came from separate films. The stall-holders, shivering from the cold, looked at him resentfully as if he should have brought more people along.

'Earrings,' said Mark. 'For my sister. That's on my list.'

They looked at sheets of amber earrings.

'Look,' said Ann, surprised. 'Here's a whole tray of *green* amber.'

Last summer Mark had bought for her secretly, on holiday with his family in Malta, a lumpy ring of green amber. She hadn't known amber could be green. It made no sense of traffic lights for a start. 'The ancient resin of conifers that grew along the shores of the Baltic Ocean fifty million years ago,' said the pamphlet that came with it, 'amber has mystical and curative properties. To the Chinese it was a symbol of courage. The ancient Greeks believed amber was the tears of the gods. Today amber is credited with a positive influence over health, especially the throat, heart and spleen.'

Ann touched the wedge of amber in its silver housing on her hand. Mark picked up a pair of earrings and turned them over. He looked completely lost: an astronaut who'd mislaid his spaceship, alone among the meterorites.

She couldn't bear to see him hurt. When he groaned in bed with heartburn after a late-night curry, she'd been known to get dressed and take the car into midnight streets to look for open chemists, get him Gaviscon. When the pain was in his feelings it was worse.

He put the earrings down. 'Let's come back here after Christmas, sweetheart, find something to match the ring.'

He looked at his list. Children, nephews, nieces; and his wife. Lucy had told him shoes to get at a Chelsea shop.

Ann shivered. She had a million things to do. She stared at Tiffany glasses with trailed-glass coils of pink and green. Two Christmasses ago she'd bought Mark one of these, a whiskey tumbler for his midnight writing in his garden shed, the only time he was ever alone.

'Nothing,' said Mark. 'Let's try Stall 9.'

Stall 9 was an unheated warehouse. A girl Mark had met at the Olympia Erotica Exhibition smiled up at him from behind a table at the back. She looked glossy and insatiable, swathed in red velvet with gelled black hair and a cleavage like frozen yoghurt. On the concrete floor a stick of incense burned in a wine-bottle.

'Well hello again,' the girl said to Mark.

'I told you I'd look you up,' he said, with instant Madeira-voice intimacy. Getting a smile from a girl made him feel suddenly, temporarily, OK. He bent over her table. Ann knew, if she asked what he was doing, he would say he was being *galant*.

'I thought Madame here would be the perfect person for your wares.'

Ann saw chilly racks of heavy dresses with just-above-nipple-necklines and a faint top-dressing of dust. Studded and spiked leather collars, foreign as a shooting-range. Taped to wire hangers, like pegged-back spaniels' ears, were rows of velvet wings.

'Wings?'

'I told you,' muttered Mark. 'It's terribly camp. But you'd look wonderful in some of this.'

'I'd look matronly and mad,' she said, looking at gathered lamé skirts.

Mark held up a burgundy velvet jacket with military collar. Everyone was silent as he did up the long frosting of black frogging down the front. The braided sides flapped round his thighs. He pirouetted, glancing back at himself as he turned. The tails swung out.

'Brilliant,' he said. 'I almost look slim. And not expensive.'

'Beautifully made,' said Ann, heartwrung. He pinned such faith on surfaces. There they stood, in an unheated catacomb in front of a swing-glass, while the word he'd said as they met still hovered in the air.

She imagined them walking about Camden Lock with a thought-bubble tonguing down to both their heads, saying LAWYER.

Reality has caught up with us at last, she thought, at the year's midnight. We are trying on fancy dress in the cold while Rome is burning, Christmas is coming and Lucy's found out, at last. Where is it going to end?

'Let's come back when it's warmer,' she said. 'You don't have to get me a Christmas present now, darling. We can have our own Christmas when all this is over. Let's get to a shop for your stocking presents. Time's getting on.'

'We'll be back,' he promised the Erotica girl.

'Happy Christmas,' she said. 'Take care.'

How does she keep warm, wondered Ann as they left.

'Camden Lock is mainly hippie junk,' she said.

'I'm not blind,' said Mark. 'That's not what's wrong with me.'

There was only one toyshop near Ann's house in Kilburn and its name was 'Happy Returns.'

'Chinese Zodiac Beanie Babies!' said a yellow Post-It on the door. 'Now in Stock!'

Ann led Mark to the back of the shop. For five years she had brought him here for exactly this purpose: to combine his rushed present-buying with a feverish squashed Christmas for the two of them.

'Here,' she said.

To the right was black – weapons, Ice Raiders, Warhammer, Tactical Combat Squad. To the left, pink princess cosmetics trimmed with fluff. In between were Crayolas in European languages (Lapices de Coor, Kleuropot Loden, Matute Colorate), and SuperBubbles.

Mark hated Ann being helpful. Anne knew this. It made him feel he needed it – which he did. 'Going shopping with Mumsie as a boy,' he'd said once, 'We'd go to a shoe-shop in the middle of Glasgow and she'd wave her hand like a queen and say, 'Shoes! Shoes for Mark!' I wanted to crawl into the shoe-boxes and die.'

But she couldn't help trying, just a little, to hurry things up.

'Bubbles?' she asked.

'I can see!' he said. 'Let me do it myself for Chrissake.'

She moved away, and watched him take down four

SuperBubbles, then one more, another two, then put one back. Own kids, nephews, nieces. Yes, yes, no, she thought. He looked so defeated; so as if every choice was bound to be wrong.

Ann drifted downstairs. Maybe where she was would look different from the cellar.

It was always damp here, full of large excited boxes – Barbie dream stables, construction toys that would drive everyone to screaming-point in five minutes. She had only once bought anything here: for Zoe's sixth birthday, a white dog on wheels that barked as it moved. Zoe named him Igwig and pulled him down the hill on his pink leash. Igwig cost thirty pounds: his bark ran down by the second block, his trailing tummy silk was black with mud ever since. But Zoe, single child of a single parent, was in heaven. 'My puppy,' she called him. My miracle.

It was a lead thing, thought Ann, conscious of Mark standing, agonized and hesitating, just above her head. The leash made Igwig hers. Where Zoe was, he had to be.

She climbed back up the stairs. Her legs felt like suitcases. The wall smelt damp. She put her hand flat to it like someone calming a horse, and the paper was soggy as a seeping wound.

Looking sulky, bulky, panicked, Mark was standing by the Brio trains clutching a scramble of packaging to his heart. She went to the till and got him a basket. He took it reproachfully. How dare you give me exactly what I need? said his eyes. He poured the toys in and went back to the shelves.

Searching for the key to being in charge, thought Ann. He was not a bad man. He had never nailed a Yorkshire Terrier's head to the floor. He was a warmhearted man who managed, most of his life, to get away with things without confronting them. A man who had betted, all his life, on style: on rules of how to behave. How you treat girls on a date, what you buy your wife for her birthday. The right way to cook steak and tip waiters. He shovelled uncertainty aside. Now his back was against a wall he hadn't believed was really there. He was in the void, and didn't want his hand held in it, thanks.

Ann moved off to a wall hung with Noddy hat and scarves, Ponyskin Fur-trimmed Tutus with a silver heart at belly button level, and Candy-Striped Birthday Candles with smily pictures of two parents blowing flames in front of awestruck children.

Every happy child and parent on the packaging is a spike in the guts, she thought. Is that my feeling, or his? If you can feel what someone else is feeling, why can't he feel you feeling it?

Sparkly Sequin Tiaras hit her with memories of ballet class and Zoe aged five.

'Oh Mark,' she said, before she could stop herself. 'What about these for the twins?'

'Look,' he snapped. 'Think what I'm going through. This may be the last Christmas I ever have with them. Leave it to me for fuck's sake.'

Shoulder to shoulder, they stared at a row of Tinkerbell Sparkle-Glitter Stick-On Nails.

'Think what I'm going through,' he said again.

Ann eased away to a swivel-rack of Matchbox Thomas the Tank Engines. I think about what he's going through all the time, she thought. I always have. It's my first base.

She could hear her friend Ellen's voice in her head.

'I don't suppose you spent those hours shopping for your own Christmas presents.'

'There wasn't time,' Ann told her. 'We were there for his.'

'All that hanging about,' said the hoarse Dublin ghost. 'Why didn't you say something?'

'Fuck off Ellen,' said Ann in her head, staring at Glow in Dark Vampire Fangs. 'He wouldn't have felt loved.'

'He doesn't seem to anyway,' said the tart voice, as Ellen faded back to the twilit hospice where Ann had said goodbye to her a year ago. Ellen, right up to when she died, had been Mark's most outspoken, least enthusiastic fan.

Joke toys were the cheapest things in the place. Zoe adored them when she was small. Ice Cube Fly. Dennis the Menace Hot Sweets.

Again Ann couldn't resist. Time was pelting by; her time

as well as his. Mark's lips were a helpless zip.

'Fake Car Scratch?'

'In Blackheath?' said Mark. 'They'd get punched on the nose. Leave me alone to do it, Annie.'

'I can't be doing with this,' Ann whispered to a basket of pink and gold Stegosasuses. 'I've got to get out of this place.'

She looked at Mark prowling the shelves in dry despair. You were my hero, she thought. For five years I've watched you hug and seduce the world. I loved you asleep in a plane, from New York, Rio, wherever - the moon, I didn't care if you were beside me. Your face crumpled against my shoulder. How you loved being seen to lock the car with the remote behind your back. The relief in our voices when we said hello. 'It's like having a second skin,' he said once. He'd come in the door, fold her into his jacket and say into her neck, 'It feels like coming home. You've made me good, Annie. You don't know how you've changed me.'

Now she felt cold and light against it all. In years and years of cherishing she had never, for a second, wanted him to leave his kids. She hadn't even imagined it to herself. She wouldn't have felt she was loving him if she had.

This is a sacramental moment, she told Star of the Sea Barbie in Aquamarine. If I let it go, it won't come again.

She remembered Mark telling her about three - no, four - girls in his office who'd got pregnant when he'd had affairs with them in years gone by.

'Not pleasant,' he'd said to Ann, 'telling them over lunch they had to have an abortion. But it had to be done.'

Had? she thought now. Have? Have it off. Have a baby. To have and to hold.

She remembered mentioning her own PA to him. 'Do you know her,' she'd asked Mark. 'Louise?'

'Have I had her?' he asked.

A joke. The sort he'd have with a man.

Despite all that, something in him called to me, thought Ann, gazing at a Young Explorer Sonic Alarm. Mark was the golden footprint in my soul. But he'll have to take his golden steps elsewhere. Whatever it was in him that called will have to holler in the wilderness from now on.

As Mark paid for the toys he held his face away from her, like a magazine he was ashamed of.

3

The wine-bar was just down from the toyshop, after Raks News and Religious Goods, Corrigans Butchers and Beirut Market.

Mark swept her in through the door like Gabriel propelling the Virgin through flaming walls of lilies. He had flurried her like this into restaurants all over the world: Portugese bars in Brazilian mountain villages, steak bars in New York, outdoor tables on mediaeval pavements of Verona, dark wet stand-up Hebridean pubs. Places he'd gone for work and brought Ann along in secret.

'We have twenty minutes to eat,' he told the waiter.

'Can you do it, in the time?' asked Ann. She hated seeing Mark critically through other people's eyes and tried to soften the impact when she saw them bristle.

The waiter was sallow and little with spiky hair like photos of Sid Vicious. Just like Neville, thought Ann, and wondered if Mark noticed.

Lucy's lover Neville was a ballad singer and music journalist married to a Texan porn queen with – so Lucy reported to Mark triumphantly the only time she met her – size eight feet. Neville wore an odd, self-deprecating beard. It began half way down his throat and stopped on the plimsoll line, as if someone hit him on the jaw with a paintbrush and the bristles stuck.

This waiter had the same scrappy chin hair, same puffy pitted skin and wetlook eyes that darted out at you and slid away at once. Ann couldn't think what Lucy saw in Neville but was very, very glad she did.

'Siddown, siddown,' said the waiter.

Australian, thought Ann, or South African. Hard to tell.

'Whatever you want, we can hack it. What do you want?'

Cream silk hangings sagged from the ceiling, painted with runny sketches of Toulouse Lautrec-like women dancing with wine glasses, bare legs, frothing petticoats and leopards. The chandeliers were frogspawn yellow globes.

Red wine came. Ann stared at it: a glass lollipop with enormous red-black bulb. She brought it up to her mouth, and looked down. The tipping surface was an eye staring back at hers.

'Ancient Greeks saw the future in basins of water,' she said. 'Catoptromancy. Mirror-prophecy. They did it in the temples. The priest looked in the reflected world for you and saw the truths you couldn't see in this one.'

Mark downed a spritzer in a gulp as if his throat had no flap to it, ordered another and heaped butter onto a piece of bread. Ann looked at the dark burn on her hand, the lopsided amber ring. It had taken weeks to get used to the weight of it. So many times they'd ended up love-making with her on her hands and knees, him over her, mouth on the nape of her neck like a tiger, their two left hands on the sheet in parallel, large and small, outer and inner, the rings they'd given each other making a single glittering line undisturbed by the bodywork panting above.

'You're going to eat all this up,' said Mark. 'You're too thin, young lady. You never eat all I give you.'

He often said this. They looked at each other over the thin rims, the exaggerated polish.

'Why do my glasses never shine like this?' said Ann.

When they had friends round, Mark made a point of washing her glasses. Once, in the middle of a dinner party, and they were changing wines, he and the other bloke had solemnly got up and re-washed and dried all the glasses with clean towels. As if women never took seriously enough the wine men brought them.

Their eyes had stared into each other and found relief and joy there over all kinds of wine on three continents. Had worked together, looked at pictures, oceans, the tops of clouds, jungles and mountains and night clubs, rock singers and friends together, seen the same thought in each other at the same time, or imagined they did; had closed and dreamed and opened into each other.

'Lucy thinks you've betrayed her,' Mark said.

'*Me?*'

'She's saying you were her friend for years, before I even met her. That you worked with her. Can that be true?'

Ann stared at him. She felt she'd never seen him before. He knew exactly – or had known, once – when and where she'd first met Lucy.

Ann had first seen Lucy in person, rather than through Mark's endless victim-of-Lucy stories, when she'd been his lover for a year. If we'd started a baby the night we began, she thought, I could have brought him in arms to the party where I met Lucy. Ann had been in a group of people with Lucy some time before she realized who she was. She sized her up guiltily: a sharp, blond woman much smaller than herself, with angry skin and glittery eyes. She listened for signs of possessiveness over Mark, any talk of 'we', and was both relieved and shocked to find none.

She's as separate from Mark as Mark from her, she thought then. He always says they are each other's exes. That must even be true. I'm not doing Lucy any harm. She doesn't want Mark in her bed, doesn't want his heart or inner thoughts. They are opposite sides of the street.

Later at that party she bumped into Mark.

'I've just met Lucy,' she said.

'Is this a wind-up?' He was feverish with love and sexual pride. The night before, his potency had at last, long last, come back.

When they had first gone to bed, all his charm and effervescence had suddenly evaporated. He was nervous; he whispered he had something to tell her, he couldn't do it properly, for years he hadn't got hard with a woman and stayed hard.

'But,' said Ann wonderingly, naked beside him for the first time. 'But all those girls.'

'Yes but I can't *fuck* them, can I?' he said, suddenly savage. Not with her, Ann realized a second later, but with himself; or rather, since he preferred to blame the outside things, with fate.

'They go down on their knees and say 'Can I give you a

blow job?" he said, 'and it's not hard. Jesus. Can you imagine what that's like? It doesn't bloody work.'

'Ssh,' said Ann. That was how it started, how it went on for months. They were in love, she was writing songs to him, they had a wonderful time in bed, but he wilted once he was in her. She tried not to take it personally. They were happy and delirious, but unfulfilled.

It was a question of trust, she thought. Trusting her; trusting himself with her. He'd been so untrustworthy, with so many women, for so long.

'Catches up with all philanderers one day,' said Ellen, when Ann asked her, a month or so later, what to do.

'How do you know?'

'Read it in the psychology column of the *Irish Times*.'

Ann never knew exactly when Ellen was pulling her leg. So easy for the Irish, to make rings around the English.

'It's all to do with guilt, chérie.'

Mark had been famously unfaithful to Lucy, ever since he'd been with her. Matthew, the first child, was an accident. They were splitting up, and Lucy was suddenly pregnant. 'Like being at a party, when you've had a fab time but you're going out the door,' said Mark once, 'and someone hauls you back saying "No mate: you're here to stay."'

The later kids, he said, were guilt-presents: Lucy wanted more. He came up with them at crisis moments. After *Private Eye* described him drapped aound a French girl at a party. 'I wasn't kissing her,' said Mark. 'I was examining her mouth.' Or after a secretary he'd been out with told tales. 'Had to sack her,' said Mark. 'Hate sacking people.'

Lucy had ridden it all out in the separate room she'd chosen the moment she walked into their first house. 'I thought we'd share a bedroom,' said Mark, 'but no. She'd never sleep the night in my bed. And for years now she won't do anything else either.'

'That's what they all say,' said Ellen when Ann told her. Ann thought it was probably true. She couldn't have gone on if it wasn't. Though she also knew Mark was incapable of not trying to make her believe him at whatever cost to truth.

Ann found she had to surprise Mark into staying hard. When he came in through the door he would attack her hungrily, a lion afraid another lion would get the carcass first. Hands all over her, tongue down her throat, hard as a gun. But if they went upstairs and lay down, he lost it. Beds mean commitment, Ann decided. The kitchen table, a long sturdy oak slab from her grandmother's verandah, was a help. She also noticed that in the bedroom, Mark was more confident, and stayed harder, if he came at her from behind. He doesn't feel confronted, she thought, like that. He's alone with his prowess. No facing the worry that his myth isn't quite up to his reality.

'He'll be fine,' she said to Ellen. 'You'll see. Well you won't. I will.'

She had to learn him like a song. She began to sound his fantasies, talk him through it till he didn't notice he was staying hard. She'd never met anyone who talked like that, all through everything, so she started talking, too, playing it as a scenario from a film. He was always turned on by words.

'What am I doing here?' she'd whisper in the dark, a street waif led up an alley by the gentleman seducer. 'What are you doing to me?'

'Oh yes, Annie,' he'd breathe above her. 'Yes.... yes.'

So they couldn't, really, have started a baby the night they began, anyway. But the night before that meeting-Lucy party, Mark's candle was suddenly re-lit. When Ann saw him in the party crowd, his psyche was running round a football pitch with its arms up from the night before, shouting 'Yes!'

'The builders,' he whispered to Ann, 'asked me for three thousand pounds this afternoon. Three thousand pounds!'

That was when Mark and Lucy were doing up their house.

'I felt like saying, 'Is that all you want? Why not take five? Take ten!''

Next day he told Ann that when he'd driven Lucy home that night, she went on about how nice Ann Daly was. Ann spent months worrying about that; then worried intermittently; then gave up. What else could she have done? Mark would have been doing the same thing, or trying to, with other people, and Lucy knew it. She was doing it herself, with Neville.

Afterwards, at other parties over the years, Lucy had come up to her to be talked to like a pony in a field looking for sugar. Ann avoided her when she could, admired her shoes, introduced her to people, as if – she'd hated that feeling – as if she were responsible for her. As if Lucy were family. Every time she'd done that was cut on her memory like letters on a glass. It hadn't felt right. But it hadn't been friendship, either. There was no betrayal.

Didn't Mark remember any of this now? Was he in as mad a state as Lucy? History, fantasy, all blurred? Where was he in his mind? Ann felt something in him she'd never felt before: a drawbridge, forged over years to protect him from this venomous relationship at the centre of his life.

'I try and think of things you say,' he told her now. 'How you tell me to calm things down, make her be reasonable. But I can't hang onto to you, I can only hear her voice in my ears, going on hour after hour – about you, your clothes, what a slag you are, she's no idea – it's so unfair….'

'Lucy knows nothing about me,' Ann said. 'Or my life. I was never her friend. I was someone she chatted to at parties.'

The Australian waiter put plates in front of them. Ann stared down at frilly ivory linguini.

'Lucy's behaving as if you still slept together,' she said suddenly. The words came out of nowhere, She hadn't realized this until she said them. 'As if she didn't have a lover of her own whom she takes to parties, spends weekends with, asks you to drive her into to town for dates with…'

'I know.' He put his fork down. 'Let's be clear about this, Annie, in all these accusations flying around. I haven't. The last time was a blow job she gave me in Scotland when we visited my sister six years ago. She wanted us to leave early – she hated being there, and my sister hates her – and when I said we could she dropped on her knees and sucked me off. Very nice too. But that's it. Long before you.'

'She must have hurt herself most,' said Ann, 'when she

eavesdropped on my messages.'

They left mobile messages for each other all the time. Ann still had one from two nights ago. 'Annie, I'm walking to the car in Charing Cross Road, it's fucking freezing, my breath is blowing white, I've just had dinner with Gerry - sweetheart, I just wanted to say I love you, I didn't ring before, I thought you'd be out with Zoe for her birthday - I just wanted to say I love you beyond anything...'

'That must have been the worst,' said Ann. 'Our messages are so conjugal, as well as passionate. Will you pick up a steak, do you know what someone said about you, all the trusting ordinary little things... '

Two weeks back, for five days Mark had kept losing his mobile. He'd found it in the laundry basket, lost it again, then it re-appeared in his jacket pocket. He hadn't thought of telling Ann.

That week had ended in a gig Ann sang in a small club, trying out new songs. Mark had come with her; Lucy's colleague Charlotte turned up too. Next day Lucy had chosen Charlotte, of all people, to confide in about Ann.

'Oh,' said Charlotte. (So Lucy, furiously, throwing glasses round the kitchen, told Mark later.) 'Ann Daly. I went to a concert of hers last night.'

'What was it like?' Lucy asked.

'Very passionate,' said Charlotte. 'And I can see - the songs were all about Mark.'

That's when the storms had really started.

'Let's have another glass,' said Mark.

'But the time – '

'Indulge me.'

Mark wasn't thinking what had upset Lucy, but what the upset had done to him.

'She doesn't want me,' he said. 'Doesn't want me around. Now she's saying we've got to live in separate houses. Where does she think the money'd come from? She even made her parents come to Sunday lunch. They *never* come to lunch! In front of them she practically stroked my cheek. She sat on my knee. She was rattling the chains. Soon as they left, she spat at me. I'm not going to lose the children, I'm not stirring from their side. She knows I'll leave her when they're grown.'

Are you sure, thought Ann. I don't believe Lucy thinks like that at all. Mark only sees people from the outside. He can't imagine anyone else's way of seeing. That's his great strength in his career: he can steamroller over everyone and not even notice. But it's also his great – great wound.

That's why he's where he is now, facing losing what he adores, the people he's surest of, his kids. Because he can't imagine Lucy's feelings from inside. To her, I'm the total sum of twelve years of everything, all the women she knew about, the thousand others she suspected.

'I have arguments with you in my head,' said Mark.' I tell you, How could you be so thoughtless? Ha. Thoughtless. It's what I call myself.'

Ann was silent. Here was the blame he'd been holding back through armfuls of plastic in the toyshop.

She'd always tried to protect them from Lucy knowing. Once, in an art gallery, they'd been sitting in front of a painting, her head on his shoulder. They loved looking into other worlds from the miracle of their own. She glanced casually away from the canvas and saw Lucy bearing down upon them, smiling to herself.

Lucy hadn't seen. Ann was sure she hadn't. She was dressed up to meet Neville, and was putting in half an hour before they met.

Whispering 'Fuck, there's Lucy,' Ann ducked from Mark's arm and out of the crowded room. Mark looked round, surprised, then looked up and saw his wife.

Ann worked her way round to a cordoned archway and saw them standing together, talking like acquaintances under the recessed lights, Mark with his hands behind his back like the Duke of Edinburgh, eyeing the bench like a ostrich looking for sand.

The weird thing was, Ann remembered now, she'd dreamed just such a meeting that very morning: that she'd been in bed with Mark, and Lucy came into the room. She'd been hidden by a swing mirror that suddenly appeared in Mark's bed – he's surrounded by mirrors even in my dreams, she thought – and ducked down the far side, swathed in ice-cream folds of hanging sheet.

I protect him even in my sleep, she thought.

'Why did you leave the gallery?' Ellen asked later. 'Why did you save him? Let him sort out his own mess.'

'He's my care,' Ann told her. 'I look after him.'

'That sort of thing should be mutual,' said Ellen. 'He's his own care. He looks out for his interests. You should be looking out for yours.'

'I want his good,' said Ann.

'You'd better want your own. It's not a brilliant way to live, Ann, letting the other person matter more than you.'

Now, as tears for him blurred her eyes, Ann thought: the only thing I've done to harm him is receive his love. I don't deserve his blame. But maybe a bit from – well, from God.

A month before, they'd been in a Museum of Drugs in New Orleans, full of hundred-year-old magic spells and medical cures. Calico voodoo dolls, snake-bite remedies, goatskin condoms, ads for Swedish leeches. Mark stalked the dream potions and love philtres; what caught Ann's eye was the first bottle of chloroform Lousiana had ever seen.

Even though Queen Victoria had tried it out successfully in childbirth, the priests of 1857 did their best to ban chloroform. It is sinful, rasped a Father in the Atchafalaya Swamp, to refuse the pain God gives. Chloroform robs God of the deep earnest cries which are His due: the despairing cries which arise in time of trouble.

Ann stared down at her mop of linguini and the black surface of House Red. She tilted the glass between her hands. Its oily swirly eye stared back up at her.

'Why call me thoughtless?' she asked. 'What have I done?'

'You let Lucy find out,' said Mark.

4

Ann stared at him.

Moral crisis? said the Ellen in her head. He wouldn't recognize a moral crisis if one tumbled in his soup. He's blaming you for the mess he's made of things. How could you know he'd lost his phone? Because he ain't trustworthy himself, he doesn't know how to trust.

You don't fight back, Ann told her, when someone's in such pain. He's still the blue snake I've loved so long. He's frightened and in my care.

He doesn't worry about things like that, said Ellen, tuning out.

Ann looked at the folds of Mark's face.

When she flew back with him from New Orleans, Lucy had already done the first bit of finding out. On journeys back, Mark always began closing off, sealing himself away from Ann to re-enter the family world. They were stuck six hours in Atlanta airport and Ann had prowled alone around the shopping mall, watched the bar TV report a stalemate in the American election, and spent most time in the memorial for Martin Luther King.

Grace of heart, all his friends had said about him. That's what Martin Luther had.

Grace of heart, she'd said to herself then. A small thing to take from such a life. But it'll do. That's what I'm going to need.

'If I split up with Lucy,' said Mark now, 'I'll have nothing. I'll lose the house.' He paused. 'I'll lose the children and –'

– he looked at her coldly over his spritzer – 'I'll lose you. Because I'll never forgive you.'

What on earth for? Ann said to herself. For being loved by you? I've got to break these bars. Like Bagheera the Black Panther in the maharajah's cage at Oodeypore.

The Jungle Book was Zoe's favourite story as a child. Her hero was Bagheera: skin like watered silk, voice like wild honey dripping from the trees; and a token of past captivity, a small secret bare patch under his chin where the collar rubbed – until, as Zoe used to shout, 'I broke the silly lock with one blow of my paw.'

Grace of heart, she thought. I've got to be bigger than the moment. But I've got to do it fast.

'Look,' she said. 'Tell Lucy if she goes to a lawyer and says you've got to leave, she won't have exactly what she's got now – the money, baby sitters, luxury – except that you're handily out of her way. Tell her you each have rights against the other. The house will have to be sold, your mortgage paid off.'

Mark's mortgage each year was more money than Ann earned in four.

'And two new places will have to be bought. She'll have to find a smaller house, pay bills which she's never done, do the shopping which she never does. She'll have to adjust the children to it all – when she can't make Matthew eat his wriggly pasta or the twins put their winter coats on, without you.'

She drew breath and sipped her wine. It tasted iodine. The bar was going on with its wine bar life, Australian waiter laughing with girl on the till, people coming in with cold plastic bags of Christmas shopping. The walls hadn't fallen.

Mark was silent. She could see him trying it out for size, picturing himself saying it. He could lie his way out of a yoghurt pot if he had to, but he always tried to hang on to how Ann put things. She watched him playing an Ann script in Lucy terms. It wouldn't work unless they were Mark's terms too – and what were those?

More iodine.

'In the evenings,' Ann went on, 'tell Lucy there'd be none of the parties she likes you to take her to, no dinner parties you cook. Tell her you want to go on doing all that, for her, and *with* her. That's very important.'

It felt ridiculous, telling the most notorious philanderer in town how to handle a woman.

'Say "with". Say it quietly, not in a shouting match. So it goes in. And then…'

Ann took a breath. From the bottom of her rib cage as her voice coach said. Support the breath, so the sound will flow.

'Then say, "Look. *I* don't want to leave. I'll stay in every night for six months. I won't go out, you can do that, I'll stay and look after the children. And I'll give Ann up."'

'She won't believe me,' said Mark at once. 'She doesn't want to hear your name anyway but she won't believe me. She said last night, "It's been going on for years hasn't it?" "No no," I said, "just a passing thing." Then she waved my phone bills in my face! She'd been through my bloody bills! She had a bunch of Vodaphone papers behind her back.

'"These tell a different story," she said. "Night after night, year after year. you were *phoning her up*. From our phone!" She pulled the fucking phone out of the wall because I'd talked to you on it. She'd never believe me if I said I wouldn't see you.'

'But I don't mean only pretend to split up,' said Ann, astonished.

She was entering Death Row, hearing trickles down the walls.

'It's got to be true, you idiot, to work.'

True was new; a strategy he'd never used. She could see him holding it to the light like a wine-taster swirling a glass. Then he spotted a snag.

'But we'd be very unhappy.'

Ann took a breath. 'Of course. But I never, never wanted you to leave your children. It wouldn't be loving you if I let you do that. If this is what it takes for you to be with them, this is what it takes.'

He thought a bit, watching her mouth as if she'd marked treasure on the map of her face with X; as if pearls might fall from her lips into the basket of walnut bread.

He signalled to the waiter, who unstuck his bottom from the bar and lazed across the floor.

'I got you all this,' said the waiter, 'in nineteen minutes flat. You said you were in a hurry. Now you've stayed an hour.'

'Two more glasses,' said Mark coldly. 'One spritzer, one House Red.'

He looked at Ann. 'Would it work?'

'It's the only thing,' said Ann. 'When Lucy sees it going on working, night after night, you there all the time, you not phoning me, not seeing me, she won't go to a lawyer. You don't realize your own power, Mark. She's totally dependant on you.'

'That's why she hates me.'

'But her dependance gives her power. You've enginereed it like that between you over the years. She can't throw you out. She lives her life through you, friends, parties, her work in your office.'

'She'd lose her job if we split up,' said Mark. 'The firm would find it doesn't really need a style consultant. I don't know what she'd do.'

'She can't do *anything* without you,' said Ann. 'Just realize that, darling. If you go away for a week and they run out of cereal, the kids just don't get cereal till you're back.'

Or so, anyway, Mark always said. It amazed Ann that Lucy seemed to run a home without carrying large shopping bags from a bus or tube, or even across a car park. Lucy had a driving licence but never drove; she got Mark to do all the shopping. Lucy ran the internet shopping for his firm, but never shopped on the Web herself.

'Just keep reassuring her,' Ann said, 'that you won't see me. I'll write her a letter if you like, promising I won't speak to you again.'

'God no. I don't know what that would do to her. She's in an unstable enough state as it is.'

But he seemed more cheerful, as if she had suggested something he could manage.

'I must go,' he said. He drained his glass, got up, looked for the bill. His coat swung over the table.

Ann left her glass half-full. She felt like her own ghost. So this was his Christmas present. Never mind Paul Smith braces: life without her, forever.

The wine bar's yellow ceiling, billowing with petticoats and leopards, leaned over her. He's looked and looked for magic all his life. It's what he feels at home with. Magic potions, to make everything alright. That's what I've given him.

She looked over her shoulder as they left, at their pushed-back chairs, her own unfinished wine.

They walked down the road. For five years they'd walked like this, continents, jungle and cities, airports, bookshops, churches, arms round each other. It still felt wonderful. Her head fitted the space between his left shoulder and neck as it always had. Clamped together, he used to say.

He loved that word, clamped.

She found she was holding his left side with the palm of her hand as if something might fall out of it, pressing the heel of her hand against the black cashmere pullover she gave him for Christmas three years ago in a compaign for buying black so he'd look slimmer, feel better about his weight. He'd taken up blackness till he thought it was his own idea, but hadn't worn the pullover. 'Not keen on V-necks,' he explained when asked why not. Two years later his daughter Suzy pulled it from the back of his chest of drawers and said, 'Why don't you ever wear this? It's gorgeous.'

It did look good on him, Ann thought, though it didn't quite curve in properly after the upshelf of the belly. It fell down straightish, uncertain what to do, like a dog that's been taken for a walk and left on the hill.

'Look,' she said. 'I'm holding your heart.'

'Have I still got one?'

'I'm holding it in.'

At the more expensive end of the road they passed tall houses, lemon and pink like Edwardian frowns, with delicate balconies, winter jasmine, a naked weeping ash.

'Gorgeous,' she said. 'All that filigree and shadow. Like New Orleans.'

'You've made me see things,' he said, and kissed her neck under her hair as if he could get through the skin to her thin marrow. Ann closed her eyes as she walked. His arm was round her. One minute more.

'I look at the world quite differently now Annie, because of you.'

Then he looked at his own car. A parking ticket in a

plastic yellow and black jacket was sellotaped to the windscreen.

'Forty quid,' he said, furious. 'And it says 'London Borough of Brent' in enormous letters. I'm so stupid. Why didn't I –? I could have put another pound in.'

Why did she have to lift the world off him where it hurt?

'Give it to me,' she said. 'Take Kilburn out of your life. I'll pay it.'

'No, why should you?'

'My wine,' she said. 'Those extra twenty minutes.'

'I bought it for you,' he said. 'I ordered it.'

He pocketed the ticket and drove them down the hill.

'So that's it,' she said. 'Five years. Average life span of a barn owl. The voyage of the *Beagle*.'

He had other things on his mind than barn owls and the origin of species.

'You owe me one though,' he said. 'I didn't come.'

'*What?*'

She thought of her frantic swivel away when she heard Zoe call, her face pushing out from between Mark's thighs – he was hard, after all – like a frog coming up from the bottom of the pond, bumping lily-pads and duckweed on the way, scrambling out from under him into her T-shirt. Then bare feet, jeans, zip – quick, quick! – and daughter sitting right there on the stairs outside the bedroom door, staring into a plate of sausages.

It was the only time in five years she'd faked it. That whole sex thing there was about making him feel better, feel in charge. But also protecting Zoe, first day of the holidays, anxious about the spitting fat. Zoe who hated fakes and laughed about Mark's clothes. 'Doesn't he ever look in a mirror?' she asked once. 'Why does he wear those awful coloured shirts?'

'I'm going to come one more time,' said Mark as he drove into the darkening air, 'in your hot dark slitheriness, young lady.'

Yes, said Ann to the fairy lights threading skeleton trees at the side of the park. He really does talk like that. And think like that too.

Sorry.

But so what? He talks and thinks other ways too. Love

does not alter when it alteration finds. I've got to honour what I loved, even if he doesn't. Even if he can't.

Years of walking round the world, looking out for things that will delight him: I can't give up on that just because he's bringing it all down to sex. They were my five years as well as his. If he imagines that ever, ever again…. That after this moment of giving him up for *him*: this self-disembowelling…

Maybe I don't like you all that much, she said to him in her head. Maybe you can't understand at all what it's meant to me, building this bower for you in my heart. Maybe I don't mind I've ended years of looking after your anxieties and wellbeing, whether people like you, what do they think of you, can you see yourself today as a hero? And you assuming, always, that what you do is the only thing. Watching you take it all, and forget about it when you're charming the rest of the world.

They drove past Queen's Park Recreation Ground. Ann watched a Staffordshire bull terrier hump on the grass, rolling piggy eyes in its brindled head. A man in a leather jacket stood holding its lead, looking up at the trees as if trying to tell the time in them. The dog shot out a golden tube of seamless turd which coiled round slowly on the grass and collapsed on itself, steaming faintly in the steely air.

Ann hated people with dogs in studded collars that looked like pit bulls. That grass was where mothers took toddlers learning to walk. She looked at the man holding the lead as if whatever was happening on the other end was nothing to do with him. He wasn't going to pick that stuff up and put it in the dog bin. No way.

Maybe, she said to the armour of twilight, as the year's darkest day swooped at her on three o'clock talons: maybe this is an enormous relief. Maybe something's already died in me. Maybe this is knowledge that's sad to have to know but you can't live a life without knowing it. Some things will happen because of what I've done today, and others won't, that's all. He wants to save his skin, even if he loses his soul.

Saffron cats' eyes up the grey hill, flanked by ochre parking lines. Air of scooped lavender under bare branches in the hospital grounds. A few torn leaves, flapping in the wind.

Mark dropped her halfway up the hospital rise, by Outpatients. Cars beeped behind. The Xmas tree seller by the bus stop shouted at them for blocking his trade.

'We're so happy together,' he said. You make everything alright, even this moment. Look, we're laughing even in a crisis.'

'Dancing on the precipice,' said Ann. She got out of the car.

This was where it stopped then, this passionate current; this life with a love at its centre like she'd never had, that made the whole world dazzle.

'We're so fab,' he said, as she bent down in, holding the car door open with her arse to say goodbye. 'We said all the right things.' He drove away.

We? thought Ann. Two geese whistled alto overhead. She heard wind clap in their wings. It's not a honking, she thought. More a reassurance, an 'Are you there?'

She looked at the green amber on her finger. Tears of the gods. She took the ring off and dropped it in her pocket. Up the rise, the red car joined a rosary of tail-lights in the Christmas queue.

—

Blue Guitar

Jean Sprackland

Wish you were here. Now.

The wind and the sun. Marram-grass whipping at my legs. An impossible gradient of deep, soft sand.

It's the highest dune on this stretch of coast. Big Balls Hill, they call it – it's actually marked on the map. We used to laugh about it every time.

Of course you are here, in a way. When I brought you here that last time I thought I'd never feel lonely in this place. But it's not so easy. I come back every day and search. I dig with my hands, sieve the sand through my fingers, looking for you.

Sand. Treacherous stuff. Every couple of years someone stumbles across a corpse, bloated and stinking. Mostly suicides, washed up on a high tide. Now and then a murder. But it's the stupidest place to dispose of a body. The dunes shrug and shiver; the sand shifts, it's alive. A year, two years later, there's an arm sticking out of the sand for someone's dog to sniff at.

Or what's left of an arm.

But people do strike lucky, make incredible discoveries. There's that story – I'd like to believe in it – about a boy, playing at the edge of the sea, who found a wedding-ring. He took it to show his mother, and it turned out to be hers, which she'd lost there twenty years before. It's that kind of magic that keeps me going.

I'm not digging deep, just crawling along, skimming off the top layer and sifting it, skimming and sifting.

Sometimes I stop and look at a handful, and I see what a fool's errand this is. It's not one thing at all, it's a handful of different colours – more shades of white and brown and black than I could have guessed at.

Then I run, like something out of a cartoon, my legs pounding away at the slope but going nowhere fast. Collapse at the top, lie on my back watching the sky, with my heart pounding and the breath scalding my throat.

You used to love coming here, in both senses of the word. 'Race you down!'

We were always very competitive. But it was pure joy, leaping off the edge and then running, almost too fast for my feet, almost losing them, hurtling down into the soft bowl between hills, where it didn't matter if I fell, where it was safe. You at my back, grabbing my T-shirt and yanking me to the ground. The weight of you knocking the air out of my chest. You tugging at the stuck zip of my jeans and –

Christ, just thinking of it, the aching again, in all the usual places and spreading, up from the small of my back, along my spine, between my shoulder-blades…

I close my eyes against the dazzling sky. *Wish you were here.*

'Mrs Shaw?'

A woman in a tight suit was handing me something wrapped in brown paper.

'What? No.' My voice was too loud for the hush of the relatives' lounge. 'We weren't married. He didn't believe in it. We didn't believe in it.'

It was surprisingly light, I nearly dropped it. It was like a Christmas present or something. I tore it open there and then, pulled out a jar made of tinted plastic, with a gold-coloured screw lid. I held it up to the window and shook gently. Not much more than half-full.

The woman in the suit was staring. At the brown paper, discarded on the swirly nylon carpet. And at me.

'I'm so sorry,' she said.

Whatever I was expecting, it wasn't this. You hated plastic. Wouldn't buy bottled water because of the plastic. Because it's not biodegradable, it just sits there in the landfill with all the disposable nappies and other shit for ever and ever. In the van, we had a piece of smoothed and oiled sycamore for a chopping-board, we bought our apple juice in glass bottles which we refilled at the healthfood shop for twice the supermarket price. We used a slightly mildewed wicker basket for the washing. We collected driftwood sculptures on the beach for the wood-burning stove; they took weeks to dry out, filled the van with a salty, foreign smell.

It wasn't as if you'd left instructions. The illness was too fast. In those last days you surprised me, didn't want to face what was coming. I was too much of a coward to bring it up. I took my lead from you, and from the relentlessly bright atmosphere of the hospital ward, nurses jollying the patients along as if it was a holiday camp. I'd have expected you to loathe every minute of that, but you went for it, the banter and the smiles. I sat beside the bed like a boring old aunt at a party. You were dying – every day your face was thinner and greyer – and all you wanted to do was joke with the porter.

'Off for a smoke? Have one for me, mate. And put something extra in it, know what I mean?'

So I never asked you any of those questions: what music you wanted at your funeral, what I should do with the ashes. You might have laughed, or cried, and I couldn't have stood either. So I made the decisions. There would be no funeral. No one would have come anyway.

Back at the van, I opened the jar, pinched a bit of the dust between my fingers and sniffed cautiously. Its faint scent reminded me of a cupboard I hid in once as a child, during a game of hide-and-seek when no one came to find me. Funny, I thought I'd be squeamish, but it was remarkably clean stuff, nothing to be afraid of. Hard to believe a human body could be reduced to such small volume. Especially your body, with its beautiful complications, its fierce impulses. I put on your donkey-jacket, tucked the jar inside it, slogged up Big Balls Hill and sowed you like seed on the wind.

It was embarrassing, if you want to know the truth. No one else seemed to notice - the dog-walkers, the joggers, the lovers - but I was embarrassed in front of myself. It's a melodramatic gesture, scattering someone's ashes. Perhaps I should say a few words? A poem? A prayer even?

But you hated ceremony of any kind, and anyway you were *dead*.

I tried not to watch myself unscrewing the lid and shaking the jar, the ashes snatched on the air, like dust off the old rag-rug when I shake it outside the van.

And the plastic jar? The least I could do was dispose of it thoughtfully, as it says on crisp packets. I dropped it in the bin by the information point, forcing myself to pause and pretend to read about the unusual breeding habits of the natterjack toad.

Then I went home.

'Houses are too permanent,' you said, as we walked along a road of semis and bungalows, passing at least half a dozen For Sale signs. 'Get a house and you start buying stuff - washing machine, carpets, lawnmower...' You made them sound like the devil's trinkets. 'You ever helped anyone move house? They have stuff in the attic, stuff in the cellar, they're clogged up with stuff like arteries clogged up with fat... that's unrestrained fucking capitalism for you.'

In theory we could have moved house whenever we wanted, gone on the road, if we'd got the brakes seen to first. But we didn't bother. It was OK here, at the back of the caravan site. We only paid a couple of hundred a year, a friend of a friend. It was quiet. We were busy staying in bed, keeping warm. There was the daily walk to the sand-dunes. And I wrote the odd piece for women's magazines – *Is There Life After 35?* and *20 Ways to Say No to your Boss* – while you sprawled on the bench, singing and playing your blue guitar.

By the way, the guitar went with you. It was the only thing you had that was truly yours. I took it out behind the van, stuffed it with paper and set light to it. It didn't burn very well. A smell of scorched varnish, and a surprising amount of metal and plastic. I scraped up the ashes with a tablespoon and added them to the jar, shook it all up together. Now you were all mixed up with little scraps of unburnt wood and bits of grass.

'What's it gonna be, babe?'
When you were playing guitar your voice changed, you acquired a West Coast drawl. You could play for hours, Dylan to Dire Straits. Sometimes it was as if you couldn't stop.
    'Don't call me babe.'
    You took a long ecstatic pull on your joint and stuck it between the strings and the fret.
    'Lay lady, lay, lay across my big brass bed...'
    'Not that, you know I hate it.'
    The van was sleepy and stoned. I rubbed my eyes and turned back to the glare of the laptop.
    'Stay lady stay, stay with your man awhile...'
    'Stop it, I mean it now. Unless you want me to throw up.'
    'Why? Why doncha like it?'
    'You know why. I told you.' I really did feel queasy.
    'Tell me again, babe. What happened to you all those long years ago? C'mon now, tell Daddy all about it.'
    'Shut up.'
    'His clothes are dirty but his hands are clean...'
    'You bastard!' I dived across the van, dashed the guitar from your hands to the floor with a splintering wrong chord. For a few seconds we just stared at each other. I watched your face, ready to fling myself at the door and escape.
    'We're on fucking fire!' You sprang off the bench and stamped on the smouldering joint, the tiny hole in the rug. Then you pulled me down with you and we were laughing and wrestling, jostling strange music from the loose guitar. The bench and the cupboard rolled us back and forth like a ship's cabin in a storm. You had a way of touching, very sure and exact...

...but I don't want to think about that. The aching, the wanting, it gets into my bones. I'm cold and tired of searching.

And what's the point? I know where you are. Everywhere, very finely scattered.

Right here, where I'm lying, at the foot of Big Balls Hill.

I just need to feel you on my skin. The jacket's going to have to come off. And the jeans, though it's freezing in this wind. I'm going to pull them off quick and businesslike, not think of you easing them over my hips, not think of your grin. I'm keeping my underwear on – if anyone sees me it'll look like a bikini.

That's good. Scooping sand all over myself. There's bound to be some of you in there.

And here comes the rain, which makes it even better. You're plastered to my arms and legs and stomach, and I'm feeling warmer already.

Under the Dam

David Constantine

1

Their first home was under the viaduct. Seth found it. His train slowed and halted, waiting for clearance into the station, and he looked down on the rows, the smoking chimneys, the back alleys, and imagined being down there looking up at a train strung out along the arches in the sky. Next day he went in among the little houses and soon found one to buy for less than it would be to rent a room in nicer places. He fetched Carrie at once, as though this opportunity were a glimpse into the heavens and might at any moment close. The back bedroom had a pretty tiled hearth but Seth was at the window craning up. The arches climbed higher than he could see, the track lay on an upper horizon out of sight. Okay, said Carrie, in a loving wonder at this renewal of his eagerness. A train crawled heavily over and away. The house trembled.

Now began a good time for both of them; different for each, but equal in its fullness. They would look back on it, separately, and marvel: that was us then! The house was solid; or if it wasn't, they never worried. The sashes rattled under the heavy trains, once a slate came loose and slithered down; but they only laughed, Seth with a kind of satisfaction. The house was never light, not with daylight, at least – how could it be? But they made it cheerful with lamps, candles, coal fires, bright paint, and with lovely things they had collected on their travels.

Carrie advertised, and got two or three pupils for the fiddle or the guitar. They came to her and played or listened in the front room, always lit and scented, under the viaduct. When a train passed overhead, they paused and smiled. Seth kept on his job at the art school, only a few hours but just about enough. In his free time he did his own work, still trying for a true style, he said, but with some hope that, if he trusted, he would feel his way. He worked, and looked about him with a lively interest, to see how the things were that he must try to answer.

Under the arches, where the little streets ended, were strange dens and businesses. Seth and Carrie had a scrap man for a neighbour. He lived behind a wall of old doors, corrugated iron and barbed wire. He was black as coal, except for a grizzly head of hair the colour of ash. He had lost the power of speech. His clients were humped old men pushing bicycles and handcarts. They brought him rolls of lead and lengths of copper piping snapped like the limbs of insects, stuff ripped out of a vacancy before the Council came to board it up. Seth sketched them from his window as they passed. They were like gleaners on the slag heaps. When Carrie bought a big brass bed and several knobs were missing, Jonah hunted out the exact replacements from a drawer. When she asked what she owed him he raised his arms and tucked down his head, to mime a fiddler. She fetched her fiddle and played him a jig. He capered like a bear, on and on, until she feared for him and paused. Then the energy left him, he slouched off into his shack. Carrie glimpsed his primus stove and mattress. Seth marvelled. The man lay smack under the tracks!

They were mostly old people under the viaduct, or who looked old. The young left if they could. The Council accommodated difficult cases there; and one or two incomers, like Seth and Carrie, lodged or settled by choice. A pub had survived very easily, a couple of corner shops by dint of bitter struggle. Carrie soon got the feeling that they were welcome. Their outlandishness was engaging. She felt people look at her and Seth with a sort of hope. Seth did a sketch of the landlord's little girl, for her birthday. Then one or two others asked him. He did it quickly, for free. They marvelled, and forcibly he had to quell in himself a rising pride. Likeness, however exact, was not enough. He saw the hands of the old miners, the broken nails, the blue-black fragments of the job inhering under the skin like shrapnel; he saw the flaky cast, like talcum powder, over their puffy faces. Then he knew his uselessness and averted his eyes.

Seth did some research on the subject of the viaduct. He learned the weight it was built to bear, and the weight that nowadays it must. He gazed up, wondering at the difference. All those blackened bricks, arches like a Norman cathedral, the iron road, the thousands of oblivious people travelling north and south. In the pub he edged the talk towards catastrophes. There was one in 1912, coaltrucks, the last two in a long line somehow derailed and hanging over the parapet, emptying. Street next to yours, somebody said. Coal through the roof, coal on the bed. Then the iron. The Company rebuilt the houses, paid for the funerals, let them keep the coal. Seth wanted more. He had read of a suicide, a man dangling from the parapet on a rope, discovered in daylight, a crowd of citizens gazing up. All night there, trembling under the trains, tolling in the breeze. Carrie watched his face becoming helpless under the pull of his wish to know. She tried to cover for him, to veil an indecency. She feared for him. But that night, thrusting a poker into the congealed coals and letting the flames out, their warmth and dancing light, he said in the story of the derailment it was the richness that overwhelmed him, the too-sudden, too-abundant giving of the fuel of life. She pulled a face, shook her head. Then he said: We'll get an allotment, they're dirt cheap, we'll grow what we like.

The streets, yards, rooms were not entirely dark. In summer the morning sun slanted in very beautifully; in fact, like a peculiar gift and grace. There were early mornings of nearly unbearable illumination: sunlight through the rising smoke, a blood redness being revealed in the substance of the arches, through a century of soot. But the allotments, higher up the dip the houses were gathered in, enjoyed an ample and more ordinary helping of daylight. Seth was given a plot on the slope facing the railway embankment, just below a ruined chapel and a few wrecked graves, just before the viaduct began its stepping over the sunken town. There was an attempt at terracing, almost Mediterranean, he said. He went up there whenever he could and Carrie joined him. He watched for her climbing the path from the houses into the allotments among the sheds and little fences. She brought a flask and a snack. Then they worked side by side. Palpable happiness, real as the heavy earth, as the tools in their hands, as the produce. So it was. She said to herself: Nothing will obliterate this.

One of Carrie's pupils was a boy of seventeen or so. He was called Benjamin and had no home to speak of. He came to their house under the viaduct, said he wanted to learn the guitar, but had no money. Could he do odd jobs for them instead? Carrie said yes. He spoke a thick vernacular. He had black eyes that seemed to be seeing things he hadn't the words to utter. Seth saw how it would be and to all that he foresaw, like Carrie, he said yes. Soon Benjamin was in love with her, muffled and bewildered by it, but with the steady helpless gaze of a passionate certitude. The best he could ever say, including both of them, but turning back helplessly to Carrie, was: You're not like people round here. Seth watched Carrie shift so almost imperceptibly in her feelings that at no point was there reason enough to halt. From pity for the incoherent child – he wrings my heart – she passed through the troubling satisfaction of being loved by him into loving him, in her fashion, in return. Seth came home once and saw them in the music room together. Benjamin was making his best attempt at the accompaniment of a familiar song. He was bent down and away from the door, anxiously watching his own fingers. Carrie was singing, and watching him. Seth saw how far along she was in the changing of her feelings. She met his eyes and knew that he knew. Afterwards she said: It doesn't make any difference. I know that, he said; but felt a difference, of a kind he could not fathom. And she added: Whatever you ask, I will always tell and whatever I tell you it will be the truth.

Seth had been planning to restore the kitchen range. It should heat, like the back boiler, from the open fire, and once would have cooked and baked for a family. But all its intricate system of flues and draughts was blocked and useless, one door hung loose, a cast iron hob below it was cracked and tilted. For weeks Seth had been brooding on his project with a secret satisfaction, as though it were the promise of a breakthrough in his drawing and painting and he must bide his time, gather his energies, make a space, and finally set to. It was all his own, all his own dreaming, that he would act on when he chose. It amazed him therefore, one afternoon when Benjamin came in from the lesson, that without thinking he took him by the arm, stood him before the hearth and said: Know anything about ranges? Benjamin blushed. Here was a large opportunity. Aye, he said. Same make as my mother's. I always did hers till my stepfather moved in. And he went on his knees before it, opened the loose door, rattled gently at the damper. No worse than you'd expect, he said. He looked up at Seth, then quickly away. In the firelight on his looks Seth saw clearly how Carrie must love him. He said: I had a mind to get it working again. You could give me a hand. His project, disclosed, shared, made over to someone else. Suddenly he was deferring to the boy, who was local and knew about these things, knew better. He tested his feelings for regret and could find none. Benjamin was rolling up his sleeves. No time like the present. There should be a rake somewhere, and wire brushes. They're out the back, said Seth. In secret he had been making his preparations. He fetched the tools, a dustsheet, a tin bucket, overalls for them both. Soon he was taking out a pail of rust and soot. Thinking Benjamin had already left, it shocked Carrie to see him in Seth's overalls, crouched close to the fire, intently working at the blocked airways. Seth came in. We've made a start, he said. Feel. She put her hand into the open oven. The warmth was coming through. A long way off baking bread, but a start. Like cleaning a spring and the water beginning again. Ben's the man, said Seth. You both look the part, said Carrie, bringing tea, their filthy hands closing round the mugs, eyes whitened through a faint mask of soot, eyebrows, hairs on the wrists lightly touched up with dirt. She felt her own cleanness like an attraction, almost too blatant. She said: Why don't I go and ask Jonah for a new door? It's the hinge, Benjamin said. The door's okay. Well, a hinge, said Carrie. Why don't you? said Seth. And to Benjamin, as she left the room: She likes asking Jonah. Five minutes later Carrie was back, with Jonah himself. Couldn't remember the make. Thought he'd better see it. His appearance in their living room was astonishing, as though an order of things had been undone. He bulked much larger, blacker, more grizzled, more indifferent to any usual manners. He glanced and nodded, tapped the cracked hob with his boot, nodded again, departed. It's sunny out, said Carrie. Strange irrelevance. Under the viaduct they seemed to be making a life that would be all interior, by lamplight, intimate. Their feelings wanted sleet and hail, early dusk, the long nights. The fire would roar, the oven would heat up tremendously, Carrie would bake a batch of loaves, there would be a kettle whispering on the hob.

They were in a hurry to finish, but it took some days. Seth would only work at it with Benjamin, at which Carrie smiled. She went to Jonah for the hinge, he had found a likely hob as well, also a battered kettle that might polish up. He beckoned her into his shack and pointed to a can of WD40 on the table. There was a notepad by it, to do his talking. He scrawled: FOR THE RUSTY NUTS AND BOLTS. And after that: YOU PLAY ME A TUNE? His oily hand had smudged the cheap lined paper. Carrie kissed him on both cheeks. A baker's dozen of tunes, she said. In town she bought the substance necessary for loosening rusty nuts and bolts, and a tin of the proper stove paint, glossy black.

Seth and Benjamin were at work, kneeling on the dustsheet side by side. Your mother must have been glad, said Seth. Why ever did he stop you? Benjamin shrugged. Whatever I liked, he put a stop to it. And after that he started thumping me. Your mother let him? Couldn't stop him. Didn't try? Little by little let the boy go, for the man, reneged on everything, betrayed him utterly, crossed over, stood against him with the incomer. Stepfather said he was a pansy, queer. Unbuckled, belted him, left him curled on the hearthrug swallowing his own snot. Then joined the mother in the room above, in the marriage bed. Benjamin said again: You're not like people round here.

It was Seth's birthday. They declared the kitchen range open for use. The burnished copper kettle boiled for tea. By evening the house smelled of bread. Red wine and brown ale shone in the firelight. Savorous things, all manner of plates and dishes, it was all their travelling gathered in. Jonah came, grinned, tapped with his dirty knuckle on the shiny iron. From somewhere in his throat came up a cheerful clucking. Two or three others were invited. Carrie played her promised thirteen tunes. After dark they went out into the yard. The arches stood supreme and along them, elongated, lay a halted train. The lights shone like scales. Nothing above until the infinitely distant constellations. When the others had gone Benjamin came to Seth and Carrie by the fire. I got you this, he said, handing Seth a thing in a plastic bag. It was the shape and weight of a bible, but cushioned to the touch and a lovely dark green and the thousand pages, closed, made a block of brilliant gold, and on the cover, ornately and goldenly inscribed, the name: Shelley. Benjamin was anxious. Okay or not? I wouldn't know. He shrugged, sorry on many counts. Seth looked from the gold to Carrie to Benjamin and bowed his head over the gold again. You've got no money, he said. It's only Oxfam, said Benjamin. And anyway I nicked it. Seth kissed him and left them by the fire. He wanted to be outside for a while, under the viaduct and the Plough, holding the book of poems. Carrie said to Benjamin: Don't go. We want you to stay.

2

In Rhayader they went first to the solicitor's, to sign. Seth had insisted that it be in Carrie's sole name, so she signed. He cradled the baby in his arms and watched. The man was polite, punctilious; if he found a client odd he would never show it. Seth felt as remote from him, fellow humans though they were, as one star is in fact from any other. All people in professions, decently dressed, decently doing their jobs, they were moving further and further away from him. He bowed his head over the sleeping child. He prayed his wife would never go from him into the icy distances while he lived. The estate agent's was a few doors along. They collected the keys. The man was jolly, heartily wished them both good luck, extended a little finger to touch the baby's cheek. Was there anything in his manner which said he was glad to be shot of the place and rather you than me?

Rhayader looked a nice town, simple on the axis of a clock tower. The waters felt very near, and the cold breath of the hills. Carrie remembered it well enough and they shopped quickly. It was late February, the daylight would soon give out, they wanted to arrive before dark.

Seth drove. Carrie held the baby on her knees, on the open map. The road climbed the river, which was rising, they heard it roar, the tyres hissed over sheets of running wet. After a while they must take a junction left, out of woodland and across the narrow reservoir, a sinuous long water whose lapping edge they clung to. So far so good. The lake seemed to double the light of the clear sky, giving them more time, a reprieve. Then, sharp right, the thin road took up with another river, doubling it exactly. Carrie opened the window. Such a din entered, the river hurtling in excess of the course at its disposal. The hills, streaked white with headlong tributaries, opened and were revealed on either side, very beautiful, terribly exposed. Seth, as so often lately, viewed himself and his enterprise with fear and pity, like a spectator. As though from high above he viewed the cumbersome white van, in which was everything he owned and loved, crawling forward at the mercy of the universe. He admired the three of them, loved them intensely, wished for their safe arrival; but remotely, as though they were fictions, actors, a lively dramatization. Carrie was in doubt. She had begun to wish it should be dark before they arrived, that he saw the place for the first time in a fresh daylight. She felt answerable, the onus on her felt as vast as the opening hills. Not that he would not like it, but that he would like it too well. Was she not siding with him against himself? Was it not a conniving in his destruction? The daylight lasted, they were far west, the stars appeared on a sky still white.

Then the road ended, they were at the dam, up under it, up against it. A stream came tumbling off the hill, the hill came steeply down in rocks, and there in the angle, between rocks and sheer black wall, on a platform reached by a raddled track, stood the house. Carrie shook her head, wondering over herself, appalled. But Seth had jumped out and stood marvelling in the cold air. He took the baby from her arms, helped her down. Home from home, he said. Well done! He was radiant. He seemed shocked back into proximity. At once he had energy, the spirits, the courage for anything. She unlocked the door, it needed a heave to open it. Never to be forgotten, the first breath of the place, the soot, the damp. The electric, he said. Can you remember where? She could. They had lights. Now for a fire, he said. I saw a wood pile. She followed him out, stood by him. He turned with his arms full of logs, faced the sheer black wall. Beloved wife, he said, I shall work here. Under the stars they lugged their brass bed from the van.

Craig Ddu was a dead end. The road stopped there, it was for Midlands Water and the few tourists. A carpark, a public toilets, a phone box, all like a failed outpost. And from under the massive wall the original river set forth again, ignominiously. True, in no time at all, fed fresh water by the free streams off the hills, it had recovered and rattled along with the dam behind it like a fading nightmare. The house itself, older than the dam, a survivor of the colossal works and shoved by them into a new relationship with the world – the house itself wanted living in. There was an acre around it and forty more vaguely up the hillside and a little way downstream. But the wall was so close and towering it seemed to Carrie that at the least diminution of their resolve they must lose the contest and be overwhelmed. Again she wondered at her choosing it for Seth. Was it vengeful? But Seth went from room to room and paced the territory blessing her name. He said his love and gratitude were as vast as the backed-up waters behind the wall. So she was reassured, but still with an anxiety that his exaltation, her doing, was itself a precipitous and dizzying thing. But they had days full of appetite and savour and at nights their love was like a miracle at their disposal. The house warmed. They owned a copse of twenty or thirty shattered firs, fuel for ever, so it seemed.

Carrie drove into Rhayader, to stock up. They needed blades, paint, sand and cement, as well as food. Seth watched her out of sight, a long while. After that, with little Gwen slung on his chest, he continued to discover how rich he was. He found a damp place in the very angle of rock and wall, a lighter green and lit up with celandines. It was a spring, and only wanted cleaning. In a stone barn he found a collapsed tractor; and a scythe, a rake, pitchforks, all wormy wood and rusted steel, that he would surely mend and put to use again. He fed Gwen, laid her down for a sleep, sat on the boards and leaned against the cot, dozing. He felt fuller than the rivers. He must have slept for a little while soundly. His face was wet with tears when he woke. Only grasp it, even a small part of it, make even a little of it able to be seen! Joyful commission, courage to come up to it! Gwen was waking. Together they went and sat in a mild sun, to watch down the length of the river and the road for Carrie coming home. Scores of rabbits browsed and scurried below them over their ragged estate. Benign neglect.

It was a week before they climbed to see the lake. They might have gone down through the carpark to the road which served the dam ordinarily; but they had seen, with a shock, a steep path, almost a stairway, starting behind their house, near the celandines and the newly discovered spring. That was the way they must go, arduous, secret, starting from their own ground. So cold, so damp – more than damp, the hillside oozed and trickled and spurted with more water than it could hold. The rocks were soft with moss, tufted with the ferns that, in their fashion, luxuriate in chill and wetness. Seth cupped the baby's head and steadied her against him, against his chest, in the warm sling. They were in an angle, almost a chimney, close into the join of dam and hillside, hard up against an unimaginable body of water behind its engineered restraint. At first, for about half the climb, they were in a shadow akin to darkness at noon, eclipsed. Seth turned whenever the stairway allowed it, for Carrie to come up. Over the bright scarf on her head he took in their new home and beyond that the river, its recovered force, its intrusion and insinuation through the resistance of the hills. How slight and at the same time vigorous and cunning they were, to climb an intricate and precipitous stairway under a deep reservoir of water, the child pressed against him felt as brave and tiny as a wren, he felt her pulse to be infused into his own, married in, blood into beating blood. The day had grandeur, like a heroic expedition, like a myth. Then they were in the sun, the low sunshine of the dawning of the spring, it warmed and illuminated the greens and the tones of gold, they climbed with a faint warmth on their backs, felt for it with their faces when they paused and turned, like a whisper of earthly everlasting life, a breath, an intimation, infinitely delicate and poignant against the immensity of the immured waters up which they climbed.

Their arrival, a last steep haul, landed them in a grave uncertainty of feeling, with no words. It was like surfacing: there lay the level water. Come up through the depths they were level now with miles of length and breadth, the far reaches winding away invisibly in many bays and inlets and the inexhaustible hills continuously contributing. The total bulk exceeded comprehension, like a starry sky. From the far head of the lake, or rather from off the hills and harrowing softly over the face of the lake, came a cold breeze. The water lapped steadily at the ramparts under them, the water came on and on, without end, hit against the stone, each wave that ceased in its particular self being at once renewed and replicated. Somewhere in the distance, out of sight, was an infinite spawning of waves against the dam. Quite suddenly their little human enterprise seemed futile. They bethought themselves fearfully of the baby, the necessary energy was lapsing out of them. There was a watchtower halfway along, locked and boarded up, but they hid in its lee, saw to little Gwen and settled then without much regret on the ugly and ordinary way to climb and descend, the waterboard's metalled road. Clouds were driving up, such hurtling clouds, you might stand and watch the world occluded in three minutes.

What are you thinking?
About the dam.
Don't.
Not badly, I wasn't thinking about it in a bad way.
What way then?
Only about the water. How it naturally wants to be level.
Not there it doesn't.
No not there. There it wants to go headlong, and be level later. Real lakes are different. They're serene in comparison. When it's too much, they overflow. That's very gentle. But the water up there, even when it's still, all the weight of it doesn't want to lie like that. It wants to be headlong.
Stop it.
Can't stop thinking. I was thinking about the waves as well.
Kiss me instead. Love me. I want you.

Carrie was feeding the baby by the window. Such a view from there, away from the dam, downstream through oaks and rowans towards the little hidden town. On the draught through the sash window she could smell a bonfire. Always a bonfire, so much to clear and burn. Seth came in, went upstairs, she heard him rummaging, floorboards and ceiling were one and the same. Peaceful feeding; the quiet view, the scent of smoke. Sometimes she dozed as the baby did. Seth went out again, she glimpsed him, what was he carrying? She dozed. Then it broke in on her. Oh no! Oh no, not that! She ran out, her dress undone, Gwen's eyes flung open wide.

He held a portfolio open on his left arm and sheet by sheet he was feeding it to the flames. Carrie halted, clutching the baby tight. He was like a man on a ledge. Should she snatch at him or quietly, quietly talk him to safety? Seth, don't, she said, soft as the small rain. He turned, his face was rapt. She hated to see it. Grief, despair, would have been easier to view in him, not rapture, feeding his work to a bonfire. No harm, my love, nothing wrong, he said in the voice of some peculiar wisdom. I see my way, I see I have to begin again. Seth, for my sake, stop it. She saw sketches and drawings, beloved likenesses, herself in the little churchyard above their allotment, a warm and vivid picture of their hearth, the burnished kettle, the rug, the glossy range. I have to, he said. One folder lay on the earth, wide open, wholly empty. Soon be over, won't take long. Then we'll begin again. They're ours, she said, they're not just yours. When they're done they belong to both of us. Herself in her sixth month, peaceable. The baby newborn. How can you? There was Jonah, seated at their kitchen table, manifestly content. And again and again, there were the heroic arches of the viaduct, striding across the town. Everything? All of it? He would not be talked into safety. Carrie made a grab for the portfolio, dislodged it from his arm, spilled out the remainder on the ground. Pictures lay under the sky, half a dozen of Benjamin. Seth's face jolted and altered, as though from a stroke. Bitch, he said in a voice like a ventriloquist's. Bitch, you are in my way, you and your bastard you are in my way. And he reached for the pitchfork, newly mended, wrenched it from the earth, raised it, stabbed and stabbed at the images and rammed home all he could of them hard into the fire. Gwen was screaming. Carrie went on her knees, scrabbling together what few sheets were left. Seth leaned on the new handle, worked the prongs free, and stood back. He saw her breasts, her weeping face, what he had done.

> Listen to the rain.
> So soft.
> And the streams, can you hear the streams?
> All of them, near and far.
> It's gone again. I'm better. I feel you have forgiven me.
> I love you. Nothing else matters. I will forgive you anything. Except the one thing which you know about. Do that and I will haunt you day and night in hell.
> Where is he, do you think?
> Who?
> Benjamin.
> I don't know.
> Does he know where we are?
> How could he?

Gwen woke. Seth went naked to her room, reached down

into her white cot, lifted her warm and snuffling against him. Carrie sat up, reached for her, all in the tranquil darkness. The baby's whimpering became a focussed hurry; then she settled into the blissful certainty of satisfaction. Seth stood by them in the dark, Carrie leaned her head against him. The baby had her hunger exactly answered. He went to the window, parted the heavy curtains, looked down. He could make out the water, like the ghost of the milky way, a soft luminance in movement. He could almost believe that the dam was a natural lake that has no wish to topple but in a measured fashion gives into the valley. Across the cold room Carrie said:

> I suppose he visits his mother.
> Did he say?
> He said he always would.
> He is very loyal. You could write to him there.
> I suppose I could look for that address.

Seth came back to bed, obliterated his face against her, dozed, woke when it was time to carry the sleeping child back to her cot. Like a little boat, he always thought, a safe little ark, into which he laid her, in which she drifted safely on the waters of her sleep, returning, calling out in the dark when next she needed a reassurance of the close connectedness and safety of her world.

The van tilted, rocked from side to side. The descent always did look perilous. Carrie, watching, was glad when he reached the girder bridge and the start of the road. There he paused, got out, waved, blew her a kiss, departed. All the way out of sight she watched him travel. Then she went indoors to prepare the house. As for herself, she made an abeyance. She feared Seth's changes. They were the abyss. Now he was marshalling events the way she most desired. Or the way she dreaded most. Or both. And between her and him, one flesh, it was never certain whose proposal they were following, either might serve the other for the self's obscure desires. She knew that much, but it appeared impenetrable and induced in her a passivity and a fatalism, under which, like a spring making for daylight, ran the irrepressible force of self-asserting life.

In the late afternoon Carrie and Gwen went down to the bridge and the junction of the little stream with the river creeping out from under the black doors of the dam. They were less in the wall's shadow there, the sunlight lingered a while longer. The rabbits fled; watched; soon resumed their trespassing. At the waterside Gwen was absorbed by all the babble and movement. A yellow wagtail flitted over and stayed close. Carrie lost her consciousness almost wholly in the child and the bobbing, darting soft-coloured bird. Her particular complexities were postponed.

At the waterside she heard the motor but could not see it. The rhythm was unfamiliar, the arrival might be somebody else, though scarcely anyone ever came so far. Having no wish to see a stranger, she took Gwen in her arms and climbed the track home. The engine still approaching made her nervous, like a pursuit. Not till she was on the level, at their usual viewing place, did she turn. The vehicle, an old estate car, long as a hearse, was riding grandly over the bridge and embarking, with great caution, on the rocky track. Seth and Benjamin. Where's the van? she asked. Seth was pleased with himself. Sold it. More seats in this. Carrie said: What about our bed, if we move? We're not moving, Seth replied. Here we are now. First job tomorrow: improve our approaches. Benjamin stood to one side, smiling, very uncertain. An army surplus haversack seemed to be all his luggage. Again that gaucheness, again his black eyes seeing more than his tongue could utter. It lurched under Carrie's heart. So here we are, to stay. Again; anew; as before; wholly new. So be it.

Then began a good time for the three of them; for the four of them, since Gwen among the childish grown-ups continued in gaiety and satisfaction with only little bouts of fret. That very evening, in a lingering daylight, in firelight and candlelight, Seth begged their forgiveness and explained as clearly as he could what he must try to do in his drawing and painting henceforth. He said: I look at you. I look from you to my hands. I can make a likeness of you but it will not be enough. It won't be what it is truly like. So my premise is failure. My axiom is that whatever I *can* do, whatever my hands *can* make, will not suffice. Carrie was anxious, wanted to halt him, she saw him raising the precipice. No, no, he said. Through what I *can* do, its manifest failure, I will feel my way towards what I should do, always by failure, I'll know what isn't right, what manifestly will not do.

Carrie stood up and stopped him softly with her fingers on his mouth. We haven't had enough music lately. She fetched the guitar for Benjamin, the fiddle for herself. Benjamin shook his head. You men, she said. So fearful. Start, it will come back. Listen to this.

Seth said he would go and stock up. Food, and we need a sledge hammer and a pickaxe, he said. Gwenny's coming with me. Back for lunch. Carrie strapped her carefully in; leaned over her, kissed him on the mouth, feeling for his tongue with her tongue. Benjamin stood in the doorway.

A bit uncertainly, Carrie first, Benjamin hanging back, they came out of the house, to greet him. They were like children, he laughed at them, how he loved them, he laughed aloud over them and him, he exulted, the life there lifting up before his very eyes filled him with a wild glee. Guess what, he said, handing Carrie the sleeping child, guess what, or perhaps you knew, and he kissed her lips, perhaps you knew already when you brought me here? What? She asked. Such a shop I did, food and alcohol for a fortnight and tools for eternity. He was handing the plastic bags out to Benjamin, overburdening him. What did I know already perhaps? Carrie asked. Shelley's down there, him and Harriet, under the second reservoir. They were alive down there and planning a thorough revolution of our ways of being in the world, in the summer of 1812. They came up here for picnics. It's all in a book, I bought a book, it's in that bag Ben's holding with the cheeses, five different cheeses. Truly, there's no end to this place. He faced the towering black wall. That wasn't here then, of course. It was a high valley with the little river hurrying down. He cupped his mouth, tilted his head and shouted at the dam. Back came the clearest sound of craziness imaginable – the sole name: Shelley, fracturing and chiming. Gods, said Seth. Did you know that as well? No, said Carrie. Benjamin stood like a beast of burden with the shopping, watching Seth and Carrie as he had under the viaduct when they appeared like an enchantment on his life. Shout, Ben, said Seth. Shout out who you are. Echo it to Rhayader that you're here. Benjamin looked called up for an ordeal. Shout, said Carrie. Stand where Seth is and shout your name. First time no sound came, none from his mouth at all. He licked his lips, raised his head, called out his name. The echoing fell away in a cadence that was utterly forlorn. Carrie ended the game. Food, she said. Then work, said Seth. Work and pray. Work and play. But work first, the chain gang. Anchor me with a ball and chain, don't let me float away.

That afternoon, with pickaxe, sledge hammer, shovel, wheelbarrow, in boots and heavy gloves, they worked at smoothing a way from the girder bridge to their platform under the dam. Parts had become like a riverbed, from frost and sun and torrents, and it was with some reluctance that Seth made them carriageable. He worked next to Benjamin, or parting and returning as the tasks required, almost without a word, in the intimacy of a shared hard labour. At first Benjamin was shy, watchful, but Seth won him over, slowly and surely into something akin to his own present state. By four the job was half done. Enough, he said. The sun was behind the dam. They went indoors, made tea, sat at the table in a too early dusk. Carrie was at the window with Gwen. Not far down the valley lay the sunlight still, the shadow advancing very slowly over it. She felt the haste more characteristic of Seth. We must show Benjamin the water, she said.

All they had seen so far cried out to be seen again, to be seen and shown, and he was the only fellow human they wanted for the revelation. The climb was eerie, chilling; the wet trickled on them as though night and blackness were exuding an icy dew. They felt the cold of the body of water through its concrete shield. But all the while, as in a seaside town when a street heads at an incline for the sea, Carrie and Seth were expecting the enormous light over the brink and treasuring it like an imminent gift for Benjamin. At the last they sent him ahead and waited, looking down over their own chimneys to the pool of sunlight on the woodland very far below. Then they joined him on the rampart of the dam. The breeze; but gentler, warmer, a zephyr if there ever was such a thing. And sunlight dancing, a shattering white radiance further than they could see, more than they could bear to contemplate. They drifted apart, drifted together, gauche and ineffectual, brimful of love and joy and their mouths silenced with shyness.

So their days rose, whatever the weather, they had work to do, they played like children, were passionately companionable. Bejamin went back to the echo, he became the master of it. He positioned Gwen on the ground to listen to the names returning strangely. He invented birds and animals, he brought them forth for her, as though from an ark.

In the evenings they read or Seth painted, Benjamin

withdrew as far as the room allowed, turned his back on them, strummed softly at the guitar and in an undertone, barely audible, hummed and mumbled some words of his own invention. Seth said aloud: Nantgwyllt went under the water in 1898. The Shelley Society lodged a formal protest. The Welsh were evicted from their homes, where they had lived for many generations. Carrie went for her bath. The clock ticked more audibly. She came in naked and kneeled on the hearthrug between her husband and her lover, bowing her head, towelling her long hair, the curve of her spine in the lamplight. She sat back on her heels, the firelight on her knees, her belly, her breasts. She slung her damp hair forward in one hank over her left shoulder. What else is under the water? she asked. The house of his cousin Thomas Grove, where he stayed in 1811, wondering what to do, when they had sent him down from Oxford for professing free love and atheism. Nothing under our dam here? Some sheepfolds, one or two cottages already given up and the ruins of a chapel at the very far end with a holy well, a hermit lived there in 1300, he had moved further and further into solitude and come this side of the hills from the Cistercian community at Strata Florida.

They trekked over hill and bog and down through woodland to a vantage point over the second reservoir from where, closely comparing Seth's old maps and the reality, they believed they must be looking on the surface under which Nantgwyllt and the house belonging to Shelley's cousin lay submerged. On a long day, first climbing the stairway that started from their liberated spring, they circumambulated the reservoir, the highest, under which, night after night, they slept, and located, to their satisfaction, the place a diver would have to sink himself who wished to visit the anchorite's roofless cell. Question, said Seth. Does the well still bubble up oppressed by tons of water? They took out the deeds of their home, Craig Ddu, and climbed the little stream, to see where they began and ended, their forty or fifty acres. But this was harder than imagining a village or a dwelling fixed for ever under sheets of water. The walls had collapsed, the bracken and sedge were over all. At the head of the stream, where it split, where its three strands were plaited together into one, there was a ruined fold, one hawthorn clinging on, its roots in rock, its shape, set by the wind, offering a threadbare roof over a waterfall. Emblem: the survivor. I don't know what we own and what we don't, said Seth. Whatever, wherever, the land was given up, for humans it was long since finished and the crows, the kites, the buzzards and the kestrels were left at liberty to scour it lot by lot.

Seth's work was changing. Carrie looked over his shoulder now and then, his concentration was intense, he did not mind. She loved to watch his hand, so quick, so deft. But what came of it troubled her. At first she thought she must make a new effort of understanding, to do him justice. He had said his way must be that of groping through failure towards the truth. But in truth she had to confess to herself that she understood him perfectly well. The lines of his art were forfeiting all insistence, one figure elided into another. One that by the shock of black curls and the steady eyes most resembled Benjamin had the bodily shape of an adolescent girl; she saw herself with Seth's short hair and features haunted by all his previous alienations. Everywhere there was doubling, tripling, echoing, fragmentation and dispersal, fleeting as Welsh weather, faithless as water. Even that she might have said yes to, and praised his courage. They were change, flux, movement, or they were dead. That was their principle, was it not? What distressed her were his trials with colour, the way he exceeded and overrode his slight outlines with a willed carelessness, like a child's smudging and genial mess, the watery colours running and giving up their selves whilst the draft of some elusive shape ineffectually showed through. But this was a man with the keenest sharpest gaze she had ever known. She had watched him when he bore on a thing and truly saw it. She knew how exact and knowing he was: when he dashed off a likeness for a favour; and in the devising and execution of a particular pleasure. So why this allowing a world in which nothing belonged, nothing had shape or fixed identity or an outline marking it off from anything else? She remembered his axiom, and it chilled her: Whatever I *can* do will not do. He was reneging on his peculiar abilities. For what?

Seth took off his boots and entered on stockinged feet, quite silently, though he had no intention of stealth. Carrie and Benjamin were sitting in the window. She was buttoning her dress, he was cradling Gwen and murmuring over her. Carrie was contemplating him and her baby with a contented love. The light from outside was on the three of them. Seth stood, he saw the beautiful ordinariness of their intimacy, the daylight fact of it. He turned, quitted the room, his movement alerted them, Benjamin came out to him as he was putting his boots back on. Seth kept his face averted. Nothing, he said. I was going to show you something. Benjamin touched him on the shoulder. What then? Seth shrugged, still averted, but walked across to the stone barn, allowing Benjamin's arm along his shoulders. And step by step he felt the virtue going out of him.

In the barn, standing still, he couldn't for the life of him remember what he had wanted to show Benjamin. He was attending dumbly to the transmutation taking place in him, a sort of petrifaction, the replacement of every atom of faith with an atom of hopelessness. He stared in stupidity at the tractor. It had slumped forward on burst front tyres. He motioned vaguely at it. The weights? said Benjamin. No, no, said Seth. Nothing. The weights, a couple of cast-iron pyramids, were still slung from their rings under the tractor's front bar. Stop you going over backwards, said Benjamin. He was staring at Seth, who at last looked him in the eyes. Tell Carrie, will you, Ben. I'm very sorry. Then he covered his face. The tears forced through his fingers, the wells of his hopeless sadness burst their strong restraint.

He curled up on the bed of love, tight as an embryo, and sobbed; he choked on his own snot; he was a grub, a grown man with his knees up to his brow, smelling his own terror and despair; in overalls, with dirty working boots, a competent man, weeping over his exile from all fellowship with love; shoved into space, into the cold and the dark of the interstellar spaces, turning for ever like a finished capsule. For an eternity, for an hour or so. After that, uncurled and lying quietly in his wife's embrace, behind the curtain of her hair, he said in a level voice he was not fit to live, he had a coward soul, he cringed in shame that he had ever associated himself – in a far-off laughable mimicry – with any of his saints and heroes, the artists and the poets. He begged in the flat, the leaden voice that she would burn every scribble of his or daub she ever found. He begged her to promise there would be nothing left, not a scrap or jot to show the world his folly and ridiculousness. And he said again that he wasn't fit to live, that on her house and home and child and love he was unfit to have the smallest claim. Then shame over these his speeches. Dumbness then, the mute inability. And a vague terror, hard to pinpoint, had to lay a finger on its whereabouts. Inside or out? The air he breathed, the wreath of atmosphere around his neck and shoulders. Or in the blood, coursing around him for as long as he was he. The nights had terrible gaps in, rents and pits, and every morning waking he felt sheeted under lead.

Ten days of this, a bad passage. He came out lachrymose and vastly sentimental. He sat with Gwen in the bedroom window like a grandfather, her hand clasped tight on his little finger as though she anchored him and nurtured him. With a large benevolence he watched Benjamin, like his own younger self, labouring at the finish of their steep track to the bridge and the beginnings of the outside world. The thistly grass was gay and innocent with rabbits, like a tapestry. Carrie, her hair coming loose from under a red headscarf, pushed manfully at the wheelbarrow. She waved, said something to Benjamin, he looked up and waved. They swam in tears as far as Seth could see.

Then his return began, unhoped for, miraculous, never biddable but somewhere in the depths of him insistent as a germination or water forcing up. He wandered about in the house and out of doors with Gwen on his hip, she was easiest to be with, he could babble at her or murmur like a breeze and what delighted her in the early summer delighted him, thistledown, dandelion clocks, forget-me-nots around their neatly stone-flagged spring whose water was a clear continuous beginning again. He viewed himself with more indulgence now, with a wry friendliness. Held up the child against the soft blue sky and intoned while she kicked and chortled: My own heart let me more have pity on; let/ Me live to my sad self hereafter kind … Brought her close, kissed her nose, went down on his heels and toddled her towards him. Her cool hands warmed in his; he marvelled with her over the unpractised action of her legs. Scooped her up to admire the woodpile, Benjamin's special pride, and the new plots set as well as possible for the growing season's sun. The stone barn, the very sight of it, tilted his spirits towards a steep collapse, so he walked away, down the slope past Benjamin and Carrie smoothing the last few yards, to the water where the wagtail liked to visit and sat there till they called him, willing his fears into submission in the happy consciousness of the child. Returning, admiring, he suddenly saw where a new plot might be dug, on the slope itself, with some terracing, almost Mediterranean; he would begin it next day.

That evening he read the Shelley Benjamin had given him. He read Mary Shelley's notes on the poems year by year, until the last. They were brave, these people, he said. It's brave just being in a place like that, so far from anywhere, facing the open sea. And Mary collecting everything afterwards and writing her notes, that's brave. What happened to Harriet? Benjamin asked. Seth made no answer so Carrie said: She went in the Serpentine. He had left her for Mary. They married and went to Italy. Seth was thinking of her heavy clothes, sodden, the mud, the weed. And her heavy belly, she was very pregnant. They didn't look after one another, Carrie said. One to another they were a catastrophe. I suppose everybody is responsible, Seth said. I mean for what he does. They left one another their own responsibility. He was feeling bolder. He was thinking about his terracing – whether to tell them or not, or make a start first thing, for a surprise.

Next morning Seth appeared at the foot of the bed. He whispered a strange sentence: The boat has come. It was early, he had parted the curtains slightly and the sun shone on the black paint and the golden brass. Carrie woke. Benjamin was asleep on her left arm. He looked, to Seth at least, much as he had lately in his drawings and paintings, only more beautiful, the black curls, the lashes. Carrie smiled, gently disengaged herself, sat up. Seth said again: The boat has come; but with his eyes on Benjamin shook his head in wonder and added the words: Sweet thief. Carrie joined him outside in the sunlight. You've been working already? Yes, he said. Come and see. He took her to the edge and pointed down to where he had begun hacking out a terrace. We shall grow what we like, he said. Carrie put his arms around her. Was I dreaming, she asked, or did you say something about a boat? I did, said Seth. That's the strange thing. But not strange at all really. Not for this place. I was working and I looked up at the dam and thought how lovely the water must be with the sun on it already. I thought I might go and swim and when I got up there I saw the boat, a little rowing boat with the oars in. It was bumping against the land where I might have gone in swimming. It's nobody's, we can use it.

Everything from the far end drifts before the wind and arrives sooner or later up against the dam or lodges in a near angle. They claimed the boat and the shipped oars until they should hear of someone who had a better claim. They made a mooring in a tiny inlet, out of sight of the rampart should anybody walk there, which was almost never, and whenever they liked, which was often, the four of them were out on the water. There was nearly always a breeze but rarely too strong to make headway against. And besides, by keeping close and following on water the path they had followed or made to the far end of the lake, they could creep along, like a yacht skilfully tacking. They packed a picnic, landed where they pleased: by two or three hawthorns, by the broken line of a drystone wall where it descended and entered the water. Poignant, these traces, these indications of a connection and a use gone out of sight. Keeping an eye on the weather – they were never foolhardy – they crossed with steady strokes the width near the far end, to experience, said Seth, the imaginable tremor of the hermit's holy well still bubbling out of the ground invisibly below. And best were their returns, scarcely rowing at all, idling down the centre, confident of safety within reach on either bank, wafted by the breeze and what felt like the bent or inclination of the water always to be coming from the west and heading, however quietly, towards the ruled line and the little tower that made the limit and the brink. It was sweet to drift like that, as though to a sheer falls but knowing they could halt when they chose, safe in a secret harbour, and disembark and descend their secret stairway into their house and home. Often they had a soft music on these returns. Carrie sat in the stern, holding Gwen and singing; Seth rowed, his eyes on them, and behind him in the bows Benjamin, become accomplished, played and murmured an accompaniment. Seth was between them, between their music. Their last such return was at full moon. They had not thought of it. They were idling down the length of the water, the music dying behind them like a wake, there was the merest breeze, and the blue of the sky was becoming pale so very gradually they were beginning to drift into nightfall before they would notice. Then Seth saw in Gwenny's face what she had seen. Her eyes were all amazement, she thrust out her pointing finger, as though she were the inventor of that gesture of an astonishment demanding to be shared, then Carrie saw too and suffered likewise a childish shock and pause or gap in her adult comprehension. Moon! The moon! White as a bone, frail as a seed, big as a whole new earth, the moon was rising over the rim of the dam, dead centre, clearing it, first with the ugly stump of tower intruding, then free, sovereign, beyond measure beautiful and indifferent. Seth turned sideways on, so all could see, and like that they drifted nearer and nearer, in silence but for the water lapping.

Carrie woke. The curtains were slightly parted, which made her think he must have stood there and looked at her. She went to find him on his terraces. There was fresh earth dug but the mattock had been flung down. She turned and called for him, the echo came back, a single note, distended. Benjamin came down. He'll be swimming, he said. Or in the boat. Look for him, will you, Carrie said. Benjamin began the climb, Carrie went indoors, dressed, saw that Gwen was still asleep. Then downstairs again, uneasy, and met with a shock, an absence: the table was cleared of his sketches, drawings, paintings; the portfolio, that had stood by it, also absent. She ran out, Benjamin was coming down from the dam, too fast. She waited by the spring, he hurried by her, not a word, averting his face. His breath was coming in sobs. He ran to the stone barn, she followed, the door was open, he took a step in, bent forward, turned to face her, ashen, smitten white. The weights, he said. He's filed them off. They're gone. He began to whimper, a queer unstoppable distress, bolted like an animal for the cliff again. Carrie fetched the child and laboured with her oblivious up the stairway to the ugly level rampart of the dam. She saw Benjamin already distant, small, making haste along the bank, visiting every inlet, in all his bearing, his sudden leaps and halts, hurting her even as he diminished with his manifest dread. How large the water, vast the hills and without bounds the sky.

Now she must wait on the dam in a steady breeze. Everything drifts that can sooner or later down the length of the water and bumps against the terminus, the ugly wall. The little boat will come, with its oars shipped, empty. Everything that can float will drift this way, the work, the distorted likenesses, they will be for a while like spawn, like a flotilla of vaguely coloured rafts, till the colours run and all weighs heavier and they sink. The boat will come. But what cannot kick free, anchored at the feet, what cannot rise on the body's insistent buoyancy, pulling towards the daylight on the will to live, that must stay where it is and in her lifetime will never rise, only toll like a bell, like a sunken, silent and useless bell. On the dam, the baby on her hip, Carrie reflects that she has said she will never forgive him.

Contributors

Steven Blyth studied Philosophy and Literature at Bolton Institute and English as a post-graduate at Manchester University. He has published three collections of poetry: *The Gox* (Redbeck) and *Baddy* and *So* (both Peterloo).

Polly Clark was born in Toronto in 1968 and brought up in Lancashire, Cumbria and the Borders of Scotland. In 1997 she received an Eric Gregory Award for her poetry. Her first collection *Kiss* (Bloodaxe) was a Poetry Book Society Recommendation.

Helen Clare's poems have appeared in *First Pressings* (Faber), *The Rialto, Ambit,* and *The North*, and won prizes in the Arvon *Daily Telegraph* Competition 2000 and the London Writers Competition 2001. She currently works for Arts Council England.

David Constantine's poetry collections include *Madder, Watching for Dolphins, The Pelt of Wasps, Caspar Hauser*, and most recently *Something for the Ghosts,* which was shortlisted for the 2002 Whitbread Poetry Prize. He is a translator of Hölderlin, Brecht, Goethe, Kleist, Enzensberger, Michaux and Jaccottet.

Matthew Francis' first collection of poetry, *Blizzard* (Faber), was shortlisted for the Forward First Book Prize and the Welsh Book of the Year and his poem, 'The Ornamental Hermit', won first prize in the TLS/Blackwell's Poetry Competition. His second collection, *Dragons* (Faber), was published in 2001.

Sophie Hannah has published four collections of poetry - *The Hero and the Girl Next Door, Hotels Like Houses, Leaving and Leaving You* and *First of Last Chances* (all Carcanet). She was Fellow Commoner in Creative Arts at Trinity College, Cambridge and a fellow of Wolfson College, Oxford. She currently teaches Creative Writing at Manchester Metropolitan University.

John Latham has published five collections of poetry, including *All Clear* and *The Unbearable Weight of Mercury* (both Peterloo Poets), and has won first prize in about 20 UK poetry competitions. He has had several plays broadcast on BBC Radio 4 and is a regular tutor to the Arvon Foundation and the Taliesin Trust.

Joanne Limburg was born in London in 1970. She studied philosophy at Cambridge, and has since gained an MA in Psychoanalytic Studies and Part 1 of a Diploma in Careers Guidance. She won an Eric Gregory Award for her poetry in 1998. Her collection *Femenismo* (Bloodaxe) was shortlisted for Forward Prize Best First Collection.

Grevel Lindop is a former Professor of Romantic Studies and British Academy Research Reader at Manchester University. His collections of poetry include *Against the Sea, Fools' Paradise, Tourists, Moon's Palette* and *A Prismatic Toy* (all Carcanet). He has also published several critical works, from *The Opium-Eater: A Life of Thomas De Quincey* (JJ Dent), to *A Literary Guide to the Lake District* (Chatto).

Originally from Fife, **Roddy Lumsden** now lives in Bristol working as a freelance writer, teacher and puzzle compiler. He has published three collections of poetry and in Autumn 2004, *Mischief Night: New and Selected Poems* is due from Bloodaxe. Also next Autumn, Chambers will publish *Vitamin Q*, a miscellany of lists and articles from his cult website of that name - now the biggest trivia site on the web.

Born in Belfast in 1972, **Sinéad Morrissey** published two collections of poetry: *There Was Fire in Vancouver* and *Between Here and There* (both Carcanet). She is currently Writer-in-Residence at Queen's University, Belfast.

Ian McMillan first made his name through his work with the Poetry Circus in the early 1980s. Since then he has become famous for his work in schools, radio, as Poet in Residence for Barnsley Football Club, and in poetry venues across the country. He has published five collections of poetry including *Selected Poems* (a Poetry Book Society Recommendation) and most recently *I Found this Shirt* (Carcanet). He recently co-hosted BBC4's nightly debate show *Big Read: Battle of the Books*.

Sean O'Brien has published four award-winning collections of poems, most recently *Downriver*, which won the 2002 Forward Prize for Best Collection. His essays have been collected in *The Deregulated Muse: Essays on Contemporary British and Irish Poetry* (Bloodaxe) and he has translated Aristophanes' *The Birds* (Methuen). He was editor of *The Firebox: Poetry in Britain and Ireland After 1945*, and currently lives in Newcastle.

Ruth Padel has won the National Poetry Competition and published five poetry collections; her most recent, *Voodoo Shop* (Chatto), was shortlisted for the Whitbread and T S Eliot Prizes. Her next, *The Soho Leopard*, is out in 2004. Her critical book *52 Ways of Looking at a Poem* (Chatto) was based on her newspaper column 'The Sunday Poem'; other non-fiction includes *I'm A Man* (Faber), on rock music, masculinity and Greek myth. She is presently writing a travel book about wild tigers.

Sheenagh Pugh's poetry has won many awards, including the Forward Prize for Best Single Poem in 1998, the Bridport Prize, the PHRAS prize, the Cardiff International Poetry Prize (twice) and the British Comparative Literature Association's Translation Prize. Her poems have been included in several anthologies, notably *Poems on the Underground* and *The Hutchinson Book of Post-War British Poetry*. Her most recent collection, *The Beautiful Lie* (Seren) was a Poetry Book Society Recommendation.

Joe Sheerin was born in Leitrim in 1941. His poems have been published in three previous books, *A Crack in the Ice* (Dolmen Press), the *Oxford Poets 2000* anthology (Carcanet), and *Elves in the Wainscoting* (Carcanet). He is a lecturer and currently lives in Brighton.

Jean Sprackland's first collection of poetry, *Tattoos for Mothers Day* (Spike), was shortlisted for the Forward Prize in 1999. Her second collection, *Hard Water* (Cape) is a Poetry Book Society Recommendation and has been shortlisted for the 2003 TS Eliot Award. She lives in Southport.

Anne Stevenson was born in England of American parents, grew up in the States but then lived in Britain for most of her adult life. She has published twelve collections of poetry, a book of essays, *Between the Iceberg and the Ship*, a recent critical study, *Five Looks at Elizabeth Bishop*, and a biography of Sylvia Plath, *Bitter Fame*. Her most recent collections are *Granny Scarecrow* and *Report from the Border* (both Bloodaxe). In 2002 she was the first recipient of a Northern Rock Foundation Writer Award, otherwise known as the Northern Booker.

Gerard Woodward is the author of three collections of poetry, *The Householder*, *After the Deafening* and *Island to Island* (all Chatto), and a shorter pamplet *The Unwriter* (Sycamore). He has received an Eric Gregory and a Somerset Maughan Award. His first novel *August* was shortlisted for the 2001 Whitbread First Novel Prize.

Cliff Yates is the author of *14 Ways of Listening to the Archers* and *Henry's Clock* (both Smiths Doorstop), winner of the Aldeburgh Poetry Festival prize. As Poetry Society poet-in-residence he wrote *Jumpstart Poetry in the Secondary School* (Poetry Society). He has received an Arts Council England Writer's Award.